BURNED

SMOKE AND FIRE BOOK 1

SUZANNE WINSLOW

MD PUBLISHING

DEDICATION

For William Winslow,
my father and first hero.
And Lisette Belisle,
my mentor and friend.

E-book Edition ISBN 9781734680102
Print Edition ISBN 978-1-7346801-1-9

1

une 2011

"**M**om!"

"I'm coming. Hold on a minute." Jenifer drained the water from the kitchen sink, dried her hands on her shorts, then shut down her laptop on the counter with a half-dozen work emails. They could wait until tomorrow.

When she got to the living room, Robbie, her six-year-old son, was hovering by the front door. Purple Popsicle colored his lips and tongue. Ketchup stained the front of his favorite Spider-Man T-shirt. He tipped his head back and gazed up at her with his father's big, beautiful hazel eyes. "Can we go outside and play now?"

"Absolutely." This was her favorite time of day. "Put your shoes on." She stepped around a pile of moving boxes and pushed the living room windows open all the way, hoping the air would cool off after dark. Later, after Robbie was asleep, she hoped to unpack a few more boxes, then call it quits for the night.

Robbie dropped down onto a box marked *Upstairs Bathroom* and yanked on his black Velcro sandals. "Can we ride bikes?"

She took in his dirty knees and shook her head. "How about we play catch instead?" She had spent most of the afternoon on the playground with her students. Her classroom was too hot on the last day of school to keep them inside. From the looks of it, Robbie's teacher had the same idea. He needed a shower, and it was already getting dark outside.

Robbie shrugged. "Okay." He jumped up to get his ball and glove from the small detached garage behind the house. Their quaint two-story colonial in Grand Rapids was half the size and almost a hundred years older than the home they had lived in before her husband, Patrick, died two years ago. The house reminded her of her parents' home outside Chicago, with its high ceilings, original maple floors, and deep front porch. She loved the new kitchen and updated bathrooms. Robbie loved riding his bike on the village sidewalks and living only a block away from their new school.

She pointed out to the street after he met her on the porch. "I want you to stay away from the road. If the ball crosses the side-walk, I'll get it. Understand?"

He nodded and raced across the yard, keeping close to the house, then spun around and threw her the ball.

She caught it, wishing Patrick could be there too. For Robbie's sake. Even after her marriage had started to fall apart, she'd never wanted her son to grow up without his father. "That was good. Now let's see you catch."

He held out his glove, flashing her a grin. His face scrunched as he caught the ball. After a few more throws, he rolled her a grounder.

"Do you want to try that?" she asked.

"Yup." He squatted down on his long legs, shaking his dark-blond hair out of his eyes, looking just like his dad. "I'm ready."

He kept his eyes fixed on the ball. Finally, she drew her arm back and rolled the ball to him. At the last second, it tipped the edge of his glove and bounced into a hedge of arborvitae along the side of the driveway. Leaping to his feet, Robbie darted underneath the clump of overgrown bushes. "I'll get it."

"Come on out. You don't know what's under there." Jenifer headed to the garage to find another ball. "We'll get it later."

Robbie's head popped out from the hedge. "I think I see it."

Jenifer turned to look at him. She put her hands on her hips. "I don't want you under there. Just wait a minute and I'll get another ball."

He dropped onto his butt, still peering under the bushes.

As soon as she walked into the garage, Robbie let out a high-pitched scream. Her heart nearly stopped when she looked back and saw a swarm of bees chasing him into the road.

"Stop!" She bolted down the driveway, panic exploding in her chest when she saw the oncoming car. "Robbie!"

Out of nowhere, a man rushed from across the street into the middle of the road. He scooped Robbie into his arms and kept running. Jenifer froze, barely able to breathe. The sound of squealing brakes cut through the air. The car skidded to a stop where Robbie had darted into the road seconds before. The man pressed Robbie's face into his chest, protecting him from the bees. He yelled for Jenifer to open her front door.

A woman jumped out of the car, shouting, "Matt!"

Frantic, Jenifer bounded up the porch steps and threw open the door as all three of them ran inside. Robbie cried, swatting at his shirt with both hands once he was back on his feet.

Hands shaking, Jenifer tugged Robbie's shirt over his head and tossed it onto the floor. Three angry welts had broken out on his arm. "Are there any bees in your shorts?"

Eyes red and watery, Robbie shook his head and grabbed at his shorts when she tried to look inside.

The man beside her put his hands on his knees and caught his breath. He reached up and looked inside his collar. When he straightened, she had to tilt her head back to see his face. The first thing she noticed was that his dark-blue eyes matched the T-shirt he wore with *Grand Rapids Fire Department* across the front.

"Is he allergic to bee stings?"

Jenifer shook her head and put her hands on Robbie's shoulders. "No. I mean, I don't know. He's never been stung before."

Through the screen door, she could see the car that had almost hit Robbie parked in the driveway across the street. A dark-haired woman in her early thirties leaned against the back of the blue Volkswagen. Arms folded over her chest, she seemed to watch Jenifer's house from behind a pair of large black sunglasses.

The man crouched down in front of Robbie. "My name is Matt Barnes. I'm a paramedic. What's your name?"

Robbie looked back at her, and she nodded for him to answer. "Robbie," he said, knuckling back tears.

"You're all right, buddy. After we get those stingers out, you'll feel better, okay?" Matt checked Robbie's breathing and then looked up at Jenifer. "Are *you* all right?" He didn't appear at all shaken, even though he'd almost been hit by the car, as well. He looked concerned, in an efficient, detached kind of way. Except for the occasional glance out the window at the woman who'd started to pace behind her car.

"I'm fine," Jenifer said, though her hands still shook on Robbie's shoulders. "I'm sorry. I didn't know about the bees. We've only been in the house a couple of days."

"I understand." Matt stood. "He'll be okay, but we should remove those stingers in his arm."

Robbie leaned in closer to Jenifer. "Is it going to hurt?"

"No," Matt told him. "I promise." He waited until she looked up again. "I have to get my bag out of my truck. I'll be right back." As soon as he opened the door, the woman outside pushed her sunglasses on top of her head and started toward him.

Jenifer thought to follow Matt. "Maybe I should talk to her."

"Jessie?" Matt turned to look at her and shook his head. "No. Believe me, her problem is not with you. It's me. It would be better if you stay here and wait with Robbie."

Jenifer wasn't sure what he meant. Not that it mattered. Still, she thought the woman deserved an explanation. "Will you tell her what happened?"

He gave her a half-smile. "I'll tell her."

Jenifer saw Matt put his head down when Jessie met him in the street. She started walking backward with her hand on his arm like she was talking to him and he wouldn't stop. When he got to the black pickup truck parked in front of her Volkswagen, he seemed to listen to her for a minute, then shook his head.

That's when Jenifer turned her head away, until she heard Jessie yell, "Fine!" loud enough to be heard from across the street. Jenifer looked again as Jessie threw her hands up in the air. "We can talk later."

Matt grabbed a black duffel-like bag from his truck as Jessie stalked back to her car and drove off. A few seconds later, he returned to Jenifer's house. She didn't mention Jessie, deciding he was probably right that Robbie wasn't the biggest problem at the moment.

Matt didn't say anything about her either as he knelt before Robbie on the floor. He took a small pair of forceps from his bag. Robbie drew back, and Matt dropped his hand. "This isn't going to hurt. I promise."

A burst of laughter from outside caught Robbie's attention. He cocked his head and looked out the door. "Is that your house?" He pointed to the big gray home across the street where three young girls rode by on their bikes.

Matt followed his gaze. "That's where I live."

Keeping his eyes on the girls, he asked, "Are you a daddy?"

Jenifer tightened her hand on her son's shoulder. He had done this once before with his pediatrician. The doctor knew he had lost his father and understood the curiosity. This man did not.

Rocking back on his heels, Matt shook his head. "No, I don't have kids." He showed Robbie the forceps again. "Are you ready?"

Robbie pinched his lips and held out his arm for Matt. He squeezed Jenifer's hand as Matt removed a stinger with the edge of the forceps.

Matt worked at a second stinger. "How old are you?" he asked in a warm, comforting voice.

"Six."

"Do you like to play sports?"

"I play baseball." Robbie slumped his shoulders. "And basketball, like my dad."

Matt exchanged a brief look with Jenifer. His eyes dropped to the gold band hanging on a chain around her neck. After he removed the last stinger, he stood. "All done."

Jenifer held out her hand. "Thank you."

"You're welcome..." Matt paused as he took her hand.

Her face grew warm when he squeezed her hand. "Jenifer. I'm sorry, I should have introduced myself. My name's Jenifer Nichols."

He smiled. "It's a pleasure to meet you, Jenifer."

Robbie blinked up at him. "Did you get stung, too?"

"No." Matt held out his arms to show him. "I'm okay."

Jenifer gave Matt a closer inspection. He wore a pair of brown cargo shorts with his T-shirt. The shorts were long and loose, the shirt untucked. The bees could have stung him almost anywhere, but from what she could see, there were no marks on his light-olive skin. "Are you sure?"

Matt stuck the forceps into one of the deep pockets in his shorts and picked up his bag. "I got lucky, I guess."

Robbie's eyes went wide when he finally noticed the fire department emblem on Matt's T-shirt. "Are you a fireman?"

Matt grinned. "Yes." The earlier detachment Jenifer noted in his eyes faded as he seemed to switch roles and become a neighbor.

"Do you drive the trucks?"

"No, but I ride in one. Does that count?" Jenifer smiled at the way Matt played along as Robbie gazed up at him with awe. Matt's grin spread. "If you come by the firehouse sometime, I'll show you around."

Robbie's mouth fell open. He looked at Jenifer with big round eyes. "Can we go?"

It was incredible to her how quickly Robbie had forgotten about the bee stings and nearly being struck by a car. Jenifer pointed to the stairs. "We'll see. Right now, you need to get into the shower. I'll be up in a minute."

Robbie's face fell. Halfway up the stairs, he stopped and looked at Matt. "Good night," he said.

Matt waved and gave him a smile. "Good night, Robbie."

After Robbie disappeared into the bathroom, Jenifer turned on the porch light and followed Matt out to the driveway. "Thank you again, for everything."

"I'm glad I was home."

So was she.

Matt walked across the grass to pick up Robbie's baseball glove as the streetlights blinked on. He brought it back to her and then kind of waited there for a second without saying anything. Like Jessie, he appeared in his early thirties. He wasn't quite as tall as Patrick had been, but he was easily over six feet. His dark-brown hair was cropped short, his light-olive skin smooth and unmarked. He had a long straight nose, a short scruffy beard, and he smelled a little like engine exhaust and sunblock.

"Are you sure I shouldn't talk to your friend?" she asked.

"That's not necessary." The lines on his forehead creased. "Jessie's okay."

Jenifer glanced up to see Robbie watching them through his bedroom window. "What did she say when you told her what happened?"

Matt cleared his throat. "She understood. She's upset with me, not you."

She eyed Robbie's glove in her hands. "Then I hope we didn't cause any more trouble between you."

"You didn't." And then, as if it were somehow important, he added, "There isn't anything between Jessie and me."

She heard the unspoken *anymore* in his voice. An uncomfortable sense of relief washed over her. Uncertain as to what caused the reaction, she tucked Robbie's glove under her arm and watched Matt head home.

A little while later, Robbie was quiet as he changed into his pajamas and climbed into bed. She thought he was just tired until she caught him staring at the picture of Patrick she kept on his bookshelf. Was he thinking about his father? God knows she did. Patrick's death often kept her awake at night. Watching her son grow up without him was the hardest thing she would ever do.

Robbie turned his head on his pillow and looked at her. "Why don't I have a daddy?"

She lay down on his bed, wrapped him up in her arms, and rested her chin on top of his head. Filled with guilt and regret, she grasped for answers. "You have a daddy. He's in heaven. And no daddy in the world ever loved his little boy more than he loved you."

As to the love Patrick had for her, she was less certain. She wished their marriage could have been different. That she had made different choices. But she would never regret loving the man who had given her a son.

As she tucked Robbie in, he asked again if they could go see the fire trucks. She promised to think about it, but she wasn't so sure it was a good idea. Matt seemed like a great guy. Her stomach fluttered when she thought about him, and that was bad. Falling for him would be worse.

One word came to mind when she even considered the possibility: punishment.

2

*J*essie was back.

Matt dropped his shirt and shorts onto the bathroom floor and blasted the hot water in the shower before he stepped in. The last time he had seen or heard from Jessie O'Connor, they were eighteen years old. She had been madder than hell at him at the time. And, he later came to believe, pregnant with his baby.

Head down, he flattened his hands on the tile wall under the rushing water and tried to clear his head.

Jessie had left Michigan and moved to Florida after they graduated high school. He was sad to hear her mother died a few weeks ago, but he'd never expected to see Jessie again. He was surprised to see she looked the same after thirteen years. She still had the sleek black hair; long, long legs; and the small, sexy smile that got him into trouble as a kid. Even her rose-scented perfume smelled familiar, bringing back memories he'd tried years to forget. When she'd cornered him in the driveway tonight, gushing about how excited she was to see him again, it rang false. And when she didn't bother to ask about the boy she almost hit with her car, he'd turned and walked away.

After a few minutes in the shower, he heard his phone vibrate next to the sink. Seconds later, the doorbell rang. He shut off the water, grabbed a towel, and wrapped it around his waist, then checked his phone. There was a text from Jessie. She was at the door. He wondered how she'd gotten his number and, more importantly, why she was even there.

Before tonight, his last desperate words to her had been *I need to know for sure.* Her parting shot had been *Go to hell.*

He didn't see a reason for anything to change now.

He tapped the phone against his forehead, frowned, then deleted the message. He'd told her earlier he was sorry about her mother, but he had to go back and check on the boy. What he'd meant was he didn't want to talk at all, but that seemed too blunt so soon after her mother's death.

Still, he didn't rush downstairs to get the door. All the lights were off except for the upstairs bathroom at the back of the house. His truck was outside, but for all she knew, he was out for the night. Not eating leftover pizza and catching a baseball game on television.

By the time he yanked on a pair of black nylon basketball shorts and started downstairs, a second text lit up his screen. She'd guessed he wasn't there and said she would come back the next day. Fine. He added her name to his contacts so he would recognize her number next time, then turned off the phone. He would take care of whatever he had to with her tomorrow.

❧

*T*he next morning, Matt tossed his gear into the back of Nate Doyle's red Jeep Cherokee for a second day of fishing. The two of them had joined the fire department about the same time ten years ago. Matt was his lieutenant now. At thirty-eight, Nate was five years older than Matt, shorter, with wide shoulders and thick red hair. He was all Irish from the green eyes and freckles to the Celtic trinity knot tattooed on his left bicep. The guy was deceptively strong, humble. And shame-lessly popular with women.

A sixteen-foot aluminum boat was trailered behind the Jeep. Matt climbed into the front seat where Nate had his head back, singing to George Strait on the radio while he waited.

Matt reached back to buckle his seat belt. "You know, your radio isn't going to blow up if you play Neil Young."

Nate sat up, looked at him, and laughed. "We listened to your music yesterday. Today, I'm driving."

"I'm not fishing next week," Matt said, slipping on a pair of black sunglasses as the sun started to rise. "I need to finish some projects around the house."

"Need any help?"

Matt caught a whiff of coffee. His stomach growled. "No, thanks. It's mostly just packing up stuff I want to get rid of."

Fiery-red hair stuck out beneath Nate's baseball cap as he pointed to the second coffee in the cupholder beside him. "What's up with your phone? I called you last night, and it went right to voicemail."

Matt nodded his gratitude as he reached for the extra coffee. "I turned it off." He dug out his phone from his pocket with his other hand and turned it back on. "Jessie's in town. I didn't want to talk to her."

Nate raised an eyebrow and turned the radio down. "She's here? You saw her?" He knew enough about Matt's history with Jessie to be surprised she would want to talk to him again.

Matt pointed his cup at Jenifer's house and told him what happened with Robbie and the bees.

Nate turned his head, checked out the house for a second, then looked back at Matt. "So why is Jessie here?"

Matt pulled the lid off his cup and drank the coffee as he scrolled through his messages. "Her mother just passed away. My guess is she's here to settle the house."

Nate turned the music back up as he pulled out of the

driveway and drove toward the lake. "What about the woman across the street? What's she like?"

Matt shook his head without looking up from his phone. "You know, you sound like my mother."

Nate snorted. "Well?" His approach to women was much different from Matt's. Single life suited him. He enjoyed playing the field. Irish Catholic and the eldest of four, he was about to become the last of his siblings to settle down after his younger brother married in October.

Matt found another text from Jessie, hit delete, and then stuck the phone back into his pocket. "Jenifer's nice," he said, trying to ignore the sudden pounding of his heart. "Maybe late twenties, brown eyes. Light-brown, wavy hair." Actually, she was beautiful, and with a smile that damn near stole his heart the moment their eyes met.

"Married?"

She had intrigued him enough that he'd stayed awake half the night wondering the same thing. "Widowed, I think." He stared out the window, recalling the gold band she wore on a chain around her neck.

Nate gave him a quick look. "You like her."

Matt shrugged and sipped his coffee, wondering whether or not she might actually be interested in him.

"You said her son's name is Robbie Nichols?" Nate scratched his chin. "I wonder if she's related to the real estate developer, Robert Nichols. If she is, you might be right that she's a widow. I think the guy's son was killed in a car accident a couple years ago. I heard about the call. It was big in the newspapers, too."

Matt kept his eyes on the road as Lake Michigan came into view. Empathy mixed with hope as he considered his chances of getting to know her better.

"Talk to her." Nate turned into the boat launch and got in line, waiting as the people ahead of them dropped their boats into the water. "See what she says."

"Maybe I will." If she was ready. If she gave him an opening, he would see what happened. Because, unlike Nate, he'd planned for a whole different kind of life than the one he had. The kind he didn't have when he was a kid. He owned the large three-bedroom home where he'd grown up, became a lieutenant with the fire department, and started to think about marriage. And kids, despite the odds. Marriage had come up with an ex-girlfriend in the past, but in the end, she'd needed a lot more than he could promise her.

Would a woman like Jenifer be different?

"What about you?" Matt finished his coffee and put the cup back in the holder. "Are you still seeing the woman you met a couple weeks ago?"

Long pause. "No. That didn't last."

"What happened?" Matt sat back and stretched out his legs. These stories were usually good.

Nate looked in his mirrors. Stalling. Finally, he said, "I got a dirty look when I ordered steak the first time I took her to dinner. I asked her what was wrong. Turns out she's vegan."

Matt grinned, trying to imagine what it would take to separate Nate from a rib eye. "What did you do?"

"She made me change my order." Nate circled the boat ramp, dropped the Jeep into reverse, and backed the boat into the water. He glanced back at Matt. "Oh, it gets better. Do you know what a Wiccan is?"

Matt laughed. "A witch?"

"That one was. Apparently, that's not true for all of them. I learned that on the second date."

Matt waited until Nate put the Jeep in Park before he got out and grabbed his fishing gear. He put his hands on the open window and looked inside. "Did you go for a third?"

Nate tugged at his ear. "No. It wasn't worth it. The two times I was in her apartment I couldn't breathe every time her cat jumped on my lap."

Incredulous, Matt said, "You're kidding. Your witch had a cat?"

"One of those long-haired Persians, smart-ass." Nate got out and unhitched the boat. "Not a black cat. It doesn't matter anyway. She didn't want to go out with me again, either."

Matt's shoulders shook with laughter. "She wasn't into Catholic carnivores?"

"Guess not." Nate pulled the fishing boat to the end of the dock, out of the way for the next launch, and Matt held the lines. Nate turned around when the guy behind him lunged to keep a small child from falling into the water. Matt stayed with the fishing boat while Nate gave the guy a hand. He lifted the 100-quart cooler the guy had been carrying with his wife and set it into their boat like it was a loaf of bread.

Onshore, two women in their early twenties stopped to watch Nate. Matt noticed one of the women give him her number when he went up to park the Jeep. The second pointed to Matt on the dock, and Nate shot him a curious look. Matt shook his head and dropped his gear into the boat where it landed with a thud. His mind was stuck on Jenifer and how much he wanted to see her again.

~

The heat and humidity over the last week finally broke by late afternoon as the temperatures hovered around the low eighties on the lake. Comfortable compared to the nineties the day before. The hot, humid weather was the reason Matt had gone home early yesterday. Otherwise, he would have stayed on the water until dark.

The thought of what might have happened to Robbie if he had made his stomach clench.

Matt had just taken another perch off his line when his phone rang in his pocket. The small boat rocked when he stood up to answer it. He blew out a breath when Jessie's name showed on the screen.

Nate reached into the cooler and handed Matt a beer. "If that's Jessie, you should probably talk to her."

"Now?"

"She'll probably keep calling if you don't."

Matt tipped his head back, thinking Nate was right, and answered the phone on the fifth ring. Jessie's voice faltered, as if she hadn't expected to hear his voice. "Matt? Where are you?"

Twisting off his beer cap, Matt sat back down and leaned against the side of the boat. He kept a watchful eye on two young kids messing around on Jet Skis in the distance. "I'm at the lake. How did you get my number?"

Jessie hesitated. "It's on a list next to my mother's phone. You must have given it to her."

He remembered now. "You're right, I did. I liked your mother." He'd empathized with Ruth O'Connor. She'd deserved better than to be abandoned by her husband and left to raise Jessie on her own. He understood the situation all too well. Ruth had stayed friendly with him over the years, making him think she never knew about the baby. He'd given Ruth his number years ago because she'd lived alone. He'd told her to call if she ever needed anything. She never did.

"She liked you, too. After I moved back to Florida, she used to call me whenever she ran into you. I remember when she told me you'd bought your mother's house and moved down the street from her again."

"What else did she say?" he asked with the uneasy feeling Jessie might have kept tabs on him over the years.

She sounded all too eager to answer. "She told me you joined the fire department and that your mother remarried a few years ago." He heard the smile in her voice when she said, "She always liked to tell me you never married."

Matt took a sip of his beer and kept silent.

When he didn't say anything, she asked, "Do you ever think about me?"

He caught Nate's eye, then dropped his head. "No." Not the way she meant, at least. "Not for a long time now."

He heard her quiet sigh. "Did you miss me after I left?"

Matt's hand tightened on the phone. His doctors had said it was nearly impossible for him to father a child after he was injured as a kid. That was the reason he'd asked Jessie for a paternity test. The request had seemed reasonable at the time. They were broken up by the time she'd told him she was pregnant. If the test had shown the baby was his, he would have asked her to marry him. God, how she had hated him for doubting her. She'd told him to go to hell, said she would have an abortion, and moved back to Florida where she'd lived when her parents were together.

"Please just tell me what you want, Jess."

"I want to talk."

Matt's head came up. "About what?"

She sighed again, this time with more frustration. "Can't you just give me a few minutes?"

"Maybe. Why don't you tell me what you want to talk about first?"

"Please, I just want to know how you're doing." Her voice turned soft and pleading. "If you're happy."

He set his beer down between his feet. A dull ache started to throb in his chest. "I'm good, Jessie. I really hope you are, too. But we don't have anything to talk about anymore." Even when they were younger, they had been incompatible. He was too practical for her, way too reserved. She had a short fuse and a flair for drama. He knew that if they had married at eighteen, they would probably be divorced by now.

"You're not happy with me. I get it. But you don't know everything."

"There's nothing left for us to talk about, Jessie."

She continued on. "I have to take care of things at my mother's house. I'll be here for a while. At least think about it. We can talk in a few days."

"No—" Matt looked down at his phone, incredulous, after the call disconnected.

Nate silently scrutinized a Styrofoam carton of minnows they used as bait.

"What?" Matt's jaw ticced as he waited for Nate to say something.

"Nothing."

"No, just say it."

Nate hooked a minnow, then flicked his wrist and cast his line. "I bet she thinks of you as her fallback."

Matt raised his head. "Her fallback?"

"You know what I mean. Maybe life didn't turn out the way she wanted it to. Now she's back and here you are." Nate's voice trailed off.

Matt frowned. He blocked Jessie's number on his phone and relegated her to the past. Because he couldn't think of one single thing she could possibly say that would make him go back down that road with her again.

3

———

*J*enifer reached for her iced coffee at the drive-through window. It nearly slipped out of her hand and spilled on the colorful macramé bracelet a student had given to her at the end of the school year. She secured the plastic lid on her cup and set it down, remembering all the tears on her last day. It was harder than she had imagined, changing schools. But at least now she'd be in the same building with Robbie for the next few years.

"Mom." Robbie kicked the back of her seat with his foot. The young man at the drive-through window held out the rest of her order.

She smiled at the guy and took her bag. "I'm sorry," she said and passed Robbie's lunch back to him as the alarm sounded from the fire department down the street. Seconds later, a single fire truck raced past.

Robbie craned his neck to look out the window. "Do you think that was Matt?"

"I don't know." She caught Robbie's eye in the rearview mirror. She was almost certain about what he was going to ask next as she waited to pull out of the parking lot. "Are you ready to go home?"

He pointed a French fry toward the firehouse. "Can we see if he's there?"

She puffed out her cheeks and looked down the street. "He might not be working today." Matt's truck wasn't in his driveway when they'd left the house that morning, but even if he was at work, there was a good chance he'd just left the firehouse.

Robbie bit into his hamburger, bobbing his head to Jimmy Buffet on the radio with his window down. "We can ask, can't we?"

Jenifer drummed her fingers on the steering wheel for a second and then turned toward the firehouse. "All right. If you see his black truck in the parking lot, we'll stop and see if he's there." She'd already made up her mind there was nothing inappropriate about accepting Matt's invitation to show Robbie the trucks. They were neighbors. If there was something going on between Matt and Jessie, well, that was none of Jenifer's business, was it?

Sure enough, three men in dark-blue uniforms stood in front of the two-story, red brick firehouse. Robbie shouted out the window when he recognized the tall, dark-haired man with his back to them. "Mom! He's there!"

Matt turned around, using his hand to block the sun from his eyes. He smiled and waved when he recognized them at the stoplight.

She waited a beat before she turned into the parking lot behind the firehouse. She could hear Robbie shoving his hamburger wrapper back into the bag and tossing it onto the seat. Matt came around the corner of the building as she parked and got out of the car.

"Hey." A warm, easy smile lit up his face. "I'm glad you're here. Can you stick around for a while?"

Before she knew it, she was smiling, too, as she opened the rear door to let Robbie out of the car. "We can stay for a little bit, if you're not busy."

"One of the trucks just left on a call, but hopefully it'll stay quiet while you're here." He led them across the parking lot to the back of the firehouse, then hurried ahead to hold the door open for them. "Come on in. I'll show you around."

Inside, Robbie's eyes roamed over the fire trucks parked inside the bay. A half-dozen large, overhead doors were open at the front of the building. Robbie tipped his head back and gazed up at the enormous truck in front of him.

"That's a fire engine." Matt pointed to the hoses. "Sometimes we call it a pumper because it carries water that can be pumped through hoses to put out a fire."

Someone snickered from the other side of the fire engine. "Are you showing off my truck, Lieutenant?"

A blond-haired man in his early thirties came around to join them. Jenifer recognized him as one of the men who'd been standing outside with Matt when they got there. The man shot Matt a grin.

Matt shook his head at him. "This is Henry Miller." Henry reached out his hand to Jenifer. "Henry, this is Jenifer Nichols and her son, Robbie."

Jenifer glanced around at the other trucks lined up inside the bay. "You work on different trucks?"

"Different trucks, different companies," Matt told her. "Henry works on the pumper."

"Which one is yours?" she asked.

Matt pointed to a smaller truck across the bay. "That one. Rescue 5. It's a heavy rescue company. We'll get calls for different types of extrications. Anything from confined space to water, working fires, accidents where someone is trapped."

Out of the corner of her eye, Jenifer saw a man with a shock of red hair come into the bay. He held up a phone to Matt. She stepped back so Matt could take the call, but he shook his head and the man turned around and walked back inside the firehouse.

Robbie inched closer to the fire engine. Henry cleared his

throat. He rested his hand on Robbie's shoulder, looking from Jenifer to Matt. "Do you mind if I show him around my truck?"

Jenifer nodded as the man with red hair came back outside and walked over to stand next to Matt.

"Sure. Go ahead." Matt took a step back as the second man reached around him to shake Jenifer's hand.

"I'm Nate Doyle." Nate smiled, his bright-green eyes hinting with mischief.

"Jenifer Nichols."

Matt touched his hand to her back, and her pulse quickened as he led her around the fire engine. "Nate and I are in the same company."

Nate was a ladies' man, she was almost positive, but with an obvious deference to Matt as he tagged along with his hands in his pockets. He was handsome, to say the least, but not in a way that drew her attention. The way Matt did.

"Mom!" Robbie called out from the front seat of the fire engine. He waved at her through the windshield and then jumped down to check out the next truck.

Matt showed Robbie around his truck last. Jenifer got a picture of Robbie draped in Matt's tan turnout coat. Henry took a picture too. After the trucks, Matt brought them upstairs to show them where he lived while he was at work.

Before they went back outside again, Henry gave Robbie an ice cream sandwich. Robbie went to go find shade, settling on a patch of grass in front of the firehouse. His face was flushed from all of the heat and excitement. Jenifer kept an eye on him from inside the bay where the air was a little cooler next to the open doors. Matt leaned a shoulder against the wall beside her. Robbie wiped his face with the back of his hand, reminding her of dinner. She shifted her gaze back to Matt, who looked to be a million miles away. "Who cooks when you're here?"

His brows drew together as if he hadn't heard her at first, then rose with his smile. "We take turns."

"Really? Are you a good cook?"

Someone snorted a laugh from deep inside the bay. Matt flicked a look over his shoulder and steered her outside. "No, not really. I make meatloaf and mashed potatoes; that's pretty much it." He rubbed his chin. "Would you and Robbie like to go to a Whitecaps game with me next Monday night?"

Jenifer had to stop and think a second, until she remembered the Whitecaps were a baseball team.

She had to give it to him. Suggesting things Robbie might enjoy seemed to make it hard for her to say no.

If he'd invited her anywhere other than to the firehouse the other night, she would have turned him down. She'd shied away from anything that might lead to a romantic relationship since her husband died. But Matt was different somehow. He was friendly without outwardly flirting with her. He made Robbie important. Included him. And by doing that, he was slowly drawing her in.

Robbie had never been to a real game before. She should've taken him long before now, but she didn't know a whole lot about baseball.

Out of earshot, Robbie stood up to throw out his ice cream wrapper. Nate called him over to one of the trucks. Matt kept his eyes on her as he waited for an answer.

"You want to take us to a baseball game?"

The corners of his mouth turned up into a bright, disarming smile. "Yes. I do."

Seconds passed as she wondered why she didn't just tell him no, even though she wanted to say yes. It was shaky ground. Patrick's death still weighed on her. Her attraction to Matt made her nervous.

Finally, she looked up at him. "Okay," she said before she could change her mind. "We'll go to the game with you."

~

*a*fter dinner that night, Matt stretched out on a black leather recliner in the dayroom at the firehouse and closed his eyes. Nate read the evening paper in the chair beside him. The television was off, and the rest of the guys were all somewhere else. One company was out on a call.

"What did Jessie want when she called?" Matt didn't open his eyes. He didn't have to ask if it was Jessie on the phone when Nate came looking for him earlier. Matt had blocked her number on his cell, and no one ever called him on the station phone.

"She wanted to know if you were here. I almost told her no, but then I thought it'd be better if you handled it."

Matt opened his eyes and looked at him. "Thanks for not saying anything in front of Jenifer."

Nate glanced over the top of his newspaper. "Did you ask her to the game?"

"She said yes."

"Did you ask her about her son's father?"

Matt pushed his recliner upright and focused on what he considered to be the most salient point. "No, but I don't believe she's married." His gut told him that the night he met her. He was even more certain now that she had come by the firehouse and then said yes to the game.

Henry came in from outside and grabbed a bottle of water from the refrigerator. He had joined the fire department about a year after Matt and Nate. The three of them became close friends after Henry's wife, Lauren, invited Matt and Nate to dinner. She liked to use them to try out new recipes for her catering business. It wasn't uncommon for Henry's father, a former firefighter turned minister, along with his mother and younger sister, Rachel, to join them for dinner. Nine years later, Matt considered them all family.

Henry walked into the room and sat in the recliner on the other side of Matt. "Are you talking about Robbie's father?"

Matt nodded. Henry looked grim. "His father died."

Matt and Nate turned and looked at him at the same time. Matt squared his shoulders. "How do you know that?"

"He told me."

"Jesus, Henry." Nate put his paper down. "You grilled a six-year-old?"

"No, I did not." Henry shot him a dirty look. "He asked me why I became a firefighter. I told him it was because my father used to be a firefighter. That's when he said his father died."

Nate had been right.

Matt's cell phone rang. He didn't recognize the number. Suspicious, he let the call go to voicemail. Seconds later, the phone pinged with a new message. Reluctantly, he listened to Jessie's voicemail. *Please, I have to talk to you. It's important. You need to call me.*

The hell he did.

4

*J*enifer stood at the bottom of the stairs with her hands on her hips and silently counted to ten. Robbie didn't see her. He was too busy watching the Yankees game on television with a juice box and bag of potato chips, obviously taking exception to the "no food in the living room" rule. He'd grabbed the chips while she took a shower. It was four thirty. Matt would be there in less than an hour to go to the game.

Robbie still didn't look up when she sat behind him. She looked over his shoulder to check the score. The Yankees were ahead by three runs at the top of the ninth inning. The other team—she had absolutely no idea who they were—was up to bat.

"You need to get into the shower," she said, then didn't know whether to laugh or get mad at him when he raised his hand for her to be quiet.

The next batter struck out. Robbie jumped to his feet, cheering loudly, and dumped his potato chips all over the clean wood floors. That was when he finally sneaked a peek back at her.

Jenifer stood and pointed to his mess. "Clean that up. And then get into the shower."

He wrinkled his brow at the warm sunlight spilling through the living room windows. "Now?"

"I have a surprise for you." She waited until this afternoon to tell him they were going to the game. Otherwise he would have made her crazy counting down the days. "You need to get cleaned up because we're going to a Whitecaps game with Matt tonight."

He grinned so hard, his face might have cracked. "Tonight?"

"Soon." She jerked her head toward the stairs. "You need to hurry up."

He looked down at his Yankees shirt. The one her Yankee fan father had given to him, having made his only grandson a fan too.

"What?"

"I have to find my Whitecaps jersey."

Jenifer shrugged and put up her hands. She had no idea which of his jerseys belonged to what team. "You're on your own, mister." She pointed up to the shower. "Just make sure you're clean when you put it on."

A little while later, Robbie sat on the front steps wearing a blue-and-white jersey and baseball cap. He was a leftie like his father and wore his leather glove on his right hand. The early July heat didn't seem to bother him at all as he waited for Matt to come home. When Matt parked in front of his house a few minutes later, Jenifer came outside, ready to leave.

As soon as Matt got out of his truck, Robbie scrambled down the porch steps to meet him. Matt caught her eye as he crossed the street to her house. "Hey." He pulled off his dark sunglasses and smiled at her. "You look great."

She glanced down at her tank top and shorts and then back at him. He wore a fire department baseball cap, cargo shorts, and a blue T-shirt. Her smile twitched. "You look nice, too."

Robbie tipped his head back and scrunched his eyebrows at

Matt. Matt clapped his hands and rubbed them together like he was embarrassed to be caught ogling someone's mother. "Are you guys ready to go?"

Jenifer took her keys from her pocket and walked over to her car in the driveway. "I'll have to drive tonight."

"You don't want me to drive?"

She looked around him at his truck across the street. He'd forgotten something important if he'd meant to drive to the game tonight. "You don't have a back seat."

Matt looked at Robbie and shook his head. "I should've thought about that. I'm sorry."

"It's okay." Robbie grabbed his hand and pulled him to the car. "Did you go to a fire today?"

"No, things were pretty slow at work." Matt opened the back door and watched Robbie buckle himself in before he checked to make sure the seat belt was secure.

Jenifer grinned when she got behind the wheel and listened to Matt tell Robbie about his day. Robbie was so engrossed he didn't bother to complain about his booster seat like he usually did. When Matt got in beside her, she said, "You're going to have to give me directions to the stadium."

"You've never been to a game?"

"No baseball games. Just basketball." She'd gone to Patrick's games in college. Games she tried not to think about right now.

Matt twisted around in his seat, giving Robbie a hopeful look. "Do you like baseball?"

Robbie adjusted his ball cap and punched his hand in his glove. "I love baseball."

"Do you have a favorite team?"

"The Yankees. They won today."

"They sure did." Matt grinned. "They beat the Reds."

Jenifer gave Matt a quick look and laughed. "The Reds?"

Matt raised a brow and pointed for her to turn right. "The Cincinnati Reds? You've never heard of them?"

Still laughing, now at herself, she said, "Oh. The *Cincinnati*

Reds." She shrugged a shoulder and lied. "I've heard of them. Aren't you from Michigan? Isn't there a team closer to home for you to follow?"

"The Tigers. I like the Yankees." Matt sank back in his seat. "Are you sure you want to go to this game?"

She smiled as the stadium came into sight. "Sure, I'm sure. It'll be fun."

～

*I*nside the stadium, Matt took her hand and guided them through the crowd. Their seats were on the lower level behind home plate, where Robbie could watch the players warm up on the field. It was a clear, balmy night. The stands filled up quickly. Queen's "We Will Rock You" played over the loudspeakers and a vendor hawked pink cotton candy in the stands behind them.

Jenifer waited with Robbie while Matt went to get hot dogs and drinks for them. She leaned back in her seat, stretched out her legs, and let the sun warm her face. It seemed forever since she'd been out like this. Relaxed, not responsible for every little thing. Something as simple as not having to debate Robbie about using the ladies' room instead of the men's room made the evening more enjoyable.

She sat up when Matt got back and helped him with the drinks. "These are great seats," she said as he handed Robbie a hot dog. She held Robbie's lemonade for him while he stood at the railing before the game. "How did you get them?"

Matt grinned and lowered his head so she could read his hat. "They give us tickets at the firehouse every now and then."

"Well, nice job, Mr. Barnes." She tapped her water bottle to his and took the hot dog he offered her. "And thank you for dinner."

"My pleasure."

Robbie finally sat between them when the game started. After a few minutes, he began to eye Matt's French fries.

Matt held his fries out for him. "Do you play baseball?"

Robbie picked out a fry, dunked it in ketchup, and nodded. "Do you play?"

"I did in college a long time ago."

Jenifer looked over at Matt. "Where did you go to school?"

"Penn State. I wanted to play baseball. My mother wanted me to get a degree. I joined the fire department after I graduated."

Embarrassed Robbie was eating Matt's dinner, Jenifer stuck her hand out to stop him from eating more French fries. Matt shook his head. "He's fine. Where did you go to school?"

"Michigan, and then Western Michigan for my master's after Robbie was born."

The mascots on the field started firing Whitecaps T-shirts into the stands with giant slingshots. Matt got to his feet with Robbie to try to catch one. "You're a teacher?"

"Third grade." Jenifer stood, put her hands high in the air, and one of the guys launching T-shirts not twenty feet away looked her straight in the eye and smiled. She caught the shirt and handed it to Robbie, and then laughed when Matt made a face like she'd cheated.

It seemed as if he'd made her smile or laugh from the moment he got to her house that night.

At the end of the eighth inning, Robbie slumped against Jenifer's shoulder. He'd fallen asleep sometime after the seventh inning, when he'd belted out "Take Me Out to the Ballgame" and entertained the crowd around them.

Matt leaned over Robbie and tapped her shoulder. "Do you want to take him home?"

"You don't mind leaving?"

"No." He stood. "Do you want me to carry him?"

She looked down at Robbie and then back at Matt. "Do you mind?"

Matt shook his head. He picked Robbie up and rested his head on his shoulder. It took him a second to arrange Robbie's long legs as Jenifer gathered up his hat and glove before they headed out to the parking lot.

When they got home, Robbie was still sound asleep. They got out of the car and Matt went to open the back door.

"You don't have to carry him again." Jenifer looked over his shoulder into the back seat. She hated to wake Robbie, but she couldn't carry him herself, and she didn't want to ask Matt to do it again. "He'll go right back to sleep this time."

"I got him." Matt lifted Robbie out of the car and carried him behind Jenifer into the house. She led him upstairs where he laid Robbie carefully onto his bed without waking him. He nodded toward the door. "I'll wait for you outside."

The nightlight at the top of the stairs cast a shadow across the doorway, leaving the rest of the room dark as Matt went downstairs. Her heart beat faster as she thought about whether or not it had been wise to go out with him tonight. Her attraction to him was strong. It made her uneasy. Wishing her life was different only made it harder.

After she tucked Robbie into bed, she went to find Matt sitting in a rocking chair under the porch light. A full moon brightened the sky. Next door, kids dribbled a basketball in the driveway and laughter followed a hard slam against the backboard. She sat in the chair beside him and said, tentatively, "I bet we were more than you bargained for tonight."

"Not at all." His bright-blue eyes turned serious. "Can I ask you a personal question?"

Jenifer leaned back into her chair and nodded.

"Where's Robbie's father?"

She took a deep breath and let it out slowly. It was harder to talk to him about her husband than she had expected. Especially when she was starting to have feelings for him. "Patrick was killed in a car accident two years ago."

Matt lowered his head and his voice softened. "I'm sorry."

"We were married for three years." She looked down at her hands folded on her lap. The night had fallen quiet after the basketball game next door ended. "We met in college."

"Are you from Michigan?"

"No, I grew up in Chicago. Patrick was from Grand Rapids. His parents still live in Forest Hills." Not far from the home she'd lived in when she was married and then sold after Patrick's death. The house had been all Patrick—much too large and extravagant for her taste. She'd meant for him to live there after the divorce, and she had no desire to keep it after his death.

"Are you close to his parents?"

"No." A heavy weight settled deep in her chest. An old wound she thought might never go away. "We had a falling out after Patrick died. Robbie still sees them sometimes." Rather than explain, she said, "Tell me about your family."

"There's not much to tell. My mother remarried a few years ago and moved to California with her husband. We're close. Her husband, Ben, is a good guy. They just live far away."

"What about your dad? Do you have any brothers or sisters?"

He shook his head. "I never met my father." He sat forward and shifted in his chair. "My parents divorced before I was born. I don't have any other family."

"Have you ever been married?"

"No."

Her mind drifted to thoughts of Jessie. The night she met Matt, he'd told her there was nothing between them. He'd also mentioned Jessie had a problem with him, and she wondered again what he had meant.

He reached over and covered her hand with his. "What are you thinking about?"

She looked down at his warm fingers engulfing hers in a gesture that felt both tender and protective. "Nothing. It's none of my business."

"Whatever it is, I'm pretty sure I want it to be your business."

A little more confident now that she wasn't crossing any lines, she asked, "Will you tell me about Jessie?"

He rubbed a hand over his mouth, failing to hide the corners that had turned down. "Jessie and I dated in high school. She moved to Florida after graduation. I never saw her again until the night you and I met."

And she still had a problem with him? "Are you still friends?"

"No," Matt said with a quick shake of his head.

Jenifer got the vague impression Jessie wasn't that simple. But it still didn't matter. It was Jenifer's past holding her back, not Matt's.

Matt gave her hand a squeeze and waited for her to look at him. "Will you have dinner with me next Saturday?"

Her stomach sank. "I'm not sure that's such a great idea."

"Why not?"

"Because I don't know if I'm ready to do this."

"Consider this a test then." The corner of his mouth lifted when she hesitated, and it seemed she might be wavering. "Please?"

He squeezed her hand again. This time sliding his fingers between hers until she found she didn't have the willpower to tell him no. "Okay. All right. I'll go to dinner with you."

He grinned at her like one of her third-grade students. "I wore you down, didn't I?"

"I have a feeling you're good at that."

His grin turned into a warm, sweet smile as he brushed his thumb over her wrist. "I have a feeling I'll have to be."

Jenifer sighed. The poor man, he was probably right.

5

_T_he next day, Jenifer picked up Robbie's baseball glove by the front door and the ticket stubs from the night before fell onto the floor. "Robbie!" She stuck the ticket stubs into her back pocket and put the glove into the coat closet as she called up the stairs. "Hurry up before your grandparents get here."

She checked her pocket one more time, making sure the tickets were out of sight. She wasn't worried Patrick's parents would see them and guess she'd been on a date, but she hid them just the same. She'd told Robbie not to mention the game to them either, but his ability to keep a secret was suspect. If he did mention Matt, she wouldn't lie. She just wouldn't volunteer personal details about her life after barely speaking to her in-laws for more than two years.

Bare-chested, Robbie leaned over the railing at the top of the stairs. "I can't find my Spider-Man T-shirt."

"Well, find something to wear because they're going to be here any minute." She looked out the front window before she went to take a pan of brownies from the oven for later. When she checked the window again, Robert and Elizabeth were parking in the driveway.

"They're here!" Robbie bounded down the stairs, yanking the missing Spider-Man shirt over his head. It was only a couple months since he'd visited with them. For her, it would be the first time since Patrick died that she'd see them for more than the five minutes it took her to drop Robbie off at their house.

She stood behind Robbie, brushing her hands nervously over her peach blouse and white cotton shorts as he opened the door.

Robert came into the house first. He was in his late fifties, six foot four, with thick silver hair and hazel eyes. Dressed casually in tan trousers and a navy-blue golf shirt, he smiled cautiously. "Hello, Jenifer."

Before she could say anything, Robbie threw his arms around his grandfather's waist. Robert bent to give him a hug. "You are getting so tall."

Behind Robert, Elizabeth kept her eyes on Robbie. She was the same age as her husband, slender, with shoulder-length hair the same dark-blond hair as her grandson. She gave Robbie a hug and a kiss, then wiped a smudge of pink lipstick the same color as her sleeveless cotton dress from his cheek. "I've missed you, sweetheart," she said.

Robbie was blissfully unaware of her bitter feelings toward Jenifer after Patrick's death. They had all made sure not to expose him to any more heartache. He'd been only three years old when his father died. He loved his grandparents. Jenifer could see how much he missed them. But until Robert had called to invite her to dinner a couple days ago, she had no idea how to bring them together.

Robbie took his grandparents by the hand. "Do you want to see my new room?"

Robert met Jenifer's eyes over the top of Robbie's head.

It came as a bit of a shock to find herself in a position of authority with her in-laws. Not that she had ever known them to be controlling or demanding in the past, at least not before Patrick died, and certainly not Robert. It was more that she'd always deferred to them, never quite putting her own influence to the test. Now, here they were, asking permission to see her home.

She drew a deep breath and stepped back with a bit more confidence. "Please. Come see inside."

Robert kissed her cheek. "It's nice to see you again, Jenifer."

Robbie pulled Elizabeth farther into the house, her gaze traveling across the living room until it settled on a black-and-white portrait of Jenifer and Robbie over the fireplace mantle. The photograph had been taken at the Nichols home as a gift for Patrick's birthday and had hung in his old study. "You have a lovely home," she said quietly.

Robbie started for the stairs. Robert let Elizabeth go first. "Are we going up to see your room?" Robert asked.

Robbie looked back over his shoulder. "Do you want to?"

As Robert smiled, his face lit up with pleasure. He put his hand at Elizabeth's back. "Absolutely we do."

Robbie showed them the entire house, including all three bedrooms and bathroom on the second floor, the updated kitchen and bathroom on the first floor, and the dark, empty basement he described as "a little scary." He led them through the dining room into the living room and finished the tour back at the front door where he sat on the wood floor and pulled on his shoes.

Once they got out to the driveway, Jenifer moved Robbie's booster seat from her car to Robert's, where he secured it into the back seat. "How long ago did you move in?" he asked, stepping aside so Robbie could climb into the car.

"I closed about a week ago." She was proud of herself for buying the house on her own. She had a career because she wanted one, not because she needed one. Patrick had been a successful real estate developer with his father's firm. She'd spent none of his three-million-dollar estate or the life insurance money. Instead, she'd put the estate into a revocable trust for Robbie. The two million dollars in life insurance was well-invested and not something she thought about often.

Robbie grumbled, buckling his seat belt when she slid in beside him. He hunched his shoulders and pouted. "I'm too big for a booster seat."

He was not too big, or too old, yet it was an ongoing argument. One she ignored now as she glanced out the window and saw Matt's truck was gone from his driveway.

Elizabeth turned around in the front seat and said to Robbie. "Are you excited to go to a new school?"

He nodded with enthusiasm and sat up straight. "I got to meet my new teacher. Mr. Ryan."

Jenifer gave him a smile. Part of the arrangement she had made when she agreed to change schools was that Robbie be assigned to Jeff Ryan's first-grade classroom. Jeff was a good teacher but even more, she wanted another strong male figure in Robbie's life. Her father spent as much time as he could with him, but her parents lived three hours away. Robert and Elizabeth lived much closer. Robert still oversaw the daily operation of his company, but Jenifer felt certain he would make time for his grandson, if only they could find a way past their estrangement.

"Grandma, guess what?" Robbie said out of the blue. "I got stung by bees."

"It was a few days ago." Jenifer lifted his arm and quickly showed Elizabeth the faded marks on his skin. "He's okay now."

Robbie pulled his arm back and locked eyes on his grandmother. "I almost got hit by a car, too."

Elizabeth blinked hard, and her face paled. Robert's eyes shot up to the rearview mirror. "What do you mean? What happened?"

Robbie pinched his lips and studied the marks on his arm as if he hadn't just scared his grandparents half to death. "Matt saved me," he said matter-of-factly.

Jenifer closed her hand over Robbie's knee. She sent him a look telling him she would finish the rest of the story. "His baseball hit a bees nest Friday night. The bees chased him into the street. Matt's a neighbor. He caught Robbie before I could when a car came down the road."

Elizabeth studied Robbie from head to toes. "But you're all right?"

"I'm okay," he said, perking up when Robert turned into a diner Patrick had pointed out to Jenifer years ago. Inside, a hostess cleared a booth for them as a waitress spotted Robert and Elizabeth at the door and rushed to greet them. Older than the other waitresses, she was short and round with a large bosom, her eyes the same bluish gray as the hair knotted on top of her head. "My two favorite customers." Her smile widened when she saw Robbie holding Elizabeth's hand. "And you brought your grandson."

Robert bent and gave the woman a familiar hug. "We did. This is Robbie and our daughter-in-law, Jenifer."

The woman didn't seem to take notice of the hesitation in Robert's voice. "Alice," she said, looking delighted to meet them. She put her hands on her wide hips and shook her head at Robbie. "You know, you look just like your daddy did when he was your age."

Jenifer swallowed past the lump in her throat. Elizabeth looked down and brushed the corner of her eye.

When the hostess returned, Alice took the menus from her and led the way to an empty booth by the front windows. She set the menus down on the table. "Take your time, and I'll be back with your water and coffee."

Robbie slid first across the red vinyl bench next to the window. Elizabeth sat next to him. Robert let Jenifer into the booth first to sit across from Robbie.

"We used to bring your daddy here for breakfast when he was a little boy," Robert said. "We've known Alice for a long time."

"Twenty years." Elizabeth picked up a red crayon and started drawing lines for a tic-tac-toe game on the back of her placemat.

Robbie picked up a blue crayon and drew a circle in the center square.

Alice returned with their water and coffee for Robert. She took their order. Her eyes met Elizabeth's when Robbie ordered macaroni and cheese. Alice smiled at him. "Your daddy used to order that when he was a little boy."

Robert sipped his coffee and watched Robbie win the first game. He didn't appear the least bit out of place. Founder and CEO of Nichols Commercial Group, one of the largest real estate companies in Michigan, he was known as an unpretentious man. One who easily checked his prominence at the door of a small family diner and assumed his role of grandfather to his only grandson. "How did your Little League do at the end of the season?"

Robbie waited for Elizabeth to draw up another game. "We came in second place."

"Your daddy played baseball," Elizabeth said. "Did you know that?"

Robbie cocked his head. Jenifer didn't know Patrick had played baseball either. He played basketball in high school, and she'd watched him play in college.

"He played baseball when he was younger," Elizabeth said without looking up. "I remember we used to go to the batting cages. We'd have contests to see who could hit the fastest ball." She laughed softly and drew a red X on the placemat. "I know he was only ten, but I still beat him every once in a while."

Alice didn't interrupt as she set their dinners on the table while Elizabeth told Robbie more stories about his father. "When he was twelve years old, he was already five and a half feet tall. One of the basketball coaches had spotted him in school and asked if he knew how to play."

Robbie gave Jenifer a puzzled look. Robert grinned and gestured toward Jenifer with his coffee mug. "That's taller than your mommy right now."

"Well, after that, Grandpa hung a basketball hoop in the

driveway. I played with your daddy almost every day. After a while, the only time I could beat him was when he let me win."

Robbie laughed around a mouthful of macaroni and cheese. Apparently, he couldn't imagine his often-reserved grandmother shooting hoops and playing keep-away with his dad. That, and he knew from photographs that Patrick was as tall as his grandfather, and Elizabeth was almost a foot shorter.

A little while later, Alice delivered the check and left four mints on the table. Robbie swiped one of the candies and tried to slide by Jenifer in the booth. "I have to go to the bathroom."

Robert got to his feet. "How about I take him?"

Alone with Elizabeth, Jenifer studied her napkin, folding it in half. And then in half again. Her eyes darted to the restroom as she wished Robbie would hurry back.

After what seemed forever, Elizabeth folded her hands on the table and leaned forward. "I'm sorry, Jenifer."

Jenifer went still.

Elizabeth's voice shook as she cleared her throat. "I never should have said those things to you after Patrick died."

Before Elizabeth could say more, Robbie started out of the restroom ahead of Robert. Elizabeth saw him and quickly dabbed her eyes with a napkin. Jenifer debated what to do, and then she stood, catching Robbie's hand before he could sit down again. All she knew for certain was if they were going to have this discussion, it would not be in front of him.

Robert returned. He glanced between his wife and Jenifer. His expression blank, he reached for the bill. "Are we ready to go?"

Robbie stuffed two more mints into his pocket, popped another into his mouth, and looked up at his grandmother. "Are you coming back to our house?"

Elizabeth gave him a small smile as she took Robert's hand and stood up from the table. "I'm not sure."

Jenifer breathed deeply, still reeling from Elizabeth's apology. "It's still early. We can have dessert at home if you'd like."

After a quick look at his wife, Robert said, "Thank you. That sounds wonderful."

Once they got back to the house, Jenifer brought Robbie's glove outside so he could play catch with Robert in the front yard. Elizabeth went to sit in one of the rocking chairs on the porch to watch. Before Jenifer went inside for dessert, she saw Matt's truck back at his house. When she returned with the brownies a few minutes later, Robert was sitting on the porch, and Elizabeth was throwing the ball to Robbie in the middle of the yard.

Robert took the plate of brownies from her and set them on the table beside him. "Thank you for agreeing to go to dinner with us tonight."

Jenifer sat in the chair beside him. Nervous to finally have this conversation, she kept her eyes on her son. "I think it's important for Robbie to spend more time with you."

"I agree. But we would have understood if you'd said no. You have every right to be angry with us. But if we can make things right, we want to try."

Jenifer couldn't imagine what had happened for Elizabeth to change her mind and want to see her again. She blamed Jenifer for her only son's death, for all the same reasons Jenifer blamed herself. Robert had vehemently denied Jenifer's involvement after the accident, but neither woman had believed him. It was Elizabeth's rage and Jenifer's guilt that had divided their family for three long years.

"How are we supposed to do this?" Jenifer asked. "Where do we even start?"

"I think that's going to have to be up to you to decide."

Elizabeth caught the ball one more time from Robbie, then raised her hands and pretended to be tired. She waved at her husband. "Your turn?"

Robert got to his feet, straightening his trousers. "Do you have another glove?" he asked Robbie.

"In the garage." Robbie spun around and raced to the top of the driveway. "Come on."

Elizabeth took Robert's seat. She seemed to gather up her courage until Jenifer heard Robbie's voice well away in the backyard. "What's happened between us is my fault. Robert was right," Elizabeth said. "I should not have blamed you for Patrick's death."

Plagued with guilt, Jenifer pressed her fingertips to her temples. "It's true. I know it's true." There was no other way to explain it.

After the accident, Robert had tried to tell them Patrick was driving from Detroit to his office in Grand Rapids, not rushing home to save his marriage like Jenifer and Elizabeth believed.

"It's not true. I didn't know you two were having trouble before he died. He never said anything to me. You never acted any differently. It was a shock to find out you had asked him for a divorce. But, please, believe me. You had nothing to do with Patrick's death. There's nothing you could have done to change what happened."

"I tried. I loved him. But we failed at marriage." Tears welled in Jenifer's eyes. "Robbie is the best part of me. I don't ever regret getting pregnant. But I can't help thinking that if Patrick and I hadn't gotten married and had raised him separately, Robbie would still have his father. And you would still have your son."

"You can't think that way. It would have torn Patrick apart not to see his son every day. And he loved you, too. He just didn't show you the way he should have." Elizabeth met Jenifer's eyes and her voice softened. "But he's gone. You have to start over again. And both Robert and I want you to be happy."

Jenifer remembered the baseball tickets in her pocket and all of the times she'd thought of Matt since last night. She still felt responsible for Patrick's death, but after talking to Elizabeth tonight, she felt a small weight lift from her shoulders.

Robbie ran around to the front of the house as the streetlights blinked on. Jenifer held out the plate of brownies for him. He grabbed one and handed another to his grandfather behind him.

Robert took a bite of the brownie, sharing a look with his wife. "We should probably head home."

Elizabeth stood and held out a hand for Robbie to walk with her to the car. Jenifer trailed behind them, watching Jessie's car turn into Matt's driveway.

Taking his keys from his pocket, Robert looked disappointed to leave. "Would it be all right if we called you again soon?"

Jenifer rested her hands on Robbie's shoulders and tried to make sense of everything that had happened tonight. "If you call tomorrow, we can talk about next weekend."

Across the street, the front lights turned on at Matt's house when he opened the front door. Out of the corner of her eye, she saw him looking at her. She touched the tickets in her pocket and hoped with all her heart everything he had told her about Jessie was true.

6

*S*aturday evening, Jenifer waited beside Robert's car as Robbie climbed into the back seat.

"Thank you again for letting him stay overnight." Robert took the Spider-Man backpack off his grandson's shoulders and set it on the seat next to him. "Elizabeth's got Patrick's room all ready for him. She's pulled out pictures, puzzles, Patrick's favorite books. I wouldn't be surprised if she hooked up the VCR to play the old Disney tapes."

"You're doing me a favor." She didn't tell them her plans when she had asked if Robbie could stay with them. It was better to keep tonight under the radar until she knew for sure she was ready for all of this. If Robert thought it curious she wore heels and a sapphire-blue sheath, he didn't say. "And I think Robbie might be even more excited about tonight than his grandmother."

Robert stuck his head into the back seat of the car. "Do you have everything?" he asked Robbie.

Nodding, Robbie dropped his baseball glove onto his lap and tried to tell him he didn't need the new booster seat they'd bought for their car.

Jenifer came around to give him a kiss goodbye as Robert got ready to leave. "I love you. Be good."

Robert braced an elbow through his open window. "We'll be home all evening." Then, almost as an afterthought, he smiled. "And have a wonderful time."

Matt came outside of his house as soon as Robert drove away. Jenifer collected her small leather bag and keys from the roof of her car. Thinking he might want to drive this time, she went to meet him at the end of his driveway.

They smiled at each other for a moment as he took her hand. "You look beautiful."

"Thank you. You're pretty handsome yourself." He wore dark jeans and a pin-striped button-down cuffed to his elbows. She discovered she had a fondness for the light scruff that darkened his face and brought out the blue in his eyes. "Will you tell me where we're going?" she asked.

"Do you mind if it's a surprise?" He sounded a bit nervous as he opened the truck door for her.

"No." She settled comfortably in her seat, excited. It was a long time since someone had tried to surprise her.

He slipped on a pair of dark sunglasses as he pulled out of the driveway. "Where's Robbie tonight?"

"He's staying with his grandparents."

He gave her a baffled look. "Your folks are in town?"

She shook her head. He must have remembered her telling him after the baseball game that she wasn't close to Patrick's parents. "He's with his father's parents."

He met her eyes, opened his mouth, then closed it again. He turned on the radio. His hand was still on the knob when Garth Brooks came on and he changed the station.

Grateful he didn't press the issue with Robbie, she teased him. "You don't like country music?"

"I'm sorry." He quickly switched the music back. "Do you like it?"

She shrugged. "I like lots of different music. Maroon 5, Ellie Goulding, Jason Mraz. What do you like?"

He glanced sideways, his fingers tapping idly on the steering wheel. "I'll tell you, but don't laugh."

Now she was curious. "Why would I laugh at the music you like?"

"Because I listen to the oldies. Stuff from the sixties and seventies. Neil Young, Seger, Creedence."

She leaned her head back in the seat and looked at him. "I like the oldies, too."

He lifted his brow like he didn't believe her. Well, he was wrong. She'd grown up listening to her father's favorite Motown music.

"Tell me, who doesn't love Diana Ross, Stevie Wonder, Marvin Gaye?"

"You like R&B? I'll have to remember that."

They drove west for about thirty minutes until Jenifer spotted Lake Michigan in the distance. Dozens of restaurants dotted the shoreline. Many of them she had been to with Patrick. Instinctively, her hand went to where she'd worn her wedding band on a chain around her neck. She'd taken it off tonight for the first time. A test, like tonight's date, to see if she was really ready to start over.

Minutes later, Matt turned into an unfamiliar marina. She let out a breath she hadn't realized she was holding. An eclectic mix of powerboats and sailboats tied to floating docks, or moored a short distance from shore, rocked gently in the warm summer breeze. Matt parked his truck at the edge of the water and narrowed his gaze out at the lake, then checked the time.

Jenifer took in the parking lot filled with cars, trailered boats, and a small clubhouse with people milling around outside. Before she could ask if they were having dinner there, his phone pinged from his pocket.

"Wait here," he said, then came around to open her door without checking his phone.

"Where are we going?"

He pointed to a large powerboat secluded at the end of a long concrete seawall.

She blocked the light with her hand and squinted into the sun. "Is that your boat?"

He smiled, and for a second, she thought he might keep her guessing. "No. It belongs to my mother's husband, Ben."

"They keep their boat in Michigan? Not California?"

"It's expensive to move, and Ben loves it too much to sell. He keeps saying he'll retire soon and they'll spend their summers here."

A breeze kicked up as they got closer to the water, and Jenifer held her hair back to see his surprise. Fifty feet or more in length, the Sea Ray was impressive with its canvas down and the lights below turned on. Beside the boat was a small table draped with a white tablecloth and topped with white taper candles. Everything was arranged under a slow setting sun as the water rippled across the bay.

She stopped and stared. "Did you do this?"

"Do you like it?"

For a moment, words escaped her. "It's beautiful."

Matt started to say something when his phone pinged again. He put his hand on the small of her back. "I'll show you around."

She gestured to his phone. "You don't want to check that?"

He gave her a cryptic smile. "No, it's okay." He led her onto the boat after she slipped off her heels and then followed her down below.

She'd half-expected to discover takeout boxes in the full-service galley after he had confessed at the firehouse he wasn't much of a cook. But the smooth granite countertops were bare, except for two wine glasses and a corkscrew, which he used to open a bottle of chardonnay he retrieved from the refrigerator.

Jenifer gazed over his shoulder to see more of the boat—dark mahogany doors, ivory leather, and polished wood floors. Matt could stand easily without his head touching the ceiling, and even with outstretched arms, he wouldn't reach the sides of the boat from where he stood.

He poured the wine and handed her a glass before he scrolled through his phone, selected Motown for music, and connected to the boat's wireless speakers. He turned on more lights and showed her the salon. She imagined quiet, peaceful mornings curled up on the leather sofa and late nights watching movies on the large flat-screen television. "Do you spend a lot of time here?"

"No, I only come down a couple of times during the summer to make sure everything's okay. Ben's daughter spends more time here than I do." He sipped his wine as he opened the doors to the two sleeping cabins to show her inside. Each had a raised queen-size bed fitted with ivory bedding and matching pillows. Bell-shaped pewter wall sconces hung on either side of two long rectangular portholes over the mocha-colored upholstered headboards. Mahogany wardrobes with pewter fittings filled an entire wall in each room.

After a quick look at his phone, he motioned her forward. "If you're ready, we can go back up."

From the boat's cockpit, Jenifer could see the two silver warming covers on the table that hadn't been there earlier. The candles flickered in the cool breeze as the sun set low in the sky. Matt stepped out onto the dock and placed the domes into the back of the boat before he held out her chair.

"This is wonderful. Thank you." Jenifer opened a cloth napkin on her lap and waited for him to sit.

"You're welcome. I had help. Do you remember meeting Henry at the firehouse?"

She nodded as she bit into a broiled sea scallop. She remembered meeting both Henry and Nate. Henry had shown Robbie the fire engine. Nate had been the one to entertain him while Matt invited them to the baseball game.

"His wife, Lauren, is a caterer. She was sending the texts earlier."

"Please tell her dinner was delicious." Jenifer shivered in the light breeze. "Does your mother know we're here tonight?"

"I told her."

"How often do you get to see her?"

"They come back a couple times a year. Ben's daughter is married with kids. She lives about an hour away, so they usually spend a few days with me before they visit his grandchildren. I try to get out to see them once or twice a year."

Jenifer watched him over her wine glass, thinking of her parents. "If you ever have kids, I bet you'll see your mother all the time."

She caught the flick of Matt's eyebrows as the breeze started to kick up.

"I'll be right back." He rose and went into the boat, then returned with the opened bottle of wine and a denim jacket.

She slipped the jacket on as he held it out for her. "Thank you."

"Tell me more about your family."

"My parents talk about moving to Michigan after they retire, but my sister and her husband live in Arizona. She's going to have a baby next year, so we'll see where they end up moving."

"You're lucky. I always wanted to have a brother or sister. Or even grandparents. My mother's parents died before I was born."

"So it was just you and your mom growing up?"

He poked a spear of asparagus and took a bite. "That's it."

Jenifer couldn't help but feel sad for him as he set down his fork and topped off their wine glasses. At least Robbie had her family, and now Patrick's.

"Don't get me wrong," he said. "For the most part, I had a great childhood."

"Have you always lived in Grand Rapids?"

"My entire life. Where did you grow up?"

"Outside of Chicago. My parents still live there."

He pushed back his chair as they finished the last of their dinner. "You're cold. Let's go back inside. I'll make coffee." He shook his head when she picked up the plates. "We can leave those here."

She glanced over her shoulder toward the parking lot some distance away. She imagined Lauren Miller wishing they would hurry up and go back inside the boat so she could clean up and go home.

Matt followed her gaze. "Lauren's not there. She won't be back for a little while."

After he made coffee, Matt passed her a cup and joined her on the sofa. For a moment, she thought he might kiss her. Did she want him to? Yes. Maybe. Or maybe she just needed to know it would be okay if he did.

She shrugged off his jacket and draped it over the side of the sofa. Sitting back, she saw a long thin scar behind his ear. "What happened there?"

He lowered his head and ran a hand over the back of his ear. "I got hit by a car when I was a kid."

A chill ran down her spine at the same time she envisioned Robbie running in front of Jessie's car. "How badly were you hurt?"

He seemed to think for a second as their eyes met. "The worst of it was a busted pelvis. Doctors said I wouldn't have kids. But then my girlfriend got pregnant in high school and told me I was the father."

Their eyes held as she gradually put all the pieces together. "Jessie?"

He nodded.

"What did you do?"

He sipped his coffee before answering. "It was the end of senior year. We'd broken up by then. I couldn't believe the baby was mine, and I asked her for a paternity test."

She could see from his grim expression he believed he'd made a huge mistake. "What did she do then?"

"She blew up. Told me it was my loss that I didn't believe her. After we graduated, she moved back to Florida, where she was originally from. She told me she was going to have an abortion."

"Do you believe now the baby was yours?"

His eyes seemed to darken with shame and regret. "I do. I saw a doctor afterward. Turns out it is possible for me to father a child. The thing is, it's not likely to ever happen again."

Jenifer set her coffee down on a side table, willing to bare of bit of her soul in return. "I'm sorry. In a way, I understand how something like that will change your life."

His thick dark brows furrowed. "You do?"

She half-smiled at his surprise, as if he perceived her as pure and innocent. "I was pregnant with Robbie when I married Patrick. We were a few years older than you and Jessie. We met my freshman year of college, and we got married near the end of my senior year."

Matt leaned forward and set aside his coffee.

"I turned Patrick down at first, too." She remembered how he had begged and pleaded with her to change her mind. He was at the end of graduate school and had a job working for his father. He'd been ready for marriage and a family. She'd still had graduate school ahead of her. A career. And a nagging doubt either of those goals would ever be a priority to him.

It turned out she was right.

"But you wanted the baby?"

"Yes." She'd never once considered ending her pregnancy. "But I'd thought it would be better if we raised Robbie separately."

"He didn't agree?"

Jenifer shook her head. Quite the contrary. "Patrick was very traditional. His parents, his father especially, always put his family first. My family is fairly traditional, too. So, in the end, tradition won out."

Matt rested his arm over the back of the sofa, angling his head so their foreheads almost touched. "You're lucky. You have Robbie."

And he had nothing.

If that was true, if that was how he felt, then empathy and compassion explained the quick jolt to her heart. Maybe it showed on her face before his arm circled her shoulders and he drew her against his chest. His soft kiss brushed her forehead, and her eyes fluttered closed. Whiskers scratched her skin when their lips touched, parted. Instinctively, she reached up and held his face in her hands. The kiss lingered, deepened, leaving her warm and breathless. A soft sigh escaped her lips when he tipped her head back, trailing warm, gentle kisses beneath her ear.

How long had it been since someone had kissed her this way? Years and years. The smell of his skin, the taste of his lips tingled up her spine. He felt so right, and then, suddenly, she couldn't do this. Passion, then guilt hammered hard at her heart. A knot tightened in her chest.

She pressed her hands against Matt's shoulders and felt him ease back. All she could hear was the quick, heavy bursts of their breath.

In that moment she knew, if Matt was a test on whether or not she was ready to start over, she had failed miserably.

"I'm sorry." His deep voice sounded thick with regret as he tipped up her chin. "I shouldn't have done that."

She stood, smoothing her hair, straightening her dress, anything to keep from looking in his eyes. "It was my fault. My mistake." She'd meant only to hold him, comfort him. Instead, she'd felt this incredible connection, then allowed herself to get lost in him.

She didn't deserve to be here with him.

He shook his head as if he understood and at the same time

knew he couldn't fix what was happening. He waited until her gaze shifted back to him. "You don't have to decide anything tonight."

"Please take me home."

He searched her eyes as he took his keys from his pocket, then went to turn off the lights and music.

She couldn't watch. She went up to the dock and put on her heels. The table and chairs were gone. Their perfect evening ruined. She squeezed her eyes shut, wishing she could change the past. Fix her mistakes—with her husband, her marriage.

And now, with Matt.

7

"*I* don't want to talk about this anymore." Matt stuck his phone between his ear and shoulder and grabbed a pizza box out of the refrigerator. He lifted the lid, counted back the days since he'd brought it home, and then tossed the whole thing into the garbage. His coffee sat cold on the counter. His empty stomach made his mood worse as he half listened to Nate lecture him.

"Have you tried talking to her? No. Because you haven't even been home since the last time you saw her."

Thinking about Jenifer made his head hurt. He'd done a pretty lousy job of managing his expectations about having a relationship with her. "Wrong. I'm home now. I was home during the week, too."

"Bullshit. Changing clothes and checking the mail doesn't count as going home."

Matt dumped the coffee down the drain and left his cup in the empty sink. After working his own shift and picking up another, that about summed his week. "What do you expect me to do? I pushed her too hard already."

"Stop hiding. You go find her. Talk to her. You work this out."

Matt scrubbed a hand over his face. He wasn't hiding from

her; he was giving her space. But whatever he called it, he'd been doing it for a week. Last night he went out after his shift. He played pool at Ernie's, the pub across the street from the firehouse. Jessie showed up around midnight. She'd hit on him, hard. Kept her answers cryptic when he'd asked why all the interest in him now before he left the bar. He could tell from her casual, breezy approach and the bright gleam in her eye that she knew about Jenifer. Hell, after just a week, the whole firehouse and half the bar knew what had happened between them.

Matt gave up. "Fine. If I see her, I'll talk to her." He had no idea what he would say, but he knew for sure he didn't want to talk to Nate about her anymore. "Right now, I need to go find something to eat." He got off the phone and grabbed his keys. Halfway out the door, he saw Jenifer standing outside her house.

Arms folded across her chest, she was looking down at a small white bookshelf and two cardboard boxes behind her car. She didn't look up when he came outside. She just stood there, head tilted to the side. Her fingers tapping against her arm. If she was thinking about putting the bookshelf into the trunk of her car, it was going to be a tight fit.

He watched her for another second or two, remembering what Nate had said, and then started across the street. Words still escaped him. He'd never had this much trouble talking to a woman in his life. But this particular woman had him all twisted up inside. "Jenifer?"

She turned to look at him, her bottom lip caught between her teeth.

"Do you need any help?"

She shook her head and a strand of wavy brown hair fell over her eyes. "Thank you, but I don't want to bother you."

His shoulders tensed. "You're not bothering me." The remoteness in her eyes, like she was trying hard not to look at him, nearly killed me. "Everything you've got there will fit into my truck. Where's it going?"

"My classroom." Her hands dropped to her sides. "If you have time, I could use your help."

"I'll be right back."

The school was only a couple blocks away. The short drive wouldn't give them a whole lot of time to talk. And even less time for him to decide what to say. After he parked his truck in her driveway, they loaded the bookshelf and two boxes into the back, then climbed into the front seat. "Robbie's not home?"

"He's at a friend's house." She shifted her gaze out the side window. "You haven't been home."

He was surprised she'd noticed. "I was at the firehouse most of the week."

She rested back against the seat and finally turned to look at him. "Thank you for doing this."

"You can ask me for help any time, you know that, don't you?"

"Yes." She sent him a sober look, then turned her face back to the window.

There was a heavy silence as they drove the rest of the way to school. He didn't think it likely she would ever come to him on her own, not if they didn't manage to work this out somehow.

The school's main doors were propped open, and construction trucks were parked alongside the bus loop when they arrived. Tarps piled high with old roofing shingles covered the sidewalk in front of the building. Matt got out of the truck, grabbed the bookshelf, and waited for Jenifer to pick up one of the open boxes filled with books before he followed her inside.

Even with all of the windows open, the warm, stuffy air smelled like ammonia and floor polish. Oldies music played at the end of the hallway. Two custodians moving desks and chairs back into a classroom said hello when Jenifer opened her door.

She set her box on a brightly colored rug in a corner of the room. Posters of books he remembered reading as a kid decorated the walls. Under the desks, sliced yellow tennis balls covered the chair feet.

"You can put that over there." She pointed to a spot next to a wooden rocking chair by the windows. "I'll get the other box."

Before Matt could tell her he would go back to the truck, an older woman in a pale-yellow suit stuck her head in the classroom. He recognized her right away. Dana Russell, his old principal, smiled and opened her arms when she saw him.

"Matthew Barnes. What a nice surprise." He grinned when she said his name the same way she had when he was eight and accidentally threw a baseball through a classroom window.

Matt gave her a hug and kissed her cheek. "I was wondering if I would get to see you today."

Dana smiled curiously at Jenifer, and damn if Jenifer didn't blush.

"You know each other?" Jenifer asked.

"I went to school here. Mrs. Russell was my principal."

"Since you two are obviously friends," Dana said to Jenifer, "maybe you could help me convince Matthew to come back in October with the fire department."

Jenifer's eyes went to Matt. A heavy weight settled in his chest. He didn't like the feeling they were about to become more neighbors than *friends*.

"We'll schedule a visit." He didn't look at Jenifer as he headed back out to the hallway. "I'll go get that last box."

It took less than an hour to finish up at Jenifer's classroom and get back to her house. Matt let his truck idle in her driveway. This was it. He studied his hands, his fingers tight on the steering wheel. "I don't want to make this any worse than it is, so I'm going to leave you alone. Not because I want to, but because I think that's what you need. I hope you'll tell me if that ever changes."

Her hand moved to the door like she wished a hole would appear and swallow her up. "I made a big mess out of this. I'm sorry."

A bad feeling washed over him as she got out of the truck. "You'll let me know?"

"Yes," she said, and then closed the door and walked away.

∾

$\mathscr{I}$t was ninety degrees outside when Matt wiped his face with the bottom of his shirt after he stowed the lawn mower back in the garage. He picked up a metal water bottle from the workbench and glanced across the street. Jenifer's car hadn't left her driveway since they got back from school that morning. No one was outside. After a few seconds, he shook his head and looked away.

Twisting off the top of his water, he considered giving Nate and Henry a call. Maybe see if they wanted to play pool at Ernie's tonight. He didn't see Jessie's car until it pulled up in front of his house. Frustrated that she kept tracking him down, he said nothing when she got out of the car and gave him a smile.

"Matt." Her flat leather sandals clipped up the driveway until she was standing next to him at the edge of the garage.

He raised his eyebrows. "Jessie." He'd done all he could to avoid a confrontation with her, but it seemed he was about to get one anyway.

Her smile faded. "We need to talk."

She'd said the same thing to him at the bar last night, then proceeded to circle around every one of his questions. Which meant to him that *she* needed to talk and wanted him to just listen.

With a subtle sideways glance, that bright gleam showed in her eyes again. Before he realized what she was about to do, she leaned in and kissed him, but only grazed his cheek when he turned his head. When he did, he saw Jenifer and Robbie riding their bikes up the sidewalk. Robbie waved to him and called out his name. Jenifer must have said something to him as they started up their driveway because neither of them turned around again.

Cursing under his breath, he caught Jessie's elbow. He had her trotting alongside him as he led her into the house before she could make things worse. He dropped his hand once they got inside and took a good three steps back. "You want to tell me what that was all about?"

She shook back her long dark hair, smoothing her hands over a short dress that looked more like a man's long white T-shirt. "Are you ready to talk to me now?"

"Fine." He squared his shoulders, intent on getting this whole thing over with fast. "What's this all about?"

She drew in a deep breath as her expression gradually softened. "I need you to tell me something." Slowly inching forward, she closed the distance between them. "What would you have done when that paternity test you had wanted so badly came back positive?"

He kept his expression even. He wouldn't lie to her, though he suspected the truth was only going to make this more difficult. "If the baby was mine, I would have asked you to marry me."

"I would've said yes."

He dropped his chin. She didn't need to drive home his mistakes for him to see them. Just as he didn't feel the need to remind her there had been nothing but a baby between them in the end. "Why are we talking about this now?"

"Because I still think about you. Sometimes I even wonder where we would be if things had happened differently."

"Jess, we've been over for a long time."

"That's what I'm trying to say to you. It doesn't have to be that way. We could try again."

Matt stared at her with disbelief. She caught his arm like she could make him see reason. "I shouldn't have left. I should have had the damn test and proved to you the baby was yours."

"Tell me," he said without pulling away, remembering when she'd told him she was pregnant in almost this same spot. "Why did you leave?"

Her lips pinched and her hand dropped to her side as if she knew what he was about to say. "Because we were young. We weren't ready for a baby."

"No. You left because we were over. And because you hated me for not believing you."

"Now do you believe the baby was yours?"

That was the hell of it. He did believe her, and there wasn't a damn thing he could do to change what happened. "Yes. I'm sorry I didn't believe you then. But I can't undo the past."

"Maybe not. But we can get part of it back. If you give us another chance."

"No." He didn't want another chance. Rather than encourage her to dig any deeper into why she thought they should be together, he reached around her and opened the door. He didn't want to hurt her feelings, but if she'd thought to pick up the pieces after Jenifer, she would be disappointed.

She sighed and turned to leave. "There's more, Matt. Just think about it."

"There's nothing to think about. You need to get on with your life," he said with a sinking feeling in his chest. "And so do I."

~

*J*enifer looked out the window when she heard a noise in front of the house. The wind had picked up a little while after Robbie went to bed, and a line of heavy clouds rolled across the sky. The air smelled like rain, damp and humid. The noise she'd heard was a neighbor's garbage can blowing into the middle of the street. She watched it for a second, debating whether she should put it back. It belonged at the neighbor's house next door to Matt, and she didn't exactly relish running into him a second time today. She checked the front of his house. Jessie's car was gone. His truck was still in the driveway, but all of his lights were off.

Since it would only take a minute, she hurried out to the street, grabbed the can, and put it back where it belonged. As she sprinted back across Matt's front yard, attempting to beat the rain, she heard a car turn onto the street. She stopped dead at the side of his driveway, hoping it wasn't him. All she could see were bright headlights. It was only when she saw the red Jeep and not Jessie's blue Volkswagen that she noticed she was holding her breath.

"Jen?" She recognized Nate after he parked in Matt's driveway and got out of the Jeep. "Are you looking for Matt?"

"No." She shook her head fast and pointed back at the neighbor's house. "I was just—" At that moment, the sky opened up, dropping a sheet of heavy rain. She bolted back across the street, Nate on her heels. By the time they ran up her porch steps, they were both soaking wet.

Embarrassed, she shook off the rain under the porch light and looked to see if Matt was sitting in the Jeep.

Nate pushed his shaggy, wet hair out of his eyes. His Charlie Daniels T-shirt stuck to his broad chest, and the bottom of his jeans were splashed with mud. "He's at Ernie's," he said, saving her the additional embarrassment of having to ask if Matt had witnessed her running across his yard. "I thought I was supposed to pick him up, but he just called to say he's already there."

Jenifer wondered if he'd caught a ride with Jessie, and her stomach twisted with jealousy.

Nate's green eyes grew sympathetic. "Are you okay?"

She plucked at her wet T-shirt. He was Matt's friend, not hers. She didn't know what to say to him. Or if she should say anything at all.

"Jen?"

She blew out a breath. What did it matter? "Are you sure you don't have to be someplace?"

He shook his head. She noticed a symbol tattooed on his arm

just beneath the sleeve of his T-shirt. "What does your tattoo mean?"

"It's a trinity knot. It's Celtic." He lifted his sleeve higher. "It's supposed to symbolize protection."

She raised a brow at the hint of Irish in his voice. "You're Irish?"

"If you ask Matt, only when I'm drunk." He grinned. "Most of the time that's when the accent comes out."

She leaned against the porch railing, brooding a bit, when Nate said his name. "I made a big mistake by letting him go."

Nate smiled, damn him. "Then tell him."

"What if it's too late?"

"What if it's not? How will you know unless you tell him how you feel?"

Her heart sank. "I miss him."

"Then make sure he knows. Call him. Ask him to come home."

"He's busy tonight."

Nate's thick red brows dipped as he checked his watch. "He's not busy. He's playing pool with Henry. And he's waiting for me to get there so Henry can go home to his wife. Truthfully, I'd rather go home, too, than go out tonight. So, please, will you give him a call?"

"Now?" Her stomach twisted again, thinking what was the use? Matt had already so much as told her goodbye this morning.

Nate nodded, then watched her go inside to get her phone.

When she came back out to the porch, Nate waited silently as she sat in the rocking chair beside him, working up her courage. Finally, she keyed *Can we talk tonight,* and then squeezed her eyes shut and hit Send. The knots in her stomach twisted even tighter as she waited to see if he would respond. Seconds later, *Yes. Give me thirty minutes* appeared on her screen and her head fell back against the chair.

Nate got to his feet and pulled his keys from his pocket. "Am I cleared to go home?"

Jenifer read the text again. "Looks like it."

He rested his hand on her shoulder. "Don't worry. Everything's going to be okay." His confidence gave her hope. But her mind drifted to Jessie.

After Nate left, she went inside and changed out of her wet clothes as she considered what she would say to Matt. She was still coming up blank when he showed up at her house less than half an hour later.

The rain turned to drizzle as the car that dropped him off pulled away. His face looked grim behind his scruffy beard and old, faded T-shirt, his blue eyes dark and serious when she met him at the door.

"I hope I didn't mess up your plans tonight," she said as he came inside.

"You didn't." He sent her a curious look and began to follow her into the living room. He waited until she took a seat on the leather sofa before he sat on the chair across from her.

She breathed deeply, let it out slowly. "I'm sorry I didn't tell you everything from the start."

"Why don't you tell me now?"

She picked up a throw pillow from the sofa and hugged it tight against her chest. "Patrick died on the same day I had asked him for a divorce. He'd driven to Detroit for a meeting that morning. It was March. There was a huge snowstorm, and he was killed driving home."

A slow, steady awareness crept over his face. "You feel responsible for the accident."

"I knew he wouldn't want a divorce, because of Robbie. I think he ended his meeting early and then drove home in the storm so he could try to convince me to stay."

"Did he tell you that he was coming home?"

She shook her head. "I didn't expect him until the next day."

"So you don't know for sure why he was on the road?"

She didn't think it was any great mystery. "Before he left that morning, he'd said he would come home as soon as he could, and we would work things out." There was no doubt in her mind that was exactly what he had done.

Matt got up from the chair and sat next to her. "Okay. What if you're right? But what if he was coming home to fix his mistakes? The mistakes he made that caused you to ask for a divorce in the first place?"

Jenifer dropped the pillow onto her lap. "You don't know that."

"You're right. I don't. But that's what *I* would've done." He covered her hand with his. "Can I ask you something?"

"Yes."

"Are you telling me this because you want to be together?"

"Are you giving me a choice?"

He squeezed her hand with a small, hopeful smile. "It was always your choice."

She shook her head slowly. "I thought maybe you and Jessie—"

"No. I want to be with you."

The certainty in his voice shored up her courage, boosted her self-confidence. Though after what she'd just told him, she needed to know. "Are you sure? I have this history of making really terrible mistakes."

He tipped up her chin and stared into her eyes. "Do you think that I'm a mistake?"

"No. I think I could be."

"I know what a mistake looks like, Jenifer. It's not you." His soft, warm lips brushed over hers. "Do you think we could try this again?"

"Yes, absolutely."

8

$\mathcal{T}$he next three weeks changed Jenifer's perception of relationships—and even love. There had been more date nights, some with Robbie, others alone. It seemed every moment she spent with Matt, she fell a little bit harder. She still hesitated at times, hid the worst of her worries and guilt from Matt. But as time went by, she was putting the past behind her. If he was disappointed by her slow, mindful pace, he didn't say.

It was five o'clock Monday afternoon when she heard his truck pull in across the street. Robbie must have seen him and gone to the door, expecting Matt to come over like he always did if Jenifer's car was home.

A few minutes later, she heard Matt come into the house, talking to Robbie. "Hey there, how was your day?"

"Okay." A baseball thudded and rolled across the wood floors. "Do you want to go outside and play catch?"

She listened for Matt's answer, expecting him to say no. He had spent the entire day at Nate's house helping him build a new deck. She imagined he was too tired and hungry to play outside with Robbie.

Instead, she heard him say, "Sure. Where's your mom?"

Robbie bounded up the stairs, probably off looking for his shoes as he called out, "She's in the kitchen."

Jenifer shut down her laptop at the kitchen table as Matt came into the doorway. She sat back in her chair, her eyes traveling over his ripped jeans, faded gray T-shirt, and old baseball cap. Suntan and stubble darkened his face.

Dressed up or dressed down, in uniform or a pair of jeans that had for sure seen better days, the man could stop her heart. More than that, he was kind, thoughtful, steady, and patient as a saint.

Matt took off his black sunglasses and smiled at her, then lowered his eyebrows when she grinned at him. "What?"

"You can always tell Robbie no, you know."

He removed the baseball cap and set it with his sunglasses on the counter. "I can play with him for a little while." Since he didn't move from the doorway, she got up and went to give him a kiss. He put up his hands and stepped back. "You don't really want to do that right now. I need to take a shower."

She rose up on her toes anyway. He smelled good, like coconut-scented sunblock mixed with hard work and the warm outdoors. His light beard scratched her cheek when she kissed him. He didn't resist when she bunched her hands into his T-shirt and dropped her feet flat on the floor, pulling him down for another kiss.

A noise at the top of the stairs had them quickly stepping back. Matt seemed to grin with some satisfaction at the disappointment on her face.

He lifted his hand, smoothing the wild waves in her hair from the humidity and turned to her folders on the kitchen table. "Are you still working?"

All of her lesson plans weren't finished yet, but she could do more tonight after Robbie went to bed. "I can stop for now."

Matt caught Robbie's shoulder when he came up from behind holding his leather glove in his hand. "Why don't I take him home with me? We'll throw the ball for a little while, and then he can play Xbox while I take a shower and you finish what you're doing."

She twisted her crazy hair into a knot on top of her head. "You don't mind?"

"No." He started to the front door behind Robbie. "When you're ready, we'll all go out to dinner, if you want."

Oh, yeah, he was a saint, all right.

After they left, she got a text from Robert asking if he could stop by on his way home from work. One more lesson plan later, she waved him through the back door into the kitchen and shut down her laptop again.

Dressed in a suit and tie, Robert kissed her cheek when she stood up from the table. She would bet his conservative gray suit was custom-tailored, but not necessarily from one of the designers Patrick had favored. Patrick's style had leaned toward trendy; his father, classic. A product of age, she supposed, but also a reflection of their distinct personalities.

Robert set a legal-size envelope on the table in front of her. "I'd like you to read this when you get a chance. It's our will."

"Okay." Concerned, she touched her hand to the envelope. "Is everything all right?"

"Everything's fine. We want you to have a copy for your files." He turned and looked around the kitchen. "Is Robbie home?"

"He's across the street. I'll call him and tell him to come back." She picked up her phone from the counter and accidentally knocked Matt's sunglasses onto the floor. She held her breath when Robert bent down to pick them up.

He hesitated, holding the sunglasses in his hand. "May I ask you a personal question?"

Jenifer gazed down at the black-framed glasses. "Of course."

His hazel eyes grew thoughtful as they moved to Matt's hat on the counter. "Are you happy?"

The question surprised her. She thought about it for a second, deciding the answer wasn't a simple yes or no. After a long moment, she said, "It's hard sometimes, especially when I think about the accident, but I'm getting there."

"Jenifer." What sounded like age-old sorrow resonated in his deep, soft voice. "You are not responsible for what happened to Patrick."

She blinked hard, staring at him with disbelief. "I don't understand how you can say that."

"I know what you think happened that day. But I'm telling you, the accident was not your fault. Nothing you said makes you responsible for his death."

She folded her arms over her chest and shook her head. There was no doubt in her mind Patrick had been driving home because she'd asked him for a divorce. "I don't believe that, and I don't know how you can either."

Robert's expression slowly mixed with pain and indecision. His eyes seemed to plead with her for some kind of blind faith and then finally filled with resignation. "Patrick wasn't driving home." His voice grew thick with grief and shame. "He was going to see his girlfriend."

Jenifer's eyes went wide. "He was having an affair?" The words burned her throat as her heart punched in her chest.

Robert looked down at the floor before he raised his head again. "I was furious with him when I found out. That was only weeks before he died. I'd told him he couldn't work for me anymore if he didn't end it. He said he would, but I didn't know he'd lied until he told me about the divorce."

Her eyes filled with tears. "You knew I had asked him for a divorce before the accident?"

"I did. I had lunch with Patrick that day. He was convinced you were going to leave him. He told me that he was going to end the affair this time, and he was going home to you. And then Elizabeth called and told me about the accident."

Jenifer dug through her memory. Tried to recall a name or face of a woman, someone who stuck out in her mind, but there was no one. "Who was she? Do you know?"

"She was a client. I never met her."

Jenifer's stomach felt sick. What else had she missed? What more didn't she know about her husband and her marriage? "Was she the only one? Were there others?"

His shoulders slumped as he shook his head. "I don't know."

"Then tell me everything you do know."

She guessed from the expression on his face he believed he was treading dangerously close to losing his grandson again. Yet he continued. "Patrick had left me a voicemail. He said the woman threatened to tell you about the affair and that he had to talk to her first before he could come home."

She squeezed her eyes shut when her phone rang. Frustrated, she grabbed it from the counter and then felt guilty when she saw Matt's name.

"Robbie sees his grandfather's car at your house," he said when she answered. "Do you want me to bring him home?"

She tried to hide the tears in her voice and failed miserably when her voice broke. "Can you give me a few more minutes?"

"Sure." He paused. "Are you all right? Do you need me to come over there?"

She did need him. But not yet. She still needed a few more answers. "I'm okay. I just need another minute or two." After the call ended, she looked back at Robert. "Why didn't you tell me all of this before?"

"Because Patrick was gone. There wasn't anything I could do to change what he had done, and I didn't want to hurt you even more. I'm sorry, Jenifer. I can see now that I was wrong."

"Does Elizabeth know?"

"I had to tell her after she blamed you for the accident." He shifted his feet and loosened his tie. "She wanted to tell you the truth as soon as she found out, hoping you would forgive her. I was the one who didn't want to tell you the truth."

Jenifer had her back to the kitchen window. She didn't see Robbie until he burst through the front door early, excited to see his grandfather. Matt was two steps behind him. He mouthed *I'm sorry* as he came into the kitchen doorway.

She nodded and wiped her eyes with the back of her hand, hoping they wouldn't ask any questions in front of Robert.

Matt had changed into a pair of brown cargo shorts and his blue fire department T-shirt. His hair was wet from the shower, but the stubble she loved remained. His blue eyes narrowed as they moved to her tear-stained face.

Robert held out his arms as Robbie charged into the kitchen. Dropping his glove on the floor, Robbie gave his grandfather a hug. "Is Grandma here, too?"

"No." Robert looked over as Matt studied Jenifer's face. "Grandma's at home."

"Do you think I could sleep at your house tonight?"

"Oh, I don't know." Robert glanced at Jenifer regretfully. "Tonight might not be a good night."

Robbie spun around to look at her. She kept her eyes on Robert. Matt stood beside her and said nothing.

It seemed Robert expected retribution. But she wasn't going to take Robbie away from them again. She was furious with Patrick, not his father. And angry with herself for not recognizing the affair. Robert had gotten stuck in the middle of it all.

"If it's okay with you," she said to Robert, "I think tonight is a good night." She could feel Matt watching her. No doubt wondering what was going on. She needed to talk to him. That would be much easier without Robbie home.

Robert straightened and nodded his head. She put her hands on Robbie's shoulders and aimed him for the stairs. "Go put your pajamas and toothbrush in your backpack." She waited until he was halfway up before she made introductions. "Robert, this is Matt Barnes. Matt, this is Robert Nichols, Robbie's grandfather."

Face impassive, Matt extended a hand to Robert. "Mr. Nichols."

"Please, call me Robert." Robert shook Matt's hand and then

turned back to Jenifer. He looked to have aged about twenty years since he'd arrived. "Thank you for letting Robbie stay with us tonight."

She didn't want to get into all the reasons why right now, so she just said, "I'll call you tomorrow before I pick him up."

Robbie hurried back downstairs with his backpack slung over his shoulder. He picked up his glove from the floor. "Love you," he said at the same time she did, giving her a quick hug and a kiss. Waving a gleeful goodbye to Matt, he spun around and shot out the door ahead of his grandfather.

Matt stood behind her as they watched them leave. "Are you all right? Why were you crying?"

She rubbed her nose with the back of her hand, feeling stupid and naïve. "Robert told me Patrick was having an affair. He said Patrick was on his way to break up with his girlfriend the night he was killed."

Matt put his hands on her shoulders and turned her around to face him. His expression hardened with anger and astonishment. "He knew his son was cheating on you? And he's just telling you now?"

"He said he was trying to protect me. I believe him. He didn't want me to be hurt by the truth."

"You *are* hurt."

"Hurt, angry, humiliated." She tried to back away, but he caught her hand. "I had thought Patrick was ambitious. I thought he spent too much time working. But it turns out he just didn't want to come home."

Matt's eyes softened. His expression turned compassionate, protective. "He was a fool. He knew it. That's why he was trying to fix the mess he'd made. Losing you would've wrecked him." He reached out and cupped her face in his hands. "I know all of this because it wasn't that long ago when I had thought the same thing myself."

9

*J*enifer dropped her head on Matt's shoulder and let out a long breath. The shock and anger she'd felt at first were gradually replaced by a fresh wave of hurt and sadness. Matt's strong arms tightened around her, making her feel wanted and loved. They stayed that way for a long while, until finally he whispered, "Let's get out of here."

She straightened, nodding, and focused hard on right now instead of thinking too much about the past.

After Matt made a quick trip back to his house, he dropped a sweatshirt beside Jenifer on the front seat of his truck. He reached over her to put the boat key into the glove box.

"We're going to the marina?"

He put on his sunglasses as he drove off. "Is that okay?"

"Sure." She looked out the window at the thin white clouds sweeping across the sky.

"What are you thinking?" he asked.

She opened the window and let the wind rush over her face. "Robbie, Patrick. His parents." The will tucked into her bag. Everything was all sort of crashing in on her at once. "Mostly, I wonder how I didn't know he was having an affair."

"You trusted him. Some people are good at deception."

She rested her head back against the seat and studied him. "Robert believes he still loved me."

The dark sunglasses hid his eyes, but a muscle ticced in his jaw. She shook her head. "You don't believe him either."

"I wouldn't say that. I think that there are different kinds of love." He slanted her a look. "Patrick's was selfish."

She thought about the kind of love she'd had for Patrick. "Maybe we'd left each other, I don't know," she said, turning her face back into the wind. She'd loved him, but she could see now that she had loved him more as Robbie's father than as a husband. What if he had loved her the same way? And when that love wasn't enough, he'd found someone new?

Matt stopped at a light. He looked left at a restaurant, and then across the street to a grocery store. When the light turned green again, he turned toward the store.

"You're hungry. Let's just go out to eat." She didn't think about it until then, but she was, too. It was already after seven. They could go to the boat later, or he could take her home after dinner.

"We can eat on the boat. I'll pick something up now." He nosed the truck into a parking spot and started to get out. "Anything special you want me to pick up?"

"Whatever you want is fine." She started to open her door to go in with him.

He waved her off. "Wait here. I'll be right back."

Her heart sank as she watched him walk into the store, his hands shoved deep into his pockets, weathering her storm again. But for how long? She knew if he turned around now, told her he'd had enough and brought her home, it would break her heart.

Fortunately, it looked like he was sticking around for a little while longer when he came out a few minutes later. He dropped two bags of groceries into the back of the truck with a thud before he got behind the wheel again.

The sun had set by the time she brought the food below and

then went to help Matt remove the boat canvas. The water rippled under the stars as she folded part of the canvas into one of the benches. No one else was out on the docks. All was quiet on a Monday night at the marina.

"Here." Matt handed her the sweatshirt he'd brought from home when she shivered in her T-shirt and shorts. "That's for you."

"Thank you." She pulled his blue fire department hoodie over her head and hitched up the sleeves. It was soft and warm and smelled like evergreen, just like him. "How long can we stay?"

He surprised her by putting the key into the ignition and starting the blower. "As long as you want." He pointed to the bow. "Can you get the bow line and jump on?"

She got out to untie the rope, then held the boat against the dock until he was ready. When he gave her a wave, she pushed off and jumped back on as he eased out of the slip. Holding the railing, she stepped along the gunwale and made her way back to him. He eased the throttle forward and the bow lifted as they headed out of the bay. Bracing her hands on the dash, she tipped her face into the wind and closed her eyes. Her hair blew wild. She breathed in deep, the cooler air filling her lungs, then exhaled, freeing her conscience and opening her heart.

The moon brightened the sky and sparkled across the water as a small cove came into view. Matt slowed the boat, steering closer to the secluded shoreline. "Does this spot look okay?"

"Perfect." She imagined it was a popular place to anchor on the weekends, but tonight they were the only boat in the cove.

Matt cut the engines and dropped the anchor from the bow. He went to set a second anchor from the stern while she went below to see what he'd picked out for dinner. One bag had potato chips and stuff for chicken salad sandwiches, the other contained a box of coffee pods and Danish pastries.

She wondered as she left the pastries on the counter if they were for dessert. Or had he thought to have them for breakfast?

She hadn't considered it before now, but suddenly she wanted to stay out on the boat all night. She was in love. She felt absolved of responsibility for Patrick's accident and, though part of her still grieved, she could now see their marriage was over long before his death.

She took the coffee out of the bag and set it with the pastries. If Matt agreed, they could have them both for breakfast in the morning.

Until then, it was easy enough to make sandwiches, find the paper plates and napkins, and grab a couple of water bottles from the refrigerator before Matt looked down at her from the back of the boat. "Do you need any help?"

She handed up the plates with sandwiches and chips. "Take these. I'll get the rest."

Up top, she set the water and napkins on the table and slid across the vinyl bench next to him. He picked up his sandwich, looking at the envelope in her hand. "What's that?"

"Robert and Elizabeth's will. He left it for me to read. That was why he was at the house tonight." She flipped through the pages of the will, giving it a cursory look, thinking it was about Robbie, and then dropped back against the bench seat when she saw her name.

"What is it?" Matt asked.

She read her name on the document again. "Robbie and I are both beneficiaries."

He caught one of the napkins before it blew away and stuck it under his plate. "That surprises you?"

It did. "I'd thought their estate would go to Robbie. He's their only family."

"Is he? What about you?"

She folded the will back up and tucked it safely into the bench behind her. "I never thought about it. Until a few weeks ago, I didn't think they even liked me."

"I can't speak to that, and I can't say I'm pleased about Robert's decision to keep the affair a secret, but I have seen the way he looks at you. The way they both do. You are their family."

Jenifer gazed at the dots of light flickering in the distance along the edge of the bay. The cove was calm and peaceful.

Matt caught her looking past his shoulder. "We won't have any trouble getting back tonight, if you're worried."

She sipped her water, then glanced down at the bottle. "Do you have plans for tomorrow?"

Shaking his head, he ate the last bite of his sandwich. Her hair caught in the breeze, and he brushed it from her eyes. "No. We can do something, if you want."

"What about tonight?" She set the bottle on the table, watching for his reaction in the moonlight. "Can we stay here?"

His eyes stayed on hers, like he was thinking about what she said, but didn't quite know how to answer.

Dessert, she thought. He'd definitely planned for dessert.

His gaze dropped as he pushed his empty plate away. "Maybe that's not such a good idea tonight."

She thought it was. She thought it was perfect, but if he wasn't sure, she wouldn't put her heart on the line again. "If you have doubts—"

He cut her off with a light kiss. "No doubts," he whispered against her lips. He nudged her off the bench as if to prove himself and then took her hand.

Anticipation stirred deep in her belly as he led her down to the aft cabin. Her eyes adjusted slowly to the soft, dim lights over the bed. His lips touched hers as they stood in the doorway. Tangling his hand in her hair, he angled her head for a deeper, more passionate kiss. Her pulse raced as his other hand skimmed the curve of her waist, teasing over her hips.

Eyes closed, she felt her heart pounding hard against his chest. She wanted him, all of him. As she surrendered, her world slowly began to right itself. Her fingers bunched at the bottom of his shirt. He held still, waiting, watching her. Always so cautious, even as desire burned in his eyes.

Spurring him on, she rose up on her toes and nipped his ear, tugging his shirt for him to raise his arms. He reached back without looking away, then yanked the shirt over his head and tossed it to the floor. Another long breathless kiss—and he'd helped rid her of her shirt and shorts. She jerked the button of his shorts and watched him kick them off as her mouth went dry. With excruciating patience, he tipped her chin up, kissed beneath her ear, the length of her throat, the soft, sensitive curve of her neck. All the while murmuring her name.

He guided her back and lifted her onto the bed, fitting her beneath him. She reached up and pulled his mouth to hers and parted his lips. A deep, low rumble sounded at the back of his throat. The tenor of the kiss changed from restrained to possessive as he settled low over her hips. His tongue touched the soft, delicate skin inside her thighs. Her back arched as her heart nearly exploded. Her hands held tight to the sheets as he slowly, tenderly laid her ghosts to rest.

~

*N*aked in his arms, Jenifer was more perfect than he had imagined. Watching her sleep before the sun came up, he marveled at the dips and curves of her soft, sweet body. Aching to touch her, her scent driving him mad, he pushed out of bed before he was tempted to wake her.

Again.

God, if he heard her cry out his name a thousand times, it would never be enough.

Wide awake, he dragged on his shorts and went to the back of the boat for air. The big boat rocked under a full moon and a warm, still sky. The vinyl bench was damp with condensation, and he wiped it down with a towel before he stretched out, arm bent under his head, staring up at the dark sky.

He'd known from the start he would fall in love with her, even if she had seemed so unattainable at first. She'd cautioned him. Her once sad brown eyes had reinforced her warning. Her husband had made a mess of their marriage; his death ripped her apart. It shouldn't have come as much of a surprise that he had cheated on her, but still, Matt was astounded. But not nearly as much as when she had asked if he wanted to spend the night with her. She'd about knocked him off his feet, and then turned the tables on him more than once during the night. It was gratifying—hell, it was exhilarating—to discover what they had with one another.

She was the one. If she still needed to be convinced, he would prove it to her. Fidelity, for him, came naturally.

He heard her first, then saw her come outside, all rumpled and sexy, wearing his blue T-shirt and a sleepy grin. God, she excited him. He started to sit up, but she flattened her hand on his chest and sat on the edge of the bench beside him.

She kissed him, her lips all warm and soft, as a riot of rich chestnut-brown hair spilled over his chest. "Couldn't you sleep?"

He tucked her hair behind her ear and smiled. She must have guessed what she looked like as she began to twist her hair up into a knot.

"Leave it." He pulled her hands down to his chest. "It proves tonight was real."

Brushing a fingertip over his bare shoulder, she asked, "What about this?"

He looked to where she touched him. He didn't remember her fingernails digging into his skin, but seeing the scratches now made him want her all over again. "More proof," he said, bringing her hand to his mouth, teasing her nails over his lips.

She blushed as she tried to pull her hand away, but he held on tight. After a second, she tilted her head up to the sky, and her eyes softened. "Have you ever made love in the moonlight?"

He dropped his head and lifted his eyes, watching her expression. He'd be damned if he would answer the question.

Instead, he tugged his T-shirt over her head, intent on making this the only time that mattered.

The corners of her mouth lifted into a sweet, sexy smile. "I haven't."

Lifting her, he curved a hand along the back of her thigh, sliding her over his hips, and placed her hands on the cushion behind his shoulders. "Then let me give you the moon."

*M*att walked into his small cramped office and slid the only other chair besides his own against the door to prop it open. It had been three years since he'd made lieutenant. The job fit him, though he'd set his sights on moving up the ranks in the future. He set a full coffee cup on top of the gray metal desk he'd bet predated the transistor radio. Morning sunlight poured through the aluminum blinds covering windows that extended across a long concrete wall and over-looked the city street below.

It was early yet. Traffic was light as he reached for the reports hanging on the bulletin board next to his desk and sat down. A picture Henry had taken of Jenifer and Robbie the first time they came to see him at the firehouse was pinned at the top of the board. From where he sat, he could see down the long narrow hallway to the bunkroom. He liked it that way. He wanted to be accessible and to keep the small space as cool as possible. Espe-cially on days like today. The single air conditioning unit installed in the bunkroom was no match for the late-August heat that had set in the day before.

The previous twelve hours of his shift were uneventful. He had no complaints. He'd sat through a class, washed his rig, and gone out on a few minor calls. He grinned as he thought about how Robbie would consider the shift a total bust.

Nate came from down the hall and stuck his head in the doorway. "Are you ready to go eat?"

Matt checked the clock on the wall outside his office. It was quarter to eight. "Almost." Jenifer had told him she had a ten o'clock meeting at school. He hoped to catch up with her before she left to drop Robbie off at his friend's house for the day.

Nate took a seat in the chair pushed up against the door. "Do you think you and Jen might want to go out to dinner tomorrow night?"

"I don't know. I can ask."

"I want you to meet someone. I'm thinking about asking her to my brother's wedding."

"Hmm." Matt tried to think of the last woman Nate had introduced to his family and came up blank.

"What, hmm? I just want you to meet her. If I bring someone to the wedding, my family's going to be all over her. I thought I'd start off easy and introduce her to you guys first."

Matt narrowed his eyes, curious. "How much do you like this woman?" That was the all-important question because Nate bringing a date to the wedding was bound to get complicated. It surprised him Nate even considered it. Then again, showing up to your younger brother's wedding alone when the rest of your family was married probably came with a different set of problems.

Nate's forehead creased. "I don't know yet."

"The wedding is what? Like, six weeks away?"

"You don't think I should bring a date, do you?" Nate hunched his shoulders as if he'd come to that conclusion already.

"I just don't think you need to decide right now. But if it makes you feel better, I'll ask Jenifer about tomorrow night." As he said this, she sent him a text that she was running late and she would have to call him later. He skimmed a couple of messages from Jessie and deleted them both.

Nate waited until he looked up. "Everything okay?"

"With Jenifer, yes." Matt put his phone back on the desk. "But Jessie's still trying to get in touch with me."

"Does Jenifer know?"

"I told her." What she didn't know was Jessie wanted him back. Because the last thing he needed was for Jenifer to question who *he* wanted to be with. He was in love with her. He was absolutely sure of it. He just needed to tell her.

"When's the last time you talked to Jessie?"

"A couple weeks ago, at Ernie's. But she keeps calling, and I keep blocking her numbers." His stomach growled, and he picked up his coffee to go get breakfast. "I'm going to have to explain things to her again. Maybe tomorrow." He pushed back his chair and got to his feet. "I'm hungry. Let's eat."

After he fixed a plate of bacon and eggs, Matt topped off his coffee and went to sit at the table with Nate and Henry. The long maple wood table easily seated twenty. A few others were eating breakfast while the rest had already started to work. Matt had a stack of reports to finish, a few calls to make, and hopefully he'd get a chance to talk to Jenifer by lunch. He'd ask her about going out with Nate tomorrow night. If she could find a babysitter for Robbie, he was pretty sure she would go. He started to ask Nate where he wanted to have dinner when the alarm sounded.

Dispatch sounded over the PA system. "Engine 17, Ladder 3, Rescue 5, report of warehouse fire. 124 Union Street."

Matt jumped up from the table ahead of Nate as more firefighters scrambled to their trucks. Beside Rescue 11, Matt yanked on his boots and turnout gear, grabbed his helmet, and jumped into the front seat with Nate at the wheel. Sirens screamed as their truck shot out of the bay behind Ladder 3 and Engine 17.

Minutes later, Matt saw whorls of black smoke billowing from the windows of a three-story warehouse. Preliminary reports stated that the warehouse stored machine parts and the fire started on the top floor. His firehouse was first on scene. Streets leading to the fire were closed off as more companies arrived.

Matt jumped out of the truck and strapped on his oxygen tank. The pumper crew on Engine 17 stretched a hose and connected it to the hydrant across the street.

A man rushed out of the burning building. He'd covered his mouth and nose with his shirt, and now he bent over coughing and pointing back at the fire. "I got two men still inside!"

Matt's captain ran over to him, then shouted out orders. "Barnes, Doyle! We got two people trapped on the second floor!"

Matt's head shot up when windows on the third floor exploded and glass shattered to the ground. The captain signaled them in, but there wasn't much time. The roof, the ceilings, all threatened to collapse as the fire burned out of control.

With twenty-four-pound air packs strapped to their backs, Matt and Nate pushed through a set of metal doors behind Henry and Engine 17. Matt ordered oxygen masks as thick smoke filled the pitch-black stairwell. Engine 17 dragged their hose up two flights of stairs where Henry directed 250 gallons of water per minute at the raging fire. The fire spread quickly, the heat blowing out windows in every direction. Matt dropped to his knees, then onto his stomach. Using the light from his helmet, he crawled on the floor in the opposite direction of Nate, searching for victims in the dark.

"I need more line!" Henry shouted from behind Matt.

Flames licked the twenty-five-foot ceiling and walls of the wide-open space. Flames engulfed hundreds of aluminum shelves loaded with metal parts packed in cardboard. It was too much fire for one hose to control. A second, even a third alarm would be called. It would take more firefighters and more equipment to knock down this fire.

Wet with sweat and water, Matt's shirt stuck to his chest in the intense heat. He swept his hands back and forth, careful with his air. Time was running out. Dark, acrid smoke hindered the search. Oxygen tanks would start to run low.

"I got one!" Nate shouted over the roar of the fire.

Matt stayed on course, low to the ground, until his hand brushed against a body. He called out, then pushed up to his knees and dragged his victim to a second team of firefighters closer to the stairwell. Ahead of him, he could see Nate's victim being carried away. Matt passed off his man to a firefighter from Ladder 3 when he heard an ominous sound in the darkness.

"Over there!" Adrenaline pumping, he signaled Henry to shoot water toward the noise as he moved back into the fire. Matt shined the light on his helmet down, saw nothing, then up, where part of the ceiling started to give way, and shouted, "Everyone out!"

There was no time. The ceiling buckled and moaned over the raging fire. Behind Matt, a crew of firefighters backed away, quickly moving toward the exit. He knew he was too close to the collapse. There was no way to miss it.

He threw his arms over his head as heavy debris buffeted his helmet, his back. Fighting to stay upright, he collided with the floor amid thick smoke and flames. His distress signal pierced the air.

Voices shouted his name. He was doused with water and dragged clear of the burning rubble, then half carried down a flight of stairs and loaded swiftly into a waiting ambulance.

~

*G*oose bumps stippled over Jenifer's skin as a gust of cool air blew through the open windows in the teachers' lounge. She had to put her hand on her notes to keep them from blowing off the table. The temperature outside dropped from stifling hot to almost cold in minutes as her principal, Dana Russell, finished an orientation for new teachers in her building. Jenifer wondered which windows she'd left open at home as dark clouds rolled across the sky. She looked up to see Dana responding to a text as everyone got ready to leave.

Dana stood abruptly and gestured for Jenifer not to leave as she gathered up her bag and started for the door. "If you have more questions," she said, ushering her teachers out to the hallway before putting her hand on Jenifer's arm, "please be sure to ask me, other teachers, or the administrative staff."

Jenifer stepped aside as the others passed, and the school's administrative assistant hurried down the hallway.

"We need to go," Dana said, hustling Jenifer down to her classroom.

Jenifer's stomach dropped. "What's wrong?" Automatically, she thought of Robbie. Without thinking, she rushed to get her bag and keys from her desk drawer.

"A call came into the office," Dana said as the secretary passed Jenifer a slip of paper. "There's been an emergency."

Jenifer read the message from the school secretary that Matt was injured at work and he'd been taken to the hospital. Her mind raced as she rushed out the door. "I have to go."

Dana took her keys from her bag. "I'll drive you to the hospital."

Lightning flashed across the sky with a loud crack of thunder as Jenifer ran through the rain behind Dana. She reread the message after they got into the car. It didn't give any details about the accident. Nate's name appeared at the bottom of the note. That Nate had called her and not Matt scared her even more.

Dana heeded stoplights, but not so much the speed limit as she passed cars driving slow in the pouring rain.

Nate didn't leave a number for Jenifer to call. She doubted he'd have his phone with him. Neither would Matt, but she called his number anyway, hoping to hear his voice, praying this was all a mistake.

You've reached Matt Barnes. Leave a message and I'll call you back.

She called two more times before they arrived at the hospital.

Jenifer stuffed the note into her bag and reached for the door. "Are you coming in?"

"No." Dana pointed to the small group of firefighters standing inside the glass doors. "It's going to be crowded in there. But I want you to call me and let me know how he's doing."

"Of course."

Jenifer rushed inside, soaked from the rain, and spotted Nate in the hallway with the other firefighters. They leaned against the wall, grim, faces dirty, smelling of sweat and smoke, still dressed in their turnout gear. Nate called her name, and everyone stood straight. His suspenders hung loose at his waist, and his thick red hair stuck out on top of his head. He eyed her skirt and blouse, then put his hands out to stop her from touching him, but she pushed them away and hugged him.

Shivering with fear, she fought back her tears. "Please tell me he's okay."

"The paramedics think he has a concussion. Maybe some cracked ribs. I talked to him after they loaded him into the ambulance. He asked me to call you." Nate dragged a hand through his damp, dirty hair, making it stick out even more. "I haven't talked to him since he got here."

Jenifer held her breath when a young woman in blue scrubs came sprinting down the hall toward them. Nate's eyes went wide. The others looked relieved to see her.

"Henry?" The woman stopped short of Nate, her expression filled with dread as she searched among the men's faces. "Where's Henry?"

Nate stared as if surprised to see her there. "He's okay, Rachel. He's not here yet."

"Who was hurt?" Rachel was younger than Jenifer, with blond hair, blue eyes, and an unmistakable affection for Henry and the other firefighters. She scanned the faces of all the men again before her shoulders slumped. "Was it Matt?"

Jenifer shifted her feet, rifling through her memory for any reference to a Rachel. All the stories Matt had told her about his family, friends, girlfriends. Everyone there seemed to know Rachel, but Jenifer came up empty.

Nate's eyes rested on Rachel for a second as he flattened a hand over his wild hair. "Yes, would you go check on him? No one's been out to tell us anything since we got here." He put his other hand on Jenifer's back and nudged her forward. "And if you see him, will you tell him Jenifer's here?"

"Of course." She reached out and gave Jenifer's hand a squeeze. "I'm Rachel, Henry's sister. I'll be right back."

Rachel disappeared around the corner as Henry came through the doors from the parking lot. He shook off the rain from his turnout gear and looked over his shoulder before he pointed back behind him. "I think we're about to have a problem."

Nate's jaw tightened as he quickly steered Jenifer toward the waiting room. A woman's panicked voice called out Matt's name. Jenifer stopped and turned around.

"Where's Matt?" Jenifer recognized Jessie as she inserted herself between the men. "Was he hurt?"

No one answered. Jessie's eyes flashed to Nate as Rachel strode back and gestured for Jenifer to follow. Jessie's face flushed bright red when Jenifer started to walk away. "Wait!"

Jenifer had no intention of waiting. Henry signaled his sister to keep going.

Jessie pushed forward, raising her voice. "I said stop!"

Nate looked about to intervene when Jenifer turned on her heel, hands fisted at her sides, and faced Jessie. Any other time, she was content to let Matt handle her his way, but that wasn't an option she had right now. "This is a bad time, Jessie."

Jessie looked past Jenifer to Rachel. "I need to see Matt."

"He asked for Jenifer," Rachel said with a hint of irritation, making Jenifer wonder if she knew Jessie.

Jessie eyed Jenifer coolly. Jenifer fought to hold it together. Nate slipped between them and crossed his arms.

"Five minutes," Jessie said, angling around Nate, calling out to Rachel as she led Jenifer away. "That's it. That's all I need."

Jenifer didn't look back as they passed through a set of metal doors and down a long narrow corridor. Matt had never come out and told her Jessie wanted to be with him. She had suspected as much after he told her about Jessie's phone calls and text messages. Given the way Jessie had just looked at her, as if she had caught Jenifer in bed with her husband, she had no doubts now.

Jenifer waited as Rachel pressed a small metal plate on the wall, then followed her through another set of doors. "Are you a doctor?"

"No, I'm a nurse. I work in the ICU. I came down to check on my brother after I heard a firefighter was brought in." The swinging doors whooshed open to the emergency department. Inside, exam rooms behind glass windows and doors ran the length of another long hallway.

Jenifer had to force herself not to push ahead of Rachel, knowing Matt was behind one of those doors.

Rachel checked in at the nurses' station. "Has Matt Barnes been taken to X-ray yet?"

"The firefighter?" The nurse sitting behind the desk checked the computer and shook her head. "No, not yet. You can go see him."

Jenifer nearly clipped the back of Rachel's heels as they went to find him. "Did you really talk to him?"

"Only for a minute. I spoke to his doctor, too. Matt suffered a concussion. Possible broken ribs. They'll know more after his X-rays." Rachel slowed down and gestured to a door with the privacy curtains drawn over the windows. "Go ahead. I'll tell the guys how he's doing. And don't worry if he's groggy. It's the pain medication."

Jenifer took a deep breath and opened the door. Her hand shook parting the curtains. She didn't know what to expect and was relieved to see him sitting up with his head leaned back against a pillow. Dressed in a mint-green hospital gown and covered with a white sheet, his arms rested at his sides. His eyes were closed. She thought maybe he was asleep until those eyes cracked open and the corner of his mouth turned up.

"Hey," he said, his voice a little rough around the edges, but still the most wonderful sound in the world to her.

Her eyes welled up as she went to stand next to his bed. Her body deflated as any semblance of courage and strength crumbled. The reality of almost losing him struck her hard.

He sent her a weak smile. "Come here."

She started to kiss his forehead, but he lifted his face and found her lips instead. "You scared me today."

He put his hand on her cheek. "Helluva day."

"Does this happen often?"

"No." He sank back against his pillow. She sat in the chair beside him, holding his hand. He looked almost the same as he had when she'd kissed him goodbye yesterday morning. His face and hands were clean, but he still smelled of smoke and sweat like Nate and the others. He was unmarked, without any tubes or wires, and she felt her fear begin to subside.

His eyes closed. She sat back to let him sleep, and he squeezed her hand. "I love you." His voice was barely above a whisper when his head lolled to the side.

"I love you," she whispered back, even though he had fallen asleep. She folded her arms on the edge of the bed and laid down her head, still holding his hand. She hoped he remembered what he had said. But if he didn't, that was all right. Because he was there—alive and whole, and hers.

$\mathcal{M}$ att crossed the cold linoleum floor in bare feet and a cool breeze on his ass, happy to be going home soon. Where he could wear sweatpants instead of a hospital gown that barely came to his knees and gaped at the back.

The pain medication had worn off. Sharp, shooting pains from bruised ribs made getting out of bed harder than he'd expected. Walking wasn't as bad. After breakfast, his nurse had offered to help him use the bathroom. He'd politely declined. He had just enough pride remaining to attempt a trip to the john all by himself.

By the time he got back into bed, he could barely manage a deep breath. His head was in better shape, though he still couldn't remember from the time they'd pulled him from the fire to when he'd arrived at the hospital.

What he did remember, though, was telling Jenifer he loved her.

The nurse returned a few minutes later with a paper cup and pitcher of water. "Are you ready for pain medication?" she asked, leaving the cup and pitcher on the table next to his bed.

He eyed the paper cup and shook his head. He didn't like the drugs. They made him feel sluggish and drowsy, like treading quicksand half asleep. He preferred wide-eyed discomfort over a dull, hazy bliss.

She wrapped a cuff around his arm and checked his blood pressure, then raised her eyebrows, reminding him of his mother when he didn't listen. "Your blood pressure is high. Probably because of the pain." She set the pressure cuff aside with a quick look at his other arm braced against his ribs. "The meds will help."

He checked the clock by the door. It was only eight. He still had a couple of hours before Jenifer said she would come back to bring him home. Reluctantly, he held out his hand. "Okay."

Sometime after his eyes closed, a chair scraped across the floor, the sound moving closer to the side of the bed. The pain was all but gone when a soft kiss pressed to his lips. "Hey."

Eyes still closed, he smiled, his voice thick with sleep. Long hair spilled over his chest as he breathed in the warm, sweet scent of roses—and he cracked his eyes open.

He managed to turn his face away before Jessie kissed him again. "What are you doing here?"

She stared at him for a second, then turned around and took something from her bag next to his bed. "I want to show you something." She unfolded a piece of paper and pushed it into his hand. "It's important."

Matt glimpsed Jenifer standing in the doorway. Shoulders straight, she gazed at the back of Jessie's head. Her hands were full with takeout coffee and a box of donuts. She wore a Cincinnati Reds T-shirt, probably meant as a joke, but there was no humor in her expression.

He scowled back at Jessie, worried Jenifer had seen the kiss. "I want you to go."

Jessie curled her fingers over his hand. "Please, look at this."

He didn't look. He wanted her gone. His head was still in a damn fog from the drugs. Crumpling the paper, he threw it onto the floor. "Just go."

Jenifer walked up behind Jessie then and set the coffee and donuts on the table next to his bed. She picked up the paper and smoothed it open. As she looked closer at it, her eyebrows pinched. Jessie tried to snatch the paper from her, but Jenifer was quick and passed it to Matt when he held out his hand, curious now. It was hard to see after being crinkled up, but it looked like a young girl with long dark hair, photocopied in black-and-white. He started to hand it back to Jenifer, but Jessie grabbed it.

"We're not doing this now," Jessie said.

"Doing what?" Jenifer asked, maybe trying her best to sound cool and disinterested, but he didn't think so.

Jessie shoved the picture into her bag and swung the strap over her shoulder. "That's none of your business."

Jenifer picked up a coffee from the table, took off the lid, and sat on the bed next to Matt. Jessie shifted her eyes to him. "You're making a huge mistake."

"How?" he asked.

Jessie sent Jenifer a sidelong glance. "Forget it. I'm not going to talk to you about this here."

"Maybe you're right that he's made a mistake." Jenifer's voice sounded to him like a challenge.

Jessie stared at her for a long moment, then turned her back and walked out the door.

Matt stared at Jenifer, too. She didn't understand. Not yet. He'd be damned if he let Jessie or anything else come between them. "We are not a mistake," he said. "Not even close."

~

*J*enifer needed to explain to Matt that she hadn't meant *they* were a mistake. The mistake, she was starting to suspect, was Matt believing that Jessie had had an abortion. She couldn't explain it. It was just a gut feeling after looking at the picture Jessie had shown him.

She sat in the chair beside his bed, trying to decide how to explain when his phone rang. She half listened to his conversation with his mother as she passed him coffee and the box of donuts, her thoughts all jumbled together in her head.

The girl in the picture looked like a young Jessie. From his reaction, Matt seemed to think so, too. She would have expected a much stronger reaction from him if he had suspected the girl might be his daughter. Doing the math quick in her head, she thought Matt's child, if he had one, would be almost fourteen years old. The girl in the picture was maybe twelve or thirteen.

What if Jessie had come to the hospital to tell him he had a daughter? She'd kissed him and no doubt wanted him back. And she had made it very clear she wasn't going to tell him anything with Jenifer there.

She glanced up and caught him watching her while he spoke on the phone. He reached out a hand and closed it over hers on the edge of the bed.

He'd said he loved her, but did he remember? Even if he did, if it came down to finding his daughter or being with Jenifer, how could she make him choose?

After the call ended, he sank back against his pillow. He looked at her as if he expected her to say something, but his eyes weren't quite focused.

"Did your mother find a flight home?"

"Yes, she's waiting for her connection in Vegas." He pushed himself up against his pillows. "Listen, we need to talk."

"About Jessie?"

He shook his head. "About us. Why would you tell her that we're a mistake?"

"That's not what I said."

"That's what I heard."

She sighed and set her coffee down, hoping to avoid a conversation about the picture before he was thinking straight again. "Well, it's not what I meant."

"I hope not. Because I meant what I said last night. I'm in love with you." He turned his hand over, sliding his fingers through hers. "I should have told you sooner, but I didn't want to pressure you. I still don't. But because of yesterday...I needed you to know."

"I love you." She stood and kissed his lips, without thoughts of the fire or Jessie or the girl in the picture. Somehow, this extraordinary man loved her and she loved him back. If her suspicions were true, and for his sake she hoped they were, she would still love him. And, hopefully, he would find a way to still love her, too.

~

*L*ater in the afternoon, Jenifer got Matt settled into the front seat of her car to bring him home. He pushed the seat back and leaned his head against the window with his eyes closed.

On the way, she called to check on Robbie at his grandparents' house. He asked about Matt. "He's doing great. I'm driving him home now."

"Are we going to sleep at Grandma's house again tonight?"

"No, I'll pick you up before dinner, and we'll watch a movie before bed."

After another minute or two of reassuring him Matt was okay, the call ended with the promise he could visit Matt the next day.

Matt turned his head and opened his eyes. "Where's Robbie?"

"He's with his grandparents. They picked him up from his friend's house yesterday, and we both spent the night with them last night."

"You slept there?"

"Elizabeth invited me to use their other guestroom. Robbie was scared when he found out you got hurt. I wanted to be there in case he woke up in the middle of the night."

Sadness filled Matt's eyes. "I wish he didn't know."

She reached out and squeezed his hand. "I couldn't not tell him. He's crazy about you. He would've figured out something was wrong."

As soon as she got him home, Matt went upstairs to take a shower. She left his front door open to let in the fresh air through the screen and opened the rest of the windows. His house was similar to hers, but larger. Cluttered, but not dirty. Patches of brown paint were brushed on one of the living room walls where he was experimenting with new colors. The furniture was an eclectic mix of old and new. A brown microfiber sectional and large flat-screen television over the fireplace were only a few years old, but the upholstered chair, maple coffee table, and formal dining room furniture were all pieces his mother had left behind when she'd sold him the house. Jenifer especially loved the formal dining table and chairs, but she thought they were a little out of character for a bachelor who ate pizza in front of the television whenever he was home alone.

She took a second and checked on her house through the screen door. She didn't hear Matt behind her until his arms tightened around her waist. "How many more days until school starts?"

"Six. We go back Wednesday after Labor Day."

"I'm going to miss you when you're gone all the time."

She rested her head back gently against his chest. "The same way I miss you?"

He moved his hands to her shoulders and turned her around to face him. "Will you finish telling me what you meant earlier about a mistake?"

The more she thought about it, the less comfortable she was sharing her suspicions about Jessie with him. "I shouldn't have said anything."

"You saw her kiss me."

Her gaze dropped to the floor as she remembered when she got to his room that morning.

He tipped up her chin with his finger. "I was asleep. You know that, right?"

"I gathered that."

"So you didn't say we're a mistake because you were mad?"

She blinked hard. "No. I wasn't mad at you." She was angry with Jessie. She stepped back. Tested the waters. "Do you think that was Jessie in the picture?"

He shrugged. "It looked like her when she was a kid."

"I thought she was older than that when you met her."

"She was. I didn't know she played sports either, but then again, her whole life changed after her father left."

After he mentioned sports, she remembered the girl in the picture wore a softball uniform. There were palm trees in the background. Jessie had lived in Florida before her father left them. It made sense for the girl to be her. But then why show the picture to Matt?

He pulled her close again. "Please don't worry about her."

"Do you trust her?"

He cocked his head. "What do you mean?"

She locked her eyes on his. "Do you trust her story about the baby?"

His hands dropped to his sides. "Are you asking me if I believe the baby was mine?"

She could see how badly he needed to believe he was the father. Could be a father. "No. I'm asking if you think there's a chance she had the baby."

Matt's head shot up. He cursed under his breath before she heard a woman's voice behind her at the door.

"Matthew?"

12

$\mathcal{M}$att saw the guilt on Jenifer's face as he squared his shoulders. He stroked a thumb over her warm, red cheeks. He could tell she was holding her breath. No way was he going to let her take responsibility for what was about to happen. Putting his lips close to her ear, he whispered, "Breathe."

Jenifer and Nate were the only two people he'd told about the baby. Not even his mother knew.

I'm sorry, she mouthed silently.

He pressed a finger to her lips, shaking his head before she turned around.

The screen door closed behind his mother as she came into the house. Worry lines carved between her brows. She pushed her suitcase against the wall and dropped her black leather bag on the floor. Her short dark hair was pulled back in a stubby ponytail, a sure sign she'd rushed out of the house. She wore white slacks, flat brown sandals, and a blue collared shirt that matched her eyes, and his, almost exactly. Average height, she was taller than Jenifer and a good six inches shorter than Matt.

"Mom." He came around Jenifer and gave his mother a hug. He held her tight, then reached behind him for Jenifer's hand.

"This is Jenifer Nichols. Jenifer, this is my mother, Sarah Zimmerman."

Jenifer reached out her free hand, a world of regret mirrored on her face. "Mrs. Zimmerman, it's a pleasure to meet you."

The formality was unnecessary. As was the guilt. His mother knew all about Jenifer and he was pretty sure she loved her already.

"Please, call me Sarah." Rather than accept Jenifer's hand, his mother drew her into a warm embrace. "I'm so happy to meet you." She stepped back, giving Matt a worried look. "You should sit down."

He checked the driveway. "How did you get here?"

"Cab." She put her hand on his back, careful not to hurt him, and led him into the living room with Jenifer. She settled in the chair that used to be hers and let out a long, deep breath. "Whose baby were you talking about?"

Matt took a seat beside Jenifer on the sectional. He looked down at the floor for a second before meeting his mother's eyes. "Mine. Jessie was pregnant when we were in high school."

His mother glanced at Jenifer, the worry lines deepening across her forehead. "Is that what Jessie told you?"

"Yes." He felt Jenifer's fingers slip between his, offering her support.

Raising her eyebrows, his mother's voice filled with confusion and doubt. "You believed her?"

"No, not at first. I asked for a paternity test and she refused."

"Is that why you broke up?"

"No, we were already broken up when she told me, but she was still furious that I didn't believe her. About a week later, she told me she had an abortion."

"Now do you believe she was pregnant?"

He sighed. The movement hurt and he pressed his arm against his ribs. "Yes." He remembered the anger and then the resentment on Jessie's face when he'd asked for the test. "I went to see a doctor afterward and found out it *is* possible I could be a father; it's just the odds are low."

"And that's why she suddenly moved back to Florida? To get away from you?"

Matt nodded. His mother turned to Jenifer. "But you don't think she had an abortion?"

Matt squeezed Jenifer's hand, wishing she wasn't involved in his problems with Jessie. "Jessie came to see me at the hospital this morning. She showed me a picture of a young girl who looks like her."

"Do you think she might be your daughter?"

He shook his head and even that hurt a little. "Why would she tell me now?"

Jenifer eyed the arm he held against his chest. "Her mother just died, and then you got hurt. She might feel alone. Or maybe she's afraid to lose you for good." Her voice dropped to a whisper. "If you have a daughter together, that might not happen."

Jesus. Was that what she thought?

His mother tipped her head. "Why didn't you tell me about the baby before?"

"Because all that would've done is hurt you. There wasn't anything you could do to change things."

"Still." Her eyes softened. "I could have been there for you."

"Do you believe the baby was mine?"

"I do," Jenifer said, sitting straighter as she turned to face him. "And after what Jessie did today, I wonder if the girl in the picture could be your daughter."

That part didn't make any sense at all to him. "Why would Jessie have the baby and then not tell me? And if she did, where's my daughter now?" The words *my daughter* stuck in his throat and hurt a hell of a lot more than his bruised ribs and banged-up head. "I talked to Jessie's mother. She never mentioned a granddaughter."

His mother stood, then wandered over to the window. "What if she gave the baby up?"

Matt's stomach suddenly felt sick. "Then that would make me just as bad as my own father, wouldn't it?"

She turned and stared at him. "What are you talking about? You didn't walk away."

"Didn't I? Jessie tells me I'm a father. I tell her I'm not. If Jenifer's right, I have a child out there somewhere I've never even thought about. The same as my father."

Their eyes met for a moment before his mother pressed her lips together and looked away.

Matt's heart slammed in his chest. "Have you talked to him?"

"No." His mother went back to sit in the chair. "I haven't talked to him. He sent me an email. He heard about the fire on the news. He wanted to know if you were all right."

Matt's headache was getting worse. "Were you going to tell me?"

"No."

"Why?"

Without looking at him, she said, "Because he asked me not to."

He scrubbed his hands over his face, not sure why what his father wanted even mattered to her. "Do you still have the message? I want to see it."

"No. I told him you're okay, and then I deleted the message like he asked. He wanted to make sure you're okay, Matt, that's all. Please, let this go."

Not likely. "Has he ever done this before?"

"No. He's never reached out in any way since you were born."

"Do you know where I can find him?"

A bleak look came over her face. "No, and please don't go looking for him."

He released Jenifer's hand and pushed to his feet. A sharp pain had him reaching for her as she rose to steady him. He dropped his eyes to his mother. "What am I supposed to do?"

"Get better, and then go find Jessie to learn the truth."

The argument about his father was one he hadn't lost to her in a long time. The need to find the man he'd alternately hated and loved his entire life had become less important as he had gotten older. It was only his father's sudden interest in him now that fired up that stubborn need again.

The pounding in his head worsened the longer he stood. "I'm going to go lie down for a little while."

His mother got up and kissed his cheek. "Get some sleep. I'll be here when you wake up."

He rested his chin on top of her head. Never able to stay mad at her for very long. "I love you, Mom."

"I love you, Matthew."

Jenifer walked with him to the stairs. She stopped at the front door. He wasn't ready for her to leave yet. "Will you come up for a minute?"

She glanced at his mother, then back at him like she was embarrassed to go upstairs with his mother there. He just smiled. His mother disappeared into the kitchen.

When they got up to his room, she pulled back the blankets for him and stood next to his bed. "I'm sorry."

"For what?"

"For bringing all of this down on you."

He sat on the side of the bed, wishing she could stay. "You didn't start anything. What happened downstairs is all my fault. I should've told my mother everything a long time ago."

She brushed her fingers through his hair, making his eyes grow heavier. He shifted her to stand between his legs and rested his head against her chest. "Do you really think the girl in the picture could be my daughter?"

She nodded and laid her cheek on top of his head. "I think you need to talk to Jessie again."

"I know. I just don't understand. She didn't want the baby."

"Maybe she changed her mind."

"And you think the fire motivated her to tell me the truth?"

"She could have been afraid you might die."

He raised his head when her breath caught, and he held her a little tighter. "I wonder if my father thought the same thing."

"Will you look for him?"

He nodded. "After I talk to Jessie."

"What about your mother? She must have a good reason for discouraging you."

He pulled her face down for a brief kiss, then got underneath the blanket. "Maybe. But whatever it is, it's not good enough anymore. If I find him and he wants nothing to do with me, at least then I'll have the satisfaction of having him tell me that to my face."

~

*C*Uhen Jenifer went back downstairs, she found Sarah sitting in a plastic patio chair on Matt's back deck. Her eyes were closed, her face tilted up to the sun. There was a strong resemblance to Matt, especially her eyes, but her skin was lighter and her face rounder. with a small, turned-up nose. Matt must have inherited his father's darker skin and long, distinctive nose.

"He's asleep," Jenifer said when Sarah sat up and opened her eyes.

"Is he okay?"

Jenifer sat on the deck stairs at Sarah's feet. "He's better. But I think he's in more pain than he says."

The corner of Sarah's mouth turned down. "I think that's always been his way. Even when he was a little boy. Always trying to fix things himself and growing up too fast."

"He told me he had a wonderful childhood."

"Did he?" Sarah's face brightened. "He was always so serious. Like he thought it was his job to take care of me, instead of the other way around."

"I imagine he regrets not taking care of Jessie, too."

Sarah sighed as she reached up and loosened her ponytail. "I never understood the two of them together. Jessie was an impulsive young woman, always making plans and then changing them again. I remember it used to drive Matt crazy. He is the most deliberate man you'll ever meet. He reads the directions to everything, plans to the smallest detail." She grinned and pointed behind her to the house. "I bet those patches of paint are still on the living room wall because he hasn't decided what to do with the floor molding and window trim yet."

Jenifer agreed.

"If you're right, I can't imagine there's anything he can or even would do if she gave the baby up. But he would want to know the truth. It's hard to think about. He's never really talked to me about it, but I'm sure he wants to be a father someday."

"He's good with Robbie. I'm sure he would be a great father."

Sarah smiled. "He talks about your son all the time."

"You should hear Robbie talk about him."

"That's good. That helps, I'm sure. He always sounds so happy when he talks about you."

Jenifer looked down and tugged a string on the hem of her shorts. "I haven't always made life easy for him."

Sarah slid forward in her chair. "I don't know about that. All I know is that you're important to him."

"I love him, and I want to protect him." Jenifer thought about the pain he was in right now and wished she could make it all go away. "I just don't know how."

"Protect his heart. If you do that, I promise you, nothing will ever truly hurt him again."

13

Two weeks after the fire, Matt met his mother at the top of the stairs and picked up her suitcase. "Does anything else need to go down?"

"No." She swatted at his hand. "You shouldn't carry that."

"I got it." His ribs were still sore when he took a deep breath, but otherwise, he'd mostly recovered from his injuries. "Are you sure you want to wait for Jenifer before we head to the airport?"

"Yes." Sarah stuck her plane ticket into her leather bag and followed him down the stairs. "It's only four o'clock. I've got at least two hours before the flight leaves."

Matt set her suitcase by the front door and checked across the street for Jenifer and Robbie. Jenifer had asked if she could go to the airport with them after school today. Matt knew it made his mother happy that she wanted to be there to say goodbye. Despite the circumstances, he was grateful for the chance to bring them together. And he had a feeling he wasn't going to be the only one his mother missed after she went home this time.

A few minutes later, Jenifer turned into his driveway and popped the trunk as they met her at the car. "I'm sorry. I tried to get home faster."

"Don't worry. We're fine," his mother said as she got into the back seat with Robbie.

"We've got lots of time." Matt put the suitcase in the trunk, then got behind the wheel after Jenifer switched seats.

She grinned and gave him a quick kiss after he slid her seat back so he could fit his long legs into the car. "Thank you for waiting." She turned around to his mother. "I wish you were staying a few more days."

Matt lifted his eyes to the rearview mirror and caught his mother's warm smile. "Maybe you can all come out and visit us sometime," she said.

"Me, too?" Robbie asked.

"Of course you, too."

Matt enjoyed listening to her talk with Robbie. They'd spent a lot of time together before school started last week. There was no doubt in his mind that Robbie had captured her heart, as well as his.

"Do you think we could go to the ocean?" Robbie asked. They'd taken him on the boat Labor Day weekend. Matt's mother had told him Lake Michigan was so big, it sometimes reminded her of the Pacific Ocean.

"If you come visit us, we'll take you anywhere you want to go."

Jenifer twisted around in her seat and looked at Robbie. "Maybe we'll go someday." The excitement in Jenifer's voice had Matt promising himself he would take them soon.

Everyone got out of the car at the airport to say goodbye. Robbie let Matt's mother kiss him on the cheek, and he gave her a hug. "You be good. I'll talk to you soon," she said to him.

Jenifer gave her the next hug. "I'm really going to miss you."

"Please take good care of my son. He needs you."

"I will."

When it was Matt's turn, he put his arms around his mother. "I love you," she said. "I need you to stay safe. I can't ever live without you."

"I love you." Matt kissed her cheek and held her tight. "I'll be okay." He got her suitcase out of the back of the car, then waved goodbye as she disappeared into the terminal.

Jenifer touched his arm. "I'm sorry you're sad. What can we do to make you feel better?"

Matt watched the glass doors slide closed behind his mother and then winked at Robbie as they all got back into the car. "How about you take me out for a pizza?"

"I think we can do that." Jenifer reached behind the driver's seat. She picked up something from the floor and looked at it before she handed it to Robbie.

Matt waited. "Everything okay?" He glimpsed into the rearview mirror and saw Robbie holding a Spider-Man action figure.

Jenifer nodded. Her eyebrows cinched. "Where did you get that?" she asked Robbie.

Robbie shrugged a shoulder. "Grandma Sarah gave it to me."

Her eyes went wide as she looked at Matt.

He kept his expression blank. Was she upset? He hadn't heard Robbie call his mother *Grandma* before now. Given the surprised expression on her face, she hadn't either. He doubted his mother would have asked Robbie to call her that without talking to Jenifer first.

"Is that okay?" Her voice dropped to a whisper. "Do you care that he called her *Grandma*?"

"No. She probably loved it." He was relieved she sounded apprehensive instead of irritated. He lowered his voice, too. "Are you okay with that?"

"I think it's sweet. As long as it doesn't bother you."

"Not at all." With the direction his thoughts were taking lately, he was more than okay with Robbie's familiarity. He was even starting to imagine them as a family someday. He hoped maybe Jenifer did, too. "I love you." And to be clear, "I love Robbie, too."

Robbie's stomach rumbled from the back seat. "I'm hungry.

When can we eat?" He stretched his legs and kicked the back of Matt's seat.

Jenifer gave Matt a wry smile. "Are you sure about that?"

"Oh, I'm very sure."

Half an hour later, they were sitting next to the window at Ernie's across from the firehouse. One side of Ernie's was a bar with a pool table and a couple of high-tops, the other side was a small Italian restaurant with great pizza. In the center of the restaurant, square tables topped with red-and-white vinyl table-cloths started to fill up and a line grew at the door. Robbie sat next to Matt in a booth with his head down, coloring a picture on his placemat while Jenifer was in the restroom. Their pizza arrived and Matt set a slice onto Robbie's plate, moving a glass of chocolate milk out of his way. He was reaching under the table for Robbie's action figure when Jenifer slid across the red vinyl bench opposite him. He could feel her staring at him before he sat up. "What's wrong?"

Robbie raised his head, looking between Matt and his mother. She broke off a slice of pizza and gave him a smile. He drank his chocolate milk and went back to coloring his picture.

She leaned forward and caught Matt's eye. *Jessie's here.* She mouthed the words to avoid getting Robbie's attention.

Matt automatically looked out to the middle of the dining room.

Jenifer tipped her head back. "No. Behind you. Closer to the bar."

Matt kept his eyes on Jenifer, not sure what to do next. Jessie ignored *his* calls now. He'd tried the last number she'd used to contact him, and he'd driven by her mother's house a few times since he got home from the hospital, hoping to talk to her about the picture. But Jessie's car was never there. He'd started to think she left town again, until he heard the guys at the firehouse had stonewalled her when she came around asking about him while he was out.

Jenifer straightened in her seat. She peered over his shoulder and kept her voice low. "She's sitting with her back to us, but the guy she's with is staring at you."

That did it. Matt looked over his shoulder and saw the guy she was with.

Well, damn.

Jenifer unwrapped her straw and took a sip of her iced tea. "He looks about twenty years old."

It wasn't a judgment so much as an observation he heard in her voice. "I think Kyle's closer to twenty-seven."

Her mouth dropped open. "You know him?"

"Kyle Owens. He's a firefighter."

She glanced at Robbie, hunched over a hidden picture game on the back of his placemat. "Do you work with him?"

Matt took another look behind him. Kyle averted his eyes. He leaned forward and said something to Jessie. "Same firehouse, different unit. But he knows who I am." He probably thought Matt was going to give him a hard time, thinking he was talking about him. Matt was willing to bet Jessie was trying. "He pulls a lot of overtime so, yeah, I have worked with him before."

Jenifer wiped her mouth with a napkin, then set it on her lap. "Does Kyle know about you and her?"

Matt pushed his plate away, unhappy about the strain Jessie kept putting on his relationship. "I doubt he knows much." He signaled the waitress and caught a glimpse of Jessie heading toward the restrooms. "Can we get dessert?"

He wanted to wait for Jessie to leave and then go talk to her out in the parking lot. If she stayed much longer, he'd give Jenifer her keys back and have her take Robbie home. He'd call Nate or Henry to pick him up when he was done. He didn't anticipate any trouble with Kyle.

Jenifer nodded and leaned back in her seat. Robbie grabbed the dessert menu from behind the napkin holder.

Matt kept an eye out for Jessie. Kyle was on his phone. He glanced over at Matt and ended the call. He left some money on top of the bill, stood, and made his way toward them. Built like a runner, he was tall and slim with dark-brown hair that some-times fell over his eyes, giving him a more youthful appearance. Right now, he not only looked young, but guilty as hell. He stopped at their table and gave Jenifer an apologetic look, then turned to Matt. "I'm sorry about all this. I didn't know who she was until she started asking questions about you. Now she's hiding out in the restroom. She's got her car. I told her I'm leaving, unless there's something else you want me to do."

Matt shook his head. "I'll take care of it." Jenifer sent Kyle a reassuring smile while Robbie read the dessert menu aloud to her. "Thanks for coming over."

Kyle left as their waitress returned. Matt got to his feet as soon as he saw Jessie walk back to her table. She turned a circle, maybe looking for Kyle, and frowned. She hung her purse strap over her shoulder and headed for the exit.

Matt took money out of his wallet and left it on the table. "I'll be right back," he said, then left to follow Jessie outside.

Jessie stalked ahead of him without looking back. A gust of wind blasted through her hair like an angry thundercloud. She'd parked her car at the rear of the building, far away from where Jenifer and Robbie sat by the window. Her key fob failed to unlock the door on the first try. That's when she spun around and huffed out a breath. "What do you want?"

"Answers."

She turned her back on him and hit the fob again. This time the door unlocked. "You're too late. You had your chance."

Matt leaned his hip against the door. "I want the truth this time. No more lies."

"The truth about what?" she shot back.

"Who was in the picture you showed me at the hospital?"

Her mouth pinched as she reached around him to open her door. "Me. Now move," she said without any conviction, like she intended it to sound like a lie.

"Why would you want to show me a picture of yourself?"

Her eyes turned as cold and flat as her voice. "Figure that out on your own."

The young girl in the grainy black-and-white picture could have easily been Jessie. But her story wasn't making any sense.

So he changed course and bluffed. "I have. It wasn't you in the picture. It was our daughter."

She jabbed a finger hard in his chest. "Now you believe the baby was yours?" Her face turned bright red. "You screwed up. You lost your chance to be a father." She yanked the door open and shoved him out of the way.

He stepped back, locking eyes with her through the open door. "Where is she?"

Jessie got behind the wheel, fumbled with her key, then stuck it into the ignition. Her chest heaved as she gripped the steering wheel. "You're insane, do you know that? Go back to your girlfriend."

"I'll find her."

Jessie turned on him, glaring as she reached for the door handle. "The hell you will. You've lost your mind."

She slammed the door closed, and he dropped back before her tires squealed out of the parking lot.

Hands fisted, he stared at the red taillights. Maybe she was right, he thought. Maybe he *had* lost his damn mind.

14

*J*enifer passed Robbie a napkin to wipe the ice cream off his chin as Jessie's blue Volkswagen sped past the window. A guy crossing the parking lot stopped short to avoid getting hit and flipped her off. Jenifer looked for Matt, worried when she didn't see him. A few seconds later, he came back inside, shaking his head as he sat next to Robbie again.

Robbie scraped the last of his ice cream in the bowl, then looked over at him. "Where'd you go?"

Matt managed a believable smile and lied like a champ. "I went to see if I left my phone in the car." He reached for the check and money he'd left on the table.

Jenifer picked up the check first and pushed his money back at him. "You forgot. We were taking you out to dinner, remember?"

He took the check from her like he didn't understand what she was talking about. "It's okay. I got this. I'll meet you guys out in the car."

Different thoughts went through her head as she watched him pay the bill. Did Jessie say anything more about the picture?

Had she been truthful about the abortion? Was he a father? Or was Jessie coldhearted enough not to tell him anything at all?

~

*a*t nine o'clock Jenifer heard Matt come back to her house. He'd gone home after dinner, she guessed to clear his head. She pulled on a T-shirt and pajama pants while she listened to Robbie get ready for bed. After he brushed his teeth, she pulled back his blanket and waited for him to turn on the loud box fan next to his nightstand. "Do you really need that thing on?" She'd meant to put the old fan back into the attic after Labor Day. But every night he turned it on before he went to sleep.

He flipped on the nightlight out in the hallway before he got into bed. "I like how it sounds." He yawned and folded his arm under his pillow after she tucked him in. "Can I keep it?"

"I suppose so." She bent to kiss his forehead. "I love you." He smelled all warm and clean when he tipped his face up to kiss her good night. Her heart melted. She had fallen in love with him before he was even born. There was nothing in the world she wouldn't do for him. And not a single day passed that she didn't wish time would stand still. His father had loved him the very same way.

If Matt felt even a fraction of that love for a daughter he'd never known, what would he do to find her?

Jenifer stood next to the bed after Robbie fell asleep. Matt loved him. He loved her. That's all that mattered. Everything else would work itself out with time.

All but one of the downstairs lights were off when Jenifer found Matt waiting for her. He leaned back against the leather sofa wearing jeans, a faded Captain America T-shirt, and a two-day beard. His legs were stretched out across the ottoman, his eyes staring up at the ceiling. He'd put up a strong front on the ride home tonight, but she knew well enough Jessie had gotten under his skin this time.

He looked over when the stairs creaked and reached out his hand when he saw her. Deep lines creased the corners of his eyes as he pulled her down next to him. "Jessie didn't tell me anything new," he said without her asking.

Jenifer curled her legs underneath her, resting her head on his shoulder. "I'm sorry."

"I shocked her, though," he said, sounding a little surprised, too, "when I asked her about my daughter."

Jenifer lifted her head to see his face. "You think she had the baby?"

He shrugged. "I think she's lying about something, but I don't know what. And even if she did have the baby, I don't think she has her now."

No. Probably not. After Matt got home from the hospital, they'd searched Jessie on the internet. There was no mention of a daughter on social media. No pictures like the one she'd shown him. But because of that picture, Jenifer was almost certain he had a daughter. It made her sick thinking Jessie had intended to tell him but then changed her mind because of Jenifer.

She started to apologize again when he hugged her a little tighter. "I love you. I don't want you to worry about any of this."

It was too late for that. "I'm worried about *you*. What are you going to do?"

"I told Jessie I would find her."

She thought of Robbie. "Then I'll help you."

"How? I don't even know where to start."

"We'll figure it out."

His gaze dropped to hers. "Are you sure you want to do this?"

She remembered his answer when she'd asked him if he was certain he loved Robbie. "Yes, I'm very sure."

With that, his eyes darkened, and she let out a quiet sigh when their lips touched. The kiss started out soft and slow, deepening as he shifted his weight so she lay beneath him. They hadn't made love since he came home from the hospital. She missed him like crazy— even as she began to worry about Robbie sleeping upstairs.

Probably thinking the same thing, Matt ended the kiss before he buried his face in her hair. "We shouldn't do this here."

It was difficult to argue with him. But the weight of his body pressing down on her mixed with the excitement of being alone with him again made her feel bold. "Please, stay. Robbie sleeps like the dead. Plus, he can't hear anything over that old fan in his room."

Matt hesitated for a second, then got to his feet and pulled her with him. She turned off the lights before she stepped around her canvas tote at the bottom of the stairs.

He reached for the bag to take with them.

She gave him a little nudge. "You can leave that there for now. It's nothing."

Well, not exactly nothing, she thought. Just something to talk to him about tomorrow.

~

*H*ours later, Jenifer woke with a start. She cracked one eye open. Robbie hovered in the doorway, backlit by the nightlight at the end of the hallway. Her eyes flew open as she covered herself with the blanket and pushed up on her elbow, trying to hide the sleeping body beside her. The room was dark except for the nightlight. The clock next to the bed read midnight.

"Hey, honey, did you have a bad dream?"

The body beside her jerked and froze.

Robbie rubbed his eyes and started into the bedroom. "Can I sleep with you?"

She felt Matt burrow deeper beneath the blanket as his hand tightened on her waist. She reached over the side of the bed and grabbed her shirt from the floor. "How about I sleep in your bed this time?"

Robbie tripped over Matt's shoes as he came farther into the room. He rose up on his toes and lifted his head, spotting the lump in the bed. "Is that Matt?"

Jenifer blew out a breath and made a futile attempt to block Robbie's view as she pulled her shirt over her head.

Robbie came to stand next to the bed and tried to look around her. "Matt?"

Jenifer reached behind and patted Matt's leg. There was no point to him suffocating now.

A muffled voice sounded from underneath the blanket. "Give me a minute, buddy, and you can sleep here."

Jenifer searched the dark for Matt's clothes. Robbie caught her hand as she got out of bed, and he led her back to his room. "It's okay. Mommy can sleep with me."

The lump stayed quiet and still.

Jenifer glanced over her shoulder, hoping Matt wasn't mad that she'd talked him into staying all night. "It's okay. Go back to sleep. We'll talk to him tomorrow."

~

*T*he next morning, Matt leaned back against Jenifer's king-size headboard and listened to Robbie's voice carry from downstairs. He rubbed a hand over his beard, stalling before he got up, and remembered that small voice in the middle of the night.

What the hell had he been thinking? He'd relied on the wrong body part to make decisions last night. Jenifer, too. Still, it felt good to have her want him there.

He reached over the side of the bed and picked up his boxers. His jeans were by the door. His shirt hung over the top of a dark maple dresser, and his shoes were strewn across the bare wood floors in an otherwise uncluttered room. It was the first time he'd slept at Jenifer's house. He'd been in her bedroom only one other time when she had shown him the house. He reached out and straightened the pale-blue quilt kicked to the bottom of the bed. It matched the color of the walls. Framed photographs of Robbie hung on the wall opposite the bed. He picked up a book from her nightstand, a romance novel, and grinned when he saw the bookmark. It was one of the tickets from when he'd taken them to the baseball game.

He put on his clothes, looking at the bedroom door. Was he supposed to go down to the kitchen and have breakfast with them like it was normal for him to be there in the morning? As much as he wanted that to be true, it wasn't. Not yet, at least.

He'd skipped a few important steps in between.

When he got downstairs, he saw Jenifer sitting with Robbie at the kitchen table. She wore jeans and his blue fire department hoodie, grading a stack of papers as the two of them talked over breakfast. She peeked up at him when he came into the doorway.

"Hey, Matt," Robbie said, cutting into his pancakes and stuffing a bite into his mouth.

Matt kissed the top of Jenifer's head, then dropped his lips to her ear. "Sleeps like the dead, huh?"

He regretted teasing her when she murmured, "I'm sorry."

She got up and went to refill her coffee cup. "We were just talking about you," she said. His heart stuck in his throat when he sat at the table across from Robbie. "I told him he might see you in the morning if we stay up too late for you to go home."

Matt nodded, even though he wasn't sure he was willing to risk getting caught in bed again. Robbie shoveled the last of his pancakes into his mouth, and syrup dripped down his chin. Matt handed him a napkin.

Robbie wiped off the syrup with a glimmer in his eyes. "Are you going to sleep here again tonight?"

Matt puffed out his cheeks and blew out the air, slanting a glance at Jenifer.

Shaking her head, she took another cup from the cabinet, filled it with coffee, and passed it to Matt. "Probably not tonight."

Robbie's face fell. Matt felt terrible. He wanted to say something to make him feel better, but it wasn't his place.

Jenifer picked up Robbie's plate and put it in the sink. "Why don't you go get dressed? When you come back downstairs, we'll decide what to do today."

"What did he say to you this morning?" Matt asked after Robbie left the room.

Jenifer leaned against the counter and shrugged, shaking her head like she didn't know how to tell him.

Matt slouched in his chair. "That bad, huh?"

She tipped her head side to side. "He asked if you're going to live with us now."

Well, hell.

He set his cup on the table, then walked over to stand with her at the counter. This wasn't the conversation he'd planned to have this morning, but there it was. Brushing her hair from her eyes, he said, "Is that something you want, someday?"

"You've got a lot on your plate right now to be thinking about that."

He lifted her hand and kissed her palm. "You are the most important part of that plate." He would prove it to her, too. "What are you doing today?"

She pointed at the stack of papers on the kitchen table. "I have to grade. When I'm done, I'll do something with Robbie."

She sounded apologetic for not including him when the last thing he wanted was to risk turning into a burden. "I'm going out with Nate in a little while. I've got a couple things to do." He sipped his coffee. "Do you think Robbie could go with us? We'll be gone a couple of hours, and you can get some work done."

Jenifer gazed at him over the top of her coffee cup. "You're asking me if you can take a six-year-old to run errands?"

He smiled at her. "I am." No doubt, babysitting was out of

his skill set, but if she was willing to give him a try, he wanted to show her that he was serious about being in a relationship with her.

"I love you." She stood on her toes and kissed his lips. "Thank you."

~

*I*t was three o'clock when Jenifer heard Matt bring Robbie home. As soon as they walked in the door, Matt handed his phone to him. He'd downloaded the Angry Birds game and let Robbie play whenever they were together. Jenifer heard the music start as Robbie hung his coat on the hook by the door. He gave her a quick wave and ran up to his room.

Sitting cross-legged on the sofa, she set her pile of papers on the coffee table. Matt looked strangely relaxed for a man who had just spent most of the afternoon with a six-year-old. "How did it go?"

He gave her a cryptic smile. "I think it went well."

"Where did you go?"

His smile grew wider when he sat next to her and gave her a kiss. "Do you trust me?"

"Of course I do."

"Then it's a surprise. You'll have to wait a few days to find out."

"Okay." She stretched her legs across his lap. The man loved his surprises. "Where's Nate?"

"He went home." Matt looked over at the stairs and then stole another kiss.

Content, she leaned over the arm of the sofa into her canvas tote and took out a small white paper bag. She set the bag on his lap and waited to hear what he would say.

"What's this?" He read the receipt stapled to the top and raised his eyebrows. "Are you starting birth control pills? Does this mean you don't want to use condoms anymore?"

She drew in a deep breath. Making love with him last night was still fresh in her mind. "I'd like to talk with you about that." Condoms lessened the intimacy she craved. She was in love with him. He was the only man in her life. In her heart, she trusted he would never stray while they were together.

Handing her back the bag, he said, "I think it's a good idea."

She looked up when she heard hurt in addition to the agreement in his voice. Not sure why he might be upset, she dropped the bag back into her tote. "It's all right. We can still use condoms."

He put his arm around her shoulders. "No, I don't want to use condoms anymore. You're right that we should use birth control pills."

"Then why do you sound sad?"

"How could I be sad? I've got you. You're everything I need."

If so, his heart belonged to her now, and because of that, she would do all she could to protect it.

15

*J*enifer watched for Matt out the front window with both hands on Robbie's shoulders. If she didn't hold him down, with all of his bouncing around, he would've bumped her chin for sure. Two weeks was a long time for a six-year-old to keep a secret, and hers was about at his limit. "He's just a little late, honey. Come have a snack and tell me about your day. I'm sure he'll be home from work soon."

With one more look out the window, Robbie trailed her into the kitchen. She knew he was anxious to see Matt. Robbie had stayed mum about the afternoon they spent together. Matt kept silent, too. The first few days, she'd been tempted to coax Robbie into telling her their secret. But that would have ruined their surprise. It was fun to watch them together, playfully keeping her in the dark. Matt had promised her on the phone last night to tell her everything after work today.

Finally, around six o'clock, a door slammed at the front of the house. Robbie charged outside.

She followed to make sure he was with Matt. That's when she saw the silver pickup truck parked in her driveway, and her heart melted.

Matt had a new truck. She guessed he'd taken Robbie to pick

it out. As far as she knew, there was nothing wrong with his old truck. Except for maybe one thing.

Still wearing his uniform, Matt opened the door and Robbie scrambled into the front seat. Matt flashed her a grin when she came out to greet him. "What do you think? Do you like it?"

"I do like it." She hugged her elbows against the cool air, dry leaves crunching under her leather boots as she circled the big four-door truck. She opened a rear passenger door and peeked inside.

Robbie looked back from the front seat. His eyes were bright as he pretended to drive. "I picked it out."

Matt dropped a kiss on her forehead when she went to stand next to him again. "I thought we needed more space," he said, answering her question before she asked.

She grinned and gave him a hug. "I love you."

Robbie climbed over the seat to sit in the back. "Can we go for a ride?"

Matt put his arm around Jenifer, keeping her warm. "Do we have plans for dinner?"

"No, but Robbie's going to spend the night at his grandparents' house."

Matt raised his eyebrows. "Maybe we can take him out to eat and then drop him off. I'd like to talk to you about something later."

She nodded. "Is something wrong?"

"I want to show you something I found the other night." His face gave away nothing as he helped Robbie out of the truck. "Come on out, buddy," he said. "I'll get changed, and then we'll go eat."

~

The house was dark when Matt brought Jenifer home after dinner.

"The bulb blew. I have to get another one," she said,

following his gaze to the front porch after he came around the truck to open her door.

"I have light bulbs at the house. I can bring one over tomorrow." He would do it for her in the morning, even though she didn't ask him to. He knew very well she could take care of it herself, but the urge to look after her was strong. For now, he settled for simple things, like changing out a light bulb.

If only the rest of his life were that simple.

Inside, Jenifer watched him as she took off her jacket. "Do you want to stay here tonight, or would you rather we go sleep at your house?"

"Here's good." It didn't matter to him where they were, as long as they were together. He walked into the living room and turned on the lights, then took the old newspaper clipping from his back pocket.

Jenifer sat next to him on the sofa. "What's that?"

He handed the piece of paper to her. "I found this in the attic the other night."

She unfolded what was left of the article. There was a photograph above it that had been more carefully cut out than the story itself. It was dated April 1993. It described the grand opening of an upscale restaurant in Grand Rapids. "I've never heard of this place," she said.

He had a vague recollection of his mother discouraging him from taking a date there years ago. Bad reviews, she'd said. "It closed a while back."

Her brows pinched when she looked closer at the picture. "The man in the middle looks a lot like you."

He'd thought so, too. Three men in the photograph were described as owners of the new restaurant. One man was tall and lean with a long straight nose, and short dark hair. He wore a tailored suit, sharp wing-tip shoes, and vague smile. He was in his early thirties, and he could have easily been Matt.

Jenifer read the caption, probably searching for a name. He'd done the same thing, but that part of the article was missing. "You found this in your attic?"

"It was in an old desk. I almost got rid of it without going through the drawers."

"Did you ask your mother about it?"

"I called her today. At first, she said she didn't know what I was talking about. So I sent her a picture of the article. I think it surprised her. It sure as hell surprised me. She told me the man in the picture is my father but not her first husband. Not the man I thought was my father."

Jenifer quietly handed the paper back to him.

"She said she met him after her husband left her. They were only together for a short time. I was born before her divorce was final. She never told the guy she was pregnant, but he found out anyway."

"Why didn't she tell either one of you?"

"She learned he'd been convicted of racketeering. She thought people he knew might be dangerous. At the very least, she believed he would be a bad influence, and she was trying to protect me."

"Did she tell you his name?"

"Nicholas Russo." Matt's gut clenched as he said the man's name for the first time. He tried to ignore the hollow feeling in his chest. "She asked me again to stay away from him."

"What do you want to do?"

Long on questions and short on answers, he stood and pulled her up to her feet, his gaze intent on hers. "I don't know yet. I'd rather forget about him, though, and just think about us tonight." Because for all of his desire to care for her, she was his rock. His refuge. A shield when he needed her. And tonight, he needed her.

⁓

*J*enifer lay in a tangle of sheets early the next morning, her languid body a testament to Matt's endless devotion. His arm rose in the dark and wrapped around her when she laid her head on his chest. He rested his chin on top of her head with a contented sigh. Since the time Robbie had walked in on them, Matt was reluctant to spend the whole night at her house. He was always sure to go home long before Robbie woke, leaving a heavy emptiness in his wake.

She stroked her hand over Matt's chest before tracing her fingertips down the dark line of his belly. "Did you sleep?"

Cold air prickled over her skin when he pulled away the sheet between them. "I always sleep when I'm with you."

The anticipation of making love with him again added to her excitement, knowing they had all morning to be together. And this time, she would make sure the pleasure was his. Tucking her hair behind her ear, she held his eyes, skirting her leg over his hips, then kissed his chest, his belly, his hip, until she felt his muscles tense and strong hands clasp around her waist as he lifted her into place.

"Tell me you want me," he said, holding her tighter, finding his rhythm. Need of a different sort crept into his voice with heartbreaking intensity. His words tightened her chest. Did he think she would leave him someday? Was he afraid to lose her, too?

Would the time ever come that *he* would leave *her*?

She leaned down and pressed her hands on either side of his head. Her hair spilled over his shoulders. Infusing her words with the deep longing that came from her heart, she whispered, "I want you." Again and again, kissing him softly on the lips each time, choosing him, loving him. Hoping that she would always be enough.

16

The day after Christmas, Jenifer sat hunched over the side of her bed, sicker than she had felt in a long time. Strong winds howled outside her bedroom window. Heavy snowfall darkened the sky. Matt's deep voice carried up from the bottom of the stairs. Her mother's voice, soft and less distinct, was probably telling him to go up and say goodbye before he left for work.

Jenifer raised her head to see him smiling as he came into the room, like he was about to tease her for sleeping late. The smile quickly faded after their eyes met.

"Are you feeling okay?" He crouched in front of her, pressing his hand to her cheek. "You look pale."

"I think I might've caught the stomach bug at school."

"I didn't notice you getting sick. When did it start?"

Her stomach roiled. For a second, she thought she would get sick again. "This morning. Right after I woke up."

He stood and pulled back the blanket for her to lie down again. "Get some more sleep. I'll tell your parents you're sick. I'm sure they won't mind keeping an eye on Robbie today."

She crawled back into bed and curled up on her side, grateful her parents planned to be there a few more days. "How are you feeling?"

He sent her a sympathetic smile as he sat next to her. "Lucky."

"Well, you better go before your luck runs out," she said, turning her head when he tried to kiss her. "I don't want you sick, too."

He took her face in his hands and kissed her forehead. "It's probably too late to worry about that." He stood when Robbie came into the doorway ahead of her mother.

Robbie frowned when he looked at Matt's uniform. "Are you going to work today?"

Matt opened his arms. "I am. But after that, I've got a couple of days off to hang out with you while you're on vacation."

Robbie stepped in between Matt's knees and gave him a hug as her mother watched. "Are you going to sleep here, too?"

Her mother grinned at Matt.

Matt dropped his head on Robbie's shoulder and gave him a hug. "You're killing me, buddy." He got up and put his hands on Robbie's shoulders and pointed him toward the door. "Mommy's sick. Let's let her sleep."

The small lines between her mother's eyebrows creased. "What's wrong?"

Jenifer made a weak shooing gesture. "Stomach bug. I don't want you to get sick, too."

"I have to go." Matt leaned over and kissed the top of her head. "Call if you need me."

By lunchtime, Jenifer was well enough to go downstairs to the kitchen and eat cereal. Her mother came up from the basement carrying an empty crate for Christmas decorations. The navy-blue sweater she wore was all dusty from the basement, and a price tag stuck to the back of her new jeans. The same height as Jenifer, she had brown eyes and short wavy hair streaked with gray. She set the crate on the floor next to the basement door. "I didn't expect to see you down here. How are you feeling?"

Jenifer reached over and pulled the tag off her mother's jeans. She threw it out, then went to load her bowl into the dishwasher. "Better. Maybe I'll get lucky and this won't last very long."

"You should go back to bed. Your dad is outside with Robbie. Matt cleaned out your driveway before he left. I'm just going to put away a few decorations for you, and then I thought I'd make beef barley soup for dinner. I already ran to the store while you were asleep."

"Soup sounds good." Jenifer leaned a hip against the counter after her mother went quiet for a second.

"Are you sure you're okay with onions and garlic?"

Jenifer shrugged. "Why wouldn't I be? They only made me sick when I was pregnant."

Her mother waited a beat. "Is there any chance?"

"A chance of what?" Jenifer pushed away from the counter as it dawned on her. "You think I might be pregnant?"

Her mother sat at the table. "Honey, two hours ago you looked like you might get sick. Now, you're eating cereal and talking about dinner. You got sick like this when you were pregnant with Robbie."

Jenifer pushed her hands through her hair. Panic rose in her chest. It never crossed her mind she might be pregnant. "We use birth control. I started new pills in September. I can't be pregnant."

"Are you sure?"

Jenifer went and slumped into the chair across from her mother. She dropped her head in her hands and took a couple of long, steadying breaths as she counted back the days. Finally, she raised her head. "I'm late. But that's not unusual for me. Especially when I'm on birth control."

"Maybe you should take a test to be sure."

Jenifer clasped her hands behind her head and closed her eyes. Now she wouldn't be able to think about anything else until she did. Glancing down at her red-checkered pajama pants and sweatshirt, she pushed her chair back from the table. "I have to get changed so I can go out to the store."

"Wait." Her mother got up and reached into the grocery bag on the counter. She handed her a pregnancy test and sat down again.

Jenifer's heart slammed in her chest as she stared down at the test. "Do you really think I'm pregnant?"

She gave a half-hearted shrug, but Jenifer could see she did. "I don't know. I just think you have that same look you had when you were pregnant with Robbie."

Jenifer turned the test over in her hands. "Will you come up and wait with me?"

Her mom's eyes reflected compassion and concern as she stood from the table. "Of course I will."

After Jenifer came out of the bathroom, she leaned against the wall in the hallway where her mother gave her hand a squeeze. "Will you go look for me?"

"Sure, I'll be right back."

When she returned, she handed Jenifer the white plastic stick showing a faint blue plus sign. "Honey, it looks like you're going to have a baby."

Staggered, tears welled in Jenifer's eyes as she pushed away from the wall. She needed to think. She was going to have two children. How was she going to tell Matt? And Robbie? What did this mean for her relationship with Matt? Did she want to raise a second child alone?

Her mom broke through her scattered thoughts, sounding worried as she followed Jenifer back downstairs. "I think you should call Matt."

Jenifer shook her head. She didn't want to tell him he was going to be a father over the phone. "I'll talk to him when he gets home tomorrow."

"How do you think he'll feel? Will he be happy?"

Jenifer looked out the living room window and watched

Robbie throw snowballs in the front yard with her father. "I don't know how he'll feel. I don't think he ever expected this to happen again."

"Again? Does he have children too?" She sounded surprised since no mention had been made of Matt's family other than his mother and Ben.

"He doesn't know for sure."

Her mom went to sit on the sofa and patted the cushion beside her. "How does he not know if he's a father?"

Jenifer blew out a breath, then sat down and told her about Jessie. When she finished, her mother folded her arms over her chest. "I don't understand what any of that has to do with your baby."

"His life's complicated right now. A baby's only going to complicate it even more."

Her mom's brow lifted. "Are you sure that's it?"

"What do you mean?"

"I mean do *you* want to have another baby?"

Jenifer's throat squeezed. "Of course I do. I love Robbie. I'll love this baby too."

"But?"

Jenifer turned her head to face her mother. "But I won't make the same mistake I made before."

"Do you think Matt will ask you to marry him?"

"I think it's likely. And I doubt he'll understand any more than Patrick did that being pregnant isn't enough reason to be married."

~

*T*he next day, Matt drove straight to Jenifer's house after work. Kate took his coat at the door. "Jenifer's in her room," she said, sounding wary as he looked up the stairs.

"How is she? Is she all right?"

Kate studied him for a moment. "She will be."

When Matt got to her bedroom, Jenifer was sitting cross-legged on the floor next to her bed, assembling some kind of pop-up Spider-Man tent Robbie had gotten for Christmas. "How are you feeling?" he asked, helping her up when she reached out a hand.

Almost immediately, she seemed to wilt as her eyes shifted to the nightstand.

He followed her gaze, and his heart slammed in his chest at the pregnancy test. Without thinking, he picked up the white plastic stick.

Jenifer sat on the edge of the bed. He wanted to hold her, but he didn't dare. She was too quiet and still, and it scared him.

"I'm sorry," she said at last.

He dragged his eyes from the pregnancy test. "Why are you sorry?"

"Because I don't know if you're ready to have a baby right now."

He sat beside her. His gut twisted, remembering when Jessie had told him she was pregnant. "You don't know if I'm ready? Or if you're ready?" The regret and uncertainty in Jenifer's eyes made him feel eighteen again.

"It's not the baby."

"What's not the baby?"

She squared her shoulders and met his eyes. "I want another child."

If that was true, then what was the problem? Unless he was the problem. "You don't want one with me?"

"That's not what I'm saying." She pushed her hands through her wavy hair, then dropped them to her sides. "I just don't know what this means for us."

He caught her hand and held it tight. "It means we belong together."

"What if it only means you're supposed to be a father?"

"You're wrong. You're the only one for me. With or without a baby." It took longer than it should have for him to see she was comparing him to her past. "Do you believe I love you?"

"Yes."

He turned her face to look into her troubled eyes. "But you doubt me."

"I don't doubt you." Her voice lacked conviction. Or maybe it was that she doubted herself. Either way, things didn't look good for him.

"You don't trust me, then."

"Yes, I do."

Heartache clashed with resentment as he fought for the words to make this right. "No. You don't trust me. You're afraid I'll be like Patrick." He dropped his head, then cursed under his breath. The woman he loves tells him she's having his baby, and he picks a fight with her. Only she looked sad instead of angry, telling him he was right.

"Having a baby changes everything," she said.

His fingers tightened around hers "I sure hope so."

Her head came up. "That's what I mean. I know you. I know what you think you have to do now."

She was right if she thought he wanted to marry her, but he sure as hell wasn't going to ask her tonight. Not this way.

"Can I ask you something?" she said.

"Anything."

"Were you in love with Jessie when you found out she was pregnant?"

His whole body went taut. "We were broken up by then. So, no, I wasn't in love with her."

"But you would have married her anyway, if you were certain the baby was yours?"

He shook his head, frustrated, knowing exactly where this was headed. "Yes, because it would have been the right thing to do."

She lifted those sad, weary eyes to his. "And you always do what's right?"

"This isn't the same thing." But it was easy to see why she thought it was. He needed to find a way to change her mind. "We're together, not falling apart."

"That doesn't always matter." She tried to take her hand away, and he tightened his hold, afraid to let her go.

"I know you were burned in the past, but I'm not Patrick." He needed her to believe in him. She needed reassurance. And he had an idea how to give it to her. "I love you. More than you seem to understand."

"I love you, too."

"Then, please, let me prove to you that you're the only one for me."

17

*J*enifer eyed the sesame seed bagel with cream cheese her mother set on the kitchen table the next morning. They were two things she'd craved her entire first pregnancy. "You remembered."

"How could I forget? You ate so many bagels the last time you were pregnant, we thought for sure Robbie was going to come out sprinkled with sesame seeds." Her mother poured two cups of coffee and set one in front of Jenifer as they sat at the table. The gray sweater her mother wore looked lovely with black jeans and the pearl necklace Jenifer's father had given her for Christmas.

Jenifer smoothed a hand over her queasy belly. She was on day two in the same black yoga pants. White toothpaste stained the M on her Western Michigan hoodie. The only thing she had going for her at the moment was fresh breath. Maybe. So far, she wasn't exactly rocking this pregnancy. "What if everything turns out to be the same as last time?"

Her mother looked over the top of her cup before she sipped her coffee. "Don't compare, Jenifer. Pregnancies, situations. Men. Each one is different. You're different now, too."

She was right. The last time Jenifer was pregnant, her whole life had fallen out of order. Family, graduate school, career. All of it out of balance. Overnight, responsibility and obligation had become more important than love and commitment.

She wouldn't settle for less again—this time, it was love or nothing.

Outside, the snowblower roared to life, and Jenifer got up to look out the window.

"It's Dad." Her mother stood and put a hand on her shoulder. "He wanted to give Matt a break this morning. We noticed he went home early last night."

Jenifer gazed out at the falling snow as her father cleared a path down the driveway. "He's got a lot to think about. We both do."

"How does he feel about the baby?"

Jenifer drank her coffee, her stomach not quite ready for the bagel, and sat back at the table. "He's happy."

The small worry lines between her mother's eyebrows returned. "What about you?"

"I want this baby, too, but I won't make the same mistake as last time. Matt's all about doing the right thing. But if he asks me to marry him…" She looked down and shook her head. "I won't do it again. Not this way."

Last night, everyone pretended nothing happened for Robbie's sake. Matt had stayed for dinner, played a little Xbox with him, and seemed in a rush to go home after Robbie went to bed.

Her mother picked up Robbie's juice box straw from the floor and threw it into the garbage. "Matt came back last night after you went to bed."

Jenifer lifted her head. "What did he want?"

"He asked if he could get something from the coat closet."

"What was it?"

Her mother shrugged and sat next to her. "I don't know." She nudged the bagel closer. "Are you in love with him?"

"Yes." She had no doubt about that.

"Do you believe he loves you?"

"Yes. But will he always love me?"

"No one can answer that question. Relationships flourish, and sometimes they fail. Because yours failed once, doesn't mean it will again. Matt loves you. I see him with Robbie. He loves your little boy. Whatever else is going on, he treats you like you're the most important part of his world."

Jenifer sat up when her phone rang in the living room. Robbie answered. Seconds later, he poked his head into the kitchen with the phone to his ear. "Are you coming over?" His voice dropped. "Oh. Okay. I'll get her." He handed her the phone as he started for the refrigerator. His grandmother stood, put her hands on his shoulders, and steered him back into the living room.

Jenifer rested her elbow on the table with her head in her hand. "Good morning."

"How are you feeling?" Matt's deep, quiet voice made her heart ache.

"Okay. I'm eating breakfast." She poked a finger at her untouched bagel.

"Can I come over?"

It made her sad that he thought he had to ask. She glanced down at the toothpaste on her sweatshirt and pushed back from the table. "Of course."

"I'll be there in a few minutes."

Jenifer hurried upstairs to go change her clothes. God only knew a dirty sweatshirt and yoga pants were no power suit. Sick or not, the last thing she needed was to appear weak and vulnerable in front of a man hell-bent on protecting the world.

Twenty minutes later, she was dressed in dark jeans, leather boots, and the black turtleneck sweater her sister had given her for Christmas. There wasn't much she could do about the hair, so she twisted it up into a knot on top of her head. Makeup mostly disguised the dark shadows under her eyes. Matt would see through it, but he'd also see that she could take care of herself.

He was talking to her father outside when she got back downstairs. Their backs were turned to her, but she could tell her father had his arms folded over his chest. The falling snow had turned to light flurries. Robbie and her mother were building a snowman in the side yard. After a short while, her father started into the garage and Matt came up the porch steps with his head down.

Jenifer opened the door for him and shuddered in the bitter cold air.

Matt kicked the snow off his boots and shook his head. "Your father hates me."

She bit back a smile. That wasn't true. He liked Matt and all the ways he doted on her. It was the pregnancy that made him nervous. "He doesn't hate you. He's worried."

"I know. We need to talk." His eyes were intense, his hand on the doorknob. "First, do you believe in me?"

Her fingers bunched around the ends of her sleeves. "I do. You're a good man."

His shoulders relaxed a bit and he smiled for the first time since he got there. "Then will you come home with me for a little while?"

The way he asked her to *come home* made her heart beat faster. Not sure why he wanted to leave, she looked outside for her mother. Robbie stood on tiptoes beside her, tying a long red scarf around his snowman's neck. Hopefully her parents wouldn't mind watching him for a little while. She grabbed her coat from the closet and pulled a knit hat from the basket by the door. Matt reached for her coat and held it out for her. He took her hat and fit it over her head, then tugged her collar up around her neck with a soft kiss. The light scruff on his face scratched her cheek.

"I love you." He rested his forehead on hers. "Everything will be all right."

While she talked with her mother about Robbie, Matt took an old baseball cap out of his jacket pocket and gave it to him for the snowman. Even now, Matt managed to make him happy with a small, simple gesture. Jenifer caught up with him at the end of the driveway. He hooked her hand through his arm when she started to reach into her pocket, then he led her across the street, leaving footprints in the snow.

Rather than decorate both their homes for Christmas, they'd put up a tree and lights at Jenifer's house and hung a wreath on his front door. Even though his house was bigger, they usually spent most of their time across the street. He often told her he wished his house felt more like a home, making her sad. Especially since his house was where he had grown up.

Jenifer pulled off her hat and caught the subtle smell of paint when they got inside. Matt helped her with her coat as she took off her boots by the door. Her gaze narrowed to the long wall behind his sectional. The patchwork of brown paint samples that had been there for months were covered over with a single shade of taupe. "When did you paint?"

Matt hung his jacket by the door and bent over to untie his boots. "After I got home last night. I stayed up late." He took her coat and laid it over the arm of the sectional.

The paint color wasn't all that was new. A brown-and-beige Persian-style area rug in the living room fit what she imagined as Matt's style when he tried. Square pillows and a chunky knit blanket folded on the sofa caught her even more by surprise. A pine-scented candle on his coffee table took the place of the game controllers he'd left at her house for Robbie.

This was not how his house looked when she was last there on Christmas Eve.

She went to sit on the sofa and studied the blank space over his fireplace. The gold-framed mirror his mother had given to him was gone. It appeared his project wasn't quite finished yet. "The room looks great. Why did you do all of this?"

He brushed snow from the top of his head, then put his hands on his hips. "For you."

Jenifer blinked. "Me? Why?"

He seemed to think for a moment as he walked over to the fireplace. Kneeling, he crumpled up pieces of newspaper and stuffed them around a pile of wood, then lit the fire. He watched the flames catch for a few seconds before he got up and sat next to her.

"I have this image of my life in my head. It's more like a puzzle with a bunch of missing pieces. Making lieutenant, buying the house, those were pieces. But they weren't enough. Nothing in my life was ever enough before you.

"I love you. I want to make a home for us. Not because of the baby, but because of how you make me feel. Because there is no one else in the world I want to come home to for the rest of my life. Your father told me a little while ago that you don't need any more empty promises. He said you could parent two children better than others raise one, and if I can't promise you forever, then I need to make room for a man who will." He lifted her hand and pressed a kiss to her palm. "I told him, and I'm telling you, I *am* that man."

A lump stuck in her throat. Her eyes filled. She wanted so much to believe this moment was about them and nothing else.

With a knowing look, Matt reached for her coat over the arm of the sofa. He put his hand inside one of the pockets. "I have thought about you every single day since the night we met." He sat back and brushed his thumb over her cheek. "I fell in love with you the night of the baseball game, and I knew I wanted to marry you the moment I woke up after the fire."

He tucked a small velvet box into her hand. "I was afraid you were going to find this before we got here. I put it in your pocket last night so that you would know I had it before now."

She could barely breathe as he dropped to his knee.

Gazing at her with those serious blue eyes, he took her hand. "Will you please marry me?"

Tears of joy and relief streamed down her cheeks. "Yes." She surrendered her heart for the very last time as he opened the box and slid a sparkling diamond ring onto her finger.

He skimmed his hands to her hips, pulling her down beside him, whispering, "I'm yours, Jenifer, now and forever."

~

*J*t was midafternoon when Jenifer woke to Matt's voice outside his bedroom door. She stretched out under the blanket and buried her face in his pillow. The fire had burned to embers before they'd finally gone upstairs and made love again. Tempted to close her eyes once more, she picked up one of Matt's T-shirts from the floor and pulled it over her head, then went to go find him when he didn't come back after a few minutes.

His voice came from the small bedroom at the top of the stairs. "She said she usually feels worse in the morning. I think she's feeling a little bit better now."

Jenifer smiled.

She found him sitting on the edge of a twin-size bed. She appreciated how he wore his jeans, zipped but with the button undone, as if he'd thrown them on in a rush. His chest and feet were bare. Day-old whiskers added to his whole sexy, disheveled, soon-to-be a husband look.

Her husband.

Clothes were piled high next to him on the bed. Boxes and plastic crates covered the floor, some full, others half-empty. Baseball pennants, movie posters, and a framed jersey hung on the dark-blue walls. A bookshelf by the closet displayed rows of baseball trophies, ribbons, and medals.

He caught her eye when she came into the doorway. "I'll call you in a few days." He pushed the clothes on the bed to the side, making room for her to sit next to him. "I'll tell her. I love you, too, Mom."

"You got ahold of her?" Jenifer sat cross-legged next to him on the bed. "What did she say?"

"They won't be home from the cruise until the end of the

weekend. She called as soon as she got my email. She said I'm a lucky man." He skimmed his thumb over her diamond. "I can't say I disagree."

Goose bumps traveled down her bare legs, and Matt covered her with a quilt from the end of the bed. "She's worried about you. She asked me how long you were sick with Robbie," he said in a tone that told her he was ashamed for not knowing. "I told her I would ask you."

"Three months, and then it was over." She rested her head against his shoulder. "I'll be all right. We'll get through it."

He rubbed his hand over the top of the quilt, warming her legs. "She offered to come home and help."

"Do you think she'll be here when the baby's born?"

He pressed a kiss on the side of her head and laughed. "I think you'll have to lock the doors to keep her away."

Jenifer glanced up at the Yankees pennants tacked on the walls and wondered what he was like as a kid. "Is this your old bedroom?"

"Can you tell?" He followed her eyes around the room. "I never finished cleaning it out."

She grinned at the mess he'd made. "What happened?"

"You happened." He flicked the tip of her nose. "You distracted me."

The understatement made her smile. "Do you think this could be Robbie's room?" Reality had set in fast since morning. She didn't doubt where they would live. Not when his home was so much larger and filled with memories from his childhood.

Matt shook his head. His eyes went to the window over the desk. "No, probably not. Besides, is this where you really want to live?"

She looked at him, surprised. "I thought that was what you would want."

"It is. But it's not just up to me. There's a lot of work we would have to do if we stay here. Everything from the furnace to the appliances is outdated."

She leaned back on her hands and thought about all the things they could do with the house. "Then we update. I want to raise our family where you grew up."

When the corner of his mouth turned up, she knew he did, too. "This wasn't always my room. When I was younger, I had the bedroom next to my mother's. She had the room I'm in now."

"Why did you switch bedrooms?"

His smile grew. "It was easier to sneak out of the house from this room."

Jenifer looked out into the hallway toward the stairs. "You did that?"

He stood and pulled her to her feet. He led her to the window where he put his hand on her shoulder and pointed to the roof over the screened porch below. "I did in high school. You didn't?"

"No." Imagining Matt sneaking out his bedroom window reminded her there was a lot they still didn't know about each other. "What did you do when you got out?"

"Not much. I met friends at the lake. We'd build a fire, play music, drink beer." He gave her an awkward grin. "Now probably isn't the best time to tell you all that."

"Why not?"

He inhaled deeply, then exhaled through his mouth. "Because I want to talk to you about becoming Robbie's father."

Her head came up. "You want to adopt him?" She'd worried until now that Matt might, in subtle ways, see the baby as theirs and Robbie as hers.

He took hold of both her hands, his expression changing from anxious to earnest. "If you'll let me."

She thought nervously about Robbie and Patrick. She wanted Robbie to have a father, but if Matt adopted him, what would that do to Patrick's parents? Robbie was the only family they had left. She didn't know what to say.

If he was disappointed she didn't give him an answer, it didn't show. "You don't have to decide right now." He gave her a crooked grin and steered her out to the hallway. "Especially since I just confessed to being a delinquent. Let's get back to your house and talk about it later."

She paused at the top of the stairs. She grinned back, content to change the subject for now. "I can't believe you broke out of the house in the middle of the night."

He turned around and walked backwards toward his room. He winked. "You wouldn't have been able to resist me back then."

She shook her head, still smiling.

He was probably right.

18

The next afternoon, Jenifer put her hand on Matt's arm and stood on her toes as he lowered his head. "You don't have to do this," she whispered.

He moved his lips close to her ear. "Yes. I do." Careful not to track snow into the house, he picked up two more suitcases to load into her parents' car.

"Thank you, Matt," her mother said, pulling on her coat and gloves, frowning at her husband after Matt went back outside.

Jenifer crossed her arms over her chest as her father watched Matt make a third trip to the car. "I wish you wouldn't do this. He thinks you don't like him."

The corner of his mouth twitched. "It's penance." Fit as a man in his thirties, fifty-five-year-old Tom Harmon was perfectly capable of carrying his own suitcases out to the car. Average height with an above-average sense of humor, he typically saw the best in everyone, though he could be overly protective and, all too often, blunt.

Robbie stuffed the last sugar cookie into his mouth and wiped his hands on his pants. He grabbed his jacket from the hook by the door and put it on. "What's penance?"

Her father put on the pulpit-face he used when he tried to be serious. "It's what happens when a man knocks—"

Jenifer sent him a sharp look, not trusting what he would say next.

"Tom," her mother snapped, obviously warning him too. She pointed at the last box to go out to the car. "It's getting late. They have things to do."

Robbie sat on the floor and pulled on his boots, giving his grandfather a curious look. "When a man knocks on what, Grandpa?"

Jenifer arched her brow. Matt had talked to her father about marrying her last night. He promised to give Matt a chance. Now was the time to start.

"Penance," he said to Robbie, acknowledging his daughter with a nod, "is when a good man knocks on the door and asks if he can help."

She smiled at Matt behind her father. He didn't know Matt had come back into the house and heard what he said.

Her mother gave Robbie a hug. "Call me later," she said over the top of his head. "And let me know how everything goes."

"I will." They had plans to tell Robbie about the baby and the wedding after her parents left. She was more concerned about the baby than the wedding. The adoption still weighed heavy on her mind.

"Don't worry. He's going to be thrilled, you'll see." Her mother kissed her cheek. "Have you talked to your mother again?" she asked Matt.

He picked up the last box and waited with Robbie to go back outside. "They're not back from their cruise yet. I'll call her tomorrow when she gets home."

Jenifer went to get her coat from the closet to follow them out to the car. Her father shook his head and gave her a hug good-bye. "It's cold and slippery out there. Stay inside." He gave Matt a serious look when he shook his hand. "You take care of them."

Matt rested his eyes on Jenifer, and her heart turned over in her chest. "Always."

From the front door, she watched Matt fit the box into the back of their car and kiss her mother goodbye. She took a deep breath and waved as her parents drove off before Robbie trailed Matt back into the house.

Robbie kicked off his boots and hung up his jacket next to Matt's. "Come sit down with me," she said as she walked over to the sofa. "We need to talk to you about something."

"What's wrong?" Robbie's eyes darted to the game system he'd played since Christmas morning. He gave Matt a woeful look. "Do you want your game back?"

"No." Matt shook his head and sat in the chair opposite them. As if he couldn't help himself, he leaned forward and said, "It looks like you get to keep it."

Robbie swung his head around to look at her, his mouth wide open.

She rolled her eyes at Matt. "What he means," she said, trying to get Robbie's attention back, "is that Matt and I are getting married, and we're all going to live in the same house."

As she expected, Robbie appeared positively gleeful. "When?"

"Soon." She put her hand on Robbie's knee. "Honey." She waited until he looked up at her. "We're going to have a baby, too. That means you're going to be a big brother."

Robbie's hazel eyes went big and round and dropped to her belly.

Matt inched forward in his chair. "How do you feel about that?"

Robbie appeared to think for a moment. "Does that mean you're going to be my dad?"

Jenifer shifted her weight against the leather cushions as Matt studied the wall over Robbie's shoulder with particular interest. "Is that what you want?" she asked, deciding Robbie should have a say in the decision. "Do you want him to be your father?"

Robbie sat up straight, his face brimming with hope. "Yes."

Jenifer met Matt's eyes. He seemed as anxious as Robbie to hear her answer. Giving him Patrick's son was probably the hardest and best decision she would ever make. After a few seconds, she nodded, and Matt got up to sit on the other side of Robbie.

Matt grinned at him. "I want that, too."

Robbie turned to face Jenifer. "Will I have two dads now?"

Jenifer looked at Matt, only this time she was waiting for him to answer as a thought about that came to mind.

"You bet," he said without missing a beat. "And you have to be pretty special for that to happen."

"Where are we going to live?"

Jenifer worried how Robbie might feel about this, too. Though Matt's house made more sense, she wasn't sure how even more change might affect Robbie. "We were thinking we could live in Matt's house," she said.

"Do you want to live there?" Matt asked.

Robbie scratched his head and scrunched his face. "Did you live there when you were six?"

Matt smiled at him. "Yes."

"Did you go to my school?"

Matt's smile grew wide. "I did."

Robbie shrugged as if the answer was obvious. "Then I think we should live at your house."

~

After Robbie went to bed, Matt settled on the sofa next to Jenifer and stretched out his legs on the ottoman. He waited for her to pick out a movie, watching as she scrolled up and down the On-Demand menu three times. Finally, he plucked the remote from her hand and picked a movie without looking at the title.

Jenifer yawned and tucked her arm through his, resting her

head on his shoulder. "You don't even know which movie you just picked out."

"It doesn't matter." He leaned over for a kiss and saw the dark circles under her eyes in the white lights from the Christmas tree. "You're going to sack out on the sofa, and then I'm going to watch a football game."

She yawned again and slapped his leg when he laughed. "I'm not going to sleep yet. It's still early."

Maybe. But that sure didn't stop her from grabbing a blanket from the back of the couch and covering their legs after he moved the ottoman closer for her feet to reach. Covered in thick socks, her small feet tented the blanket, while his stuck out at the end. She was always freezing. Even now in flannel pants and one of his thermal shirts with the sleeves pulled down over her hands.

He touched his thumb to her diamond ring underneath the cuff. "You're tired. Maybe you should go to bed. We'll make plans tomorrow about moving you guys across the street."

"You're going to sleep here until we move, aren't you?"

That suited him just fine now that Robbie knew they were going to be a family. "You're okay with that?"

"I don't want to sleep alone anymore. Not when you're home." She turned her head and kissed him underneath his ear. "Is everything okay?"

He let his gaze drift from her ring, to her belly, and finally, to those beautiful caramel-brown eyes staring up at him. "How could it not be?"

She sat up and fixed the blanket over their legs. "I just mean that everything's happening so fast. Would it be better if we slowed things down?"

"No." He laid his hand on her flat belly and tried to imagine what she would look like in a few months. "I don't want to slow anything down."

"Including the adoption?"

He angled his head back to look at her. And so that she could see he was serious. "Especially the adoption."

"Okay. I'll call an attorney this week. But can I ask you something first?"

"Anything." He imagined she had a lot of questions about the adoption. He anticipated them. Yes, he loved Robbie. Yes, he would always be Robbie's father, even if something happened to their marriage—not that anything ever would. No, he would never think of the child she was carrying as his only "real" child.

He was prepared to answer any questions she had to ask him.

Her face flushed a little. "Would you consider having Robbie keep his last name?"

Slowly, he picked up the remote and turned off the television. That was a question he hadn't expected. "You want him to keep his name? Why?"

"Because I have you, Robbie, and our baby. You have us. Forever. Robbie is the only family Robert and Elizabeth have left."

"I would never take him away from them."

"I know." She sounded rushed and apologetic, as if she was afraid to offend him. "But it might feel that way. And they've already lost too much."

He got up and crossed the room. Bracing his hands over the fireplace, he stared down at the floor. "You don't think it would be strange to him to have a different last name?"

"We'll explain to him why." She sank back against the cushions. "Did you mean what you said to him about having two fathers?"

Matt turned around with his hand on the mantle. "He will have two fathers. I don't care for the way Patrick treated you, but from what you've told me, he was a good dad. He loved Robbie. Robbie deserves to know that."

"He could keep a part of Patrick by having his name. Robert

147

and Elizabeth wouldn't feel like they've lost him again. If we give them this one important thing."

"What about you?" Nichols was Patrick's name. Matt wanted her to belong to him. It made him feel like a damn caveman, but while he could entertain the idea of sharing his son with another man, he would not share his wife. "What name will you use?"

"Barnes," she said, with another yawn as she got up to stand next to him. "Will you just think about it? We don't have to decide tonight."

"I will think about it." He put his hands on the sides of her face and kissed her forehead. "You should go to bed. I'll be up in a little while."

"We'll talk in the morning?"

"Sure. Get some sleep." He watched her go upstairs, visibly exhausted as the wood steps creaked beneath her feet. When he heard the bedroom door close, he sat down again and closed his eyes.

He had made up his mind about Robbie's name almost as soon as she'd asked. Robbie should keep his name, more for his sake than anyone else's. What troubled Matt was the uncertainty about the kind of father he would be. Russo had left him without an example to follow. Was that good or bad? What would his life have been like if his parents had stayed together? Or if Russo had stuck around at all?

Robbie's situation was entirely different. Patrick had acknowledged him and loved him. He didn't leave his son by choice.

Sometime later, Jenifer's quiet voice sounded from the top of the stairs. "Are you down there?"

He cracked one eye open and saw it was after midnight. "Sorry. I fell asleep." He pushed to his feet and turned off the television and Christmas lights. "Are you okay?"

"I'm fine. Just looking for you."

After he took off his clothes and got into bed, she curled up next to him. He rolled onto his side and wrapped her up in his arms. Now that he was awake, he wanted to talk. About Robbie, and maybe his father. And then, he wanted her.

Hope faded quickly after she tucked a cold foot between his legs, sending a shiver up his spine as he felt her fall back asleep.

Strangely, that was enough.

❧

Sunlight spilled through the bathroom window as Jenifer rinsed her face over the white pedestal sink. Matt's guilt-ridden expression when she'd gotten out of bed stuck in her head. There was no way to ease him into morning sickness, or any chance of disguising it.

She brushed her teeth as a light tap sounded at the door. "Can I come in?"

She looked out to the hallway where he was leaning against the railing at the top of the stairs. Blurry-eyed and wearing nothing but a scruffy beard and a loose pair of jeans, he appeared half-asleep. He worried about her, she knew, but something more was bothering him this morning. Robbie's name was a likely culprit.

"Come back to bed. It's still early." She walked around him to peek into Robbie's room. He was still sound asleep, and she closed his door.

Matt started downstairs. "I'll be there in a minute."

Concerned about him now, she followed behind him, wishing she wore more than a T-shirt after she shivered at the bottom of the stairs. He rubbed her arms, frowning down at her bare legs. "Go wrap up in your blanket on the sofa. I'll make you something to eat."

Cold and queasy, she went to lie down in the living room while the sun continued to rise. As she settled against the leather cushions, she admired the warm, cozy room, imagining the home she and Matt would create together. One filled with love and trust. A commitment they could both count on.

The sound of bare feet on the wood floors made her look up. Matt came around the corner with a plate of toast and a cup of coffee in his hands. A water bottle stuck out of the back pocket of his jeans.

After setting the coffee and toast on the coffee table, he pulled the water from his pocket and sat next to her. "I'll have to pick up more bagels for you, and I wasn't sure about the coffee. So I brought water, too."

"Thank you." She studied his quiet expression as she reached for the water. "Do you want to talk?"

He grabbed the bottle and twisted off the cap for her. "I thought about what you said last night, and I think Robbie should keep his last name."

She considered the toast and decided it was better to wait a little longer before she gave it a try. "Are you sure?"

He nodded and tucked the blanket around her legs. "If this were just about me, I would want him to have my last name. But this is about him. If I do this right, and he accepts me as his father, then that's all that matters."

"Don't you see? He already thinks of you as his father."

Matt picked up the coffee and stared into the cup. "It's a wonder how I got so lucky."

"Will you tell me what else you're thinking?"

He answered with a shrug. "It's New Year's Eve."

She tapped his cup with her bottle. "I guess that means I'm driving tonight."

"We don't have to go anywhere. Everyone will understand."

"I want to go." She flashed him a grin. "You said Nate has a new girlfriend. I want to meet her."

Matt looked dubious. "I'm not sure about the girlfriend part."

She flapped her hand in the air. "Either way, I'd like to meet her." Their plans to be at a hotel party tonight seemed an excellent way to announce their engagement and the baby to everyone. "Besides, Robbie's going to his friend's house tonight. We should take advantage and have some fun."

Matt set his coffee back on the table. "If that's what you want."

"Is something else bothering you?"

"No." He shifted, turning her with him so he could rub her back. "I'm worried about you, that's all."

She understood. Because she was worried about him, too.

19

"Won't you at least think about it?" Jenifer shrugged into her black wool coat and watched Matt fix his tie before Nate picked them up a Matt's house. He owned one suit, black, tailored to his wide shoulders, slim waist, and long legs. She picked out his white dress shirt and red paisley tie. He'd managed the black belt and leather loafers all on his own.

Even agitated and uncooperative, he made her heart race.

Matt dropped his hands and shook his head. "I won't use the money from Robbie's trust fund to work on the house."

She frowned and tried one more time to explain about the money. "I'm not referring to his trust fund. I'm talking about life insurance money. Money that was left to me. Robbie's inheritance is an entirely different fund."

Matt shook his head again and pulled on his dress coat. There was no real anger behind his stubborn expression. "No. We're not spending *that* money on *this* house." His voice sounded willful, exasperated, and proud.

Jenifer gave in. There was nothing wrong with his '80s kitchen. It certainly wasn't worth offending or antagonizing him.

His mouth drew tight as his eyes traveled over the oak-veneered cabinets, the blue-tiled countertops, then down to the beige-patterned linoleum floor. He let out a heavy sigh and walked over to stand with her by the counter. "You're right about the kitchen. We'll look at the numbers. I can do most of the work myself."

He knew about the two million dollars of life insurance money, and the last thing she wanted was for it to become a problem for them. "Does the money bother you?"

"No." He squared his shoulders and put his hands into his coat pockets. "It doesn't bother me. But I would prefer it if we live on the money you and I make."

She wanted that, too, and what he said reminded her of something she'd been thinking about. "How would you feel if I took next year off? I would go back the following year."

His brows arched. "You're okay with that?"

She took a pair of black leather gloves from her pocket and put them on. "I am." Matt knew that her working at all had been a point of contention with Patrick. She'd fought long and hard for her career. Even so, she wouldn't have given up the first year home with Robbie for anything in the world.

"We'll more than manage." He put his hands on her shoulders and rested his chin on top of her head. "Will you be able to work while you're sick?"

"Yes." It wouldn't be easy, though. Long, exhausting days lay ahead for sure. But she knew because of Robbie that it would be worth every minute in the end.

Matt buttoned his coat after he looked out the window. "Nate's here." He looked down at her four-inch heels "You're wearing those in the snow?"

She smiled at the mixed emotions in his voice. He had admired the silver heels when she'd first put them on, asking if maybe she would wear them after they got home tonight. At the moment, he seemed to prefer different footwear even though he'd cleared the driveway and it wasn't snowing anymore. "I'm not wearing boots, so forget it," she said.

"Come on, then." He held out his hand begrudgingly. "I don't want you falling and making the night memorable."

She dropped a gloved hand in his and walked with him out to Nate's Jeep. The sky was clear and the air so cold she hurried to slide across the back seat before Matt got in behind her and closed the door.

Nate turned around and introduced the woman sitting beside him before the overhead light dimmed. "Caroline, this is Matt Barnes and Jenifer Nichols."

Caroline twisted in her seat to face them. "Caroline Fitzpatrick. Pleasure to meet you." In her late twenties, Caroline was lovely. And had her fair skin and bob of auburn hair not revealed her heritage, her strong Irish accent would have surely given her away.

"Where are you from?" Matt asked, sounding to Jenifer as if he suspected the answer.

"Dublin." She tucked a stray hair behind her ear. "I've just come to the States a short time ago."

Jenifer inched forward, intrigued, and ignored the curious look Matt shot Nate in the rearview mirror. "How did you meet Nate?"

Caroline flashed Nate the sweetest smile as he started to drive toward the city. "Nate's sister introduced us Christmas Eve. She's acquainted with my family here."

Finding the story utterly romantic, Jenifer started to hope Nate might actually find love this time. "Do you like it here?"

Caroline let out what sounded like a soft, wistful sigh. Her face glinted in the city lights as the Jeep slowed in traffic. "I do, but this is all very new to me."

Jenifer caught the cautionary look from Nate to Matt in the rearview mirror. Matt cleared his throat, laying his hand on her leg. Jenifer silently asked him *what?* when she saw Nate sit up straight with his eyes back on the road.

Matt only shook his head and covered her hand with his.

After a few minutes, Nate looked back in the mirror. First at

Matt, then Jenifer. "Do you guys mind if we leave early tonight? I told Caroline we have to work early tomorrow morning."

Light from the street caught Matt's face when Jenifer nodded at him. "That works for us," he said.

The corner of her mouth lifted. She'd swear he just peeked at her heels. It was going be a long night. It would be a miracle if she managed fulfill whatever fantasy he was having over there, no matter what time they got home. It wouldn't have surprised her if Nate had planned to spend the night at the hotel. Until she met Caroline. Now she got the impression there was something about Caroline that kept Nate on his best behavior.

~

*I*nside the hotel, Matt took Jenifer's coat and gloves, then stuck the gloves into one of her coat pockets. Her silver cocktail dress sparkled in the light with its high scooping neckline and low plunging back. He watched as she covered her left hand with the right one, hiding her ring until they shared their news. "Will you wait here for me? I'll be right back," he asked.

Nate helped Caroline with her coat and gestured Matt to the coatroom. Matt strode behind him through the high-ceiling lobby, passing an enormous Christmas tree decked out with red ribbon and white sparkling lights. Leather chairs were clustered into small seating areas where Jenifer went to sit with Caroline. Christmas music played in the background. The smell of pine and leather mixed with all of the excitement of the holidays.

When they were far enough away, Nate slowed down and looked at Matt. "This is my sister's doing. Christmas Eve she waltzes into my parents' house with Caroline's aunt and uncle. They're friends from Ireland. Oh, and look, they brought their niece, fresh off the island." He ran a hand over his wavy red hair, staring hard at Matt. "I mean, really fresh."

Looking over his shoulder, Matt couldn't tell why Nate had a problem with the beautiful redhead in an emerald-green dress. "I like her. She seems nice. Why don't you give her a chance?"

Nate grabbed a hanger when they got to the coat closet and pointed it at him. "That's the thing. She's *too* nice for me."

"What are you talking about?" Matt tilted his head toward Jenifer in the lobby. "What's wrong with nice? Jenifer's nice."

Nate hung up Caroline's coat, and then his, before he took the two draped over Matt's arm. "Yeah, well, Jenifer wasn't almost a nun six months before you met her."

Incredulous, Matt leaned around Nate and looked at Caroline again. He laughed, but only for a second. "You're dating a nun?"

Nate's jaw flexed. "She's not a nun. She was studying to become one. That's what they told me Christmas Eve. I don't know how long she was in before she quit. Or whatever you do when you leave a convent." He put his hands in the air. "Still, what am I supposed to do?"

Matt drew a blank.

"You're not helping."

"You're right. I'm sorry."

"Forget it." Nate shook his head and started back to the lobby. "Maybe I should just give this a chance."

"She deserves that much. So do you." Matt turned his head, looking for Jenifer, and accidentally walked into the elderly woman in front of him. "I'm sorry." He threw out his arms and caught her before she fell over. "Are you okay?"

The woman came up to his chest and weighed no more than a hundred pounds. She smiled with forgiveness as she regained her balance. "Yes. Yes, of course." Dressed in a glittering black gown with a knot of silver hair, she tipped her face up to look at him, and her smile faded. Her hands tightened on Matt's wrists as she turned to the older gentleman behind her. The man's eyes met Matt's for a brief second before he looked away.

"Come, Anna." The man gently withdrew her hands. "Stai bene."

"I'm sorry," Matt said again, wondering if he'd just been cursed out in Italian.

Nate clapped a hand on his shoulder. "I wouldn't worry. I don't think she's hurt. You just startled her."

Jenifer and Caroline met them by the Christmas tree and walked with them into the formal dining room. Several guests gathered by a white marble fireplace flanked by floor-to-ceiling windows. The view overlooked a cold, snowy Lake Michigan. Waitstaff dressed in black trousers and white tuxedo shirts served canapés, shrimp, and smoked salmon to mingling guests. Frank Sinatra's voice crooned in the background.

"Everything okay?" Jenifer asked when Matt pressed his hand to her back, searching for Henry and Lauren.

He put his lips close to her ear as Nate and Caroline veered off. "I'll tell you later."

Henry had staked out a table near the fireplace. From across the room, Nate appeared to be making introductions as Caroline sat beside Lauren at the table. Henry waved to someone and Nate turned around. His face went blank. Henry's sister, Rachel, came over to give her brother a hug before she kissed Nate's cheek. The man beside her shook everyone's hand. Then Henry pointed to Matt and she waved.

Matt watched as Nate seemed to give Rachel what passed as a friendly smile. Nate waited until after Rachel and her date moved away before he sat at the table. He caught Matt's eye, his brows pinched together, and held up his finger asking for a beer.

Matt glanced at Henry. Henry stared at Nate. Nate had never acknowledged his feelings for Rachel, and Henry never asked. Caroline, bless her heart, showed the patience of a saint.

Matt took Jenifer's hand and started for the bar. Maybe his life wasn't so crazy after all. "Would you like a drink?"

She nodded, looking behind him. "Those people over there are watching you."

He turned and followed her gaze to a table by the windows. The woman he'd run into earlier quickly looked away.

As he explained what happened, Jenifer leaned against the bar. Her attention seemed divided.

"You're staring," he said, ordering their drinks, wishing she would look the other way.

She touched his arm, tilting her head for him to turn around. "Maybe you should look again."

He kept his eyes forward and passed her two glasses of ice water, the second for Caroline, not knowing what she liked to drink. "Why?"

She peered over the edge of her glass. "Because one of the men at that table looks a lot like you."

Curious now, he lowered his head and looked behind him. He studied the three men at the table, the older gentleman he saw earlier and two men in their fifties. They all looked alike, with dark hair, olive skin, and a distinctive nose. A woman also in her fifties and two younger women Matt's age rounded out the table. They appeared to be a family, and all but one of them slanted a look in his direction.

Jenifer inched closer. "Do you see the man in the dark-gray suit?"

Matt sipped a beer the bartender set in front of him and looked again. "You think that's Russo?"

"Maybe." She rubbed a hand over his coat sleeve. "Are you okay?"

Matt's heart hammered in his chest. If he had to guess, he would say the man studiously gazing out the window, the one in the gray suit, could be his father.

"I'm fine," Matt lied, tipping the bartender and picking up the second beer for Nate. He held out his arm for Jenifer to walk her to the table. He didn't want her caught in the middle of all this. If that was Nicholas Russo, sitting with family who might belong to Matt, too, then it was up to his father to make a move.

"There you are," Henry said when they got to the table. "Everything all right?"

Matt grinned, unwilling to let anything dampen their news.

"Everything's great." Before they sat, he handed Nate his beer and pulled Jenifer close to his side. "Especially now that we're getting married."

Henry's face broke into a grin. "That's great news."

Henry's wife, Lauren, came around the table to give them each a hug. "I'm so happy for you."

Nate stood and raised his glass. "Congratulations, my friend."

Even Caroline beamed.

The man in the gray suit looked on.

"Even better." Matt lifted Jenifer's hand to his lips. He kissed her palm, hardly able to believe what he was about to say. "We're going to have a baby."

Mouths fell open in stunned silence. A hand clapped on his shoulder. He barely noticed, focused on Jenifer's eyes sparkling with the kind of love he thought he would never find. Reminding him that no matter what happened, they would always have each other.

20

"We'll ask your father to marry us," Matt said to Henry when everyone sat again.

Henry put his arm around his wife's shoulder. "You know he'll do it. He's still disappointed he wasn't ordained when we got married."

Lauren leaned forward and folded her arms on the edge of the table. "Have you set a date yet?"

Matt understood Jenifer wanted to plan a bigger wedding, for his sake. But he didn't want to wait long. "We'll talk to Henry's dad and see when he can do it, but hopefully it'll be soon."

Nate shook his head like he still couldn't believe the news. "When is the baby due?"

"I'll find out next week, but it should be sometime in the middle of summer," Jenifer said.

Lauren raised her wine glass and toasted them. "Our Matt is going to be a daddy."

"Times two," Jenifer said, smiling as she held up two fingers. "Robbie is a lucky little boy."

Matt believed the privilege was his.

After dinner was over, he took Jenifer's outstretched hand as the DJ played her favorite song.

She sent him a cheeky little grin and walked backward, pulling him through a small crowd to the dance floor. "Dance with me?"

"Always." He gathered her into his arms, breathing in her warm, soft scent as Jason Mraz sang about never giving up. Matt couldn't have agreed with him more. He tightened his arms around her, welcoming the distraction from being watched since he'd stood at the bar. She had looked over her shoulder during dinner as if she'd felt it, too. Neither of them mentioned Russo to the others.

Jenifer turned her face up to look at him. "Are you going to say anything to those people tonight?"

He trailed his hand down her back, teasing his fingers over her soft skin. "No, I don't think so."

If he knew for sure the man was Nicholas Russo, and they were alone, he would approach him. Confronting him in front of others without evidence was not the way he would handle the situation.

As they danced, Jenifer started to lean a little heavier in his arms. She laid her head on his shoulder and stifled a yawn. He'd thought to ring in the New Year and then leave, but he felt her fading early. It was time to take her home. He spotted Nate across the room, suit coat draped over the back of his chair, engrossed in a conversation with Caroline and Lauren. Henry sat a couple tables over, talking with his sister and the man Henry had introduced to Matt earlier as a former boyfriend.

As the song ended, Matt caught Jenifer's hand and started back to the table. "Let's find Nate and see if he's ready to leave soon."

Jenifer lifted his wrist, looking at his watch. "It's only ten o'clock."

"He won't mind. We'll tell him you're tired. He'll understand. He wanted to leave early anyway."

"Matt?" a man's voice called from behind them.

Matt stopped and looked at Jenifer.

"Can I talk to you for a minute? I'm Nicholas Russo."

Matt's heart punched in his chest. He put a protective hand on Jenifer's arm and nudged her away. "Please. Go sit with Nate and Henry. I'll be there in a minute."

He glanced over to see his father walk out of the crowded dining room. Matt shook his head when she asked if he wanted her to stay. "It looks like he wants to do this alone." And until he knew more, he didn't want Jenifer anywhere near the man.

Matt waited until she got to the table before he went to go find Russo. He was waiting at the end of a short hallway past the kitchen doors. A sharp bite of resentment tempered his excitement over meeting his father after all this time.

Tall and rigid with olive skin and thick, dark hair streaked with silver, Nicholas Russo was an imposing man. Wearing a well-tailored, conservative gray suit, he resembled an expensive lawyer more than a felon. Deep lines creased his forehead as Matt approached him.

A waiter passed through the kitchen doors, stealing a look in their direction. Russo moved to shield Matt from view and the man retreated into the dining room.

Matt straightened and swallowed his pride at the obvious reluctance on his father's face. He wanted answers, but he wasn't about to beg for them. "We don't have to do this."

His father's dark-brown eyes expressed warning. "People are going to notice you after this."

Matt bristled. "Is that a problem for you?"

"No. But it might be a problem for you if people learn that you're my son." Russo hesitated. "You know that, don't you?"

"Yes." Matt thought about the people with his father tonight. Especially the woman he'd walked into in the lobby. "Can I ask you something?"

Russo's expression grew resigned. "Yes."

Matt gestured toward the dining room. "Is that your family with you tonight?"

Russo nodded. "My mother, your grandmother," he said as if he were trying out the words for the first time, "recognized you right away. She wasn't going to let me leave here tonight without talking to you."

Your grandmother. How many times as a kid had he wished to have a grandmother? Or a grandfather? All while the father he did have wanted nothing to do with him. "You don't want to talk to me?"

A smile hinted at his lips. "Because of your mother. She told me she would have my head if anyone ever found out you're my son."

"How did you find out about me?"

"A mutual friend told me she was pregnant. I'd tried to convince her to let me be a part of your life, but she wouldn't have it. I'd been arrested again. She didn't trust me. So I kept my distance like she asked, but I didn't stay away."

"What did you do?"

His father hung his head like he couldn't decide how to answer, then after a few seconds, he looked back up at Matt. "I know that your mother rarely missed a game from the time you first hit a tee ball until you made captain of your high school baseball team. I watched those games from a distance. But once you went to Penn State?" His smile turned proud. "Well, those were the games to see. Especially that championship game. And your mom, God bless her, she had a hard time traveling to watch you play back then."

Matt dropped his arms to his sides, unable to believe what he was hearing. "You watched me play baseball?"

Russo drew a long breath and nodded. "As often as I possibly could."

Matt didn't get it. Why would his father travel to see his games and not talk to him? "I was older by then. You should have said something to me."

"I promised your mother."

"But you still watched me play?"

"I watched you do a lot of things." He fisted a hand to his mouth and blew out his breath. "After you got hit by that car, I thought I'd sooner face Sarah than never have the chance to be close to you. You were only ten years old. I think she understood. The first night you were in the hospital, she left your room for a few minutes and a nurse let me in to see you. You were so small. The cast they put you in looked like it swallowed you whole." Sorrow and regret filled his eyes. "I went to prison shortly after that. I didn't see you again until after you were in high school."

Matt scratched his chin. He couldn't remember anything that happened right after the accident. He certainly didn't remember seeing his father at the hospital.

Russo snorted. "By the way, your haircut when you were sixteen was atrocious. And that Mustang you got a good deal on when you were seventeen? That was mine."

Matt's head came up. He remembered that car. He'd bought it from a girl about his age. Tall, thin, dark hair. He glanced out at the table where his family sat. He'd probably bought the car from one of his cousins.

Russo continued. "I watched you graduate high school and college. I was proud when you joined the fire department. You have always made better choices than I did. But for what it's worth, I think you could have done a lot better than that one girlfriend in high school."

Matt stared at his father. "You know about Jessie?"

"I know about the baby, too." This time, Russo looked out into the dining room, presumably at Jenifer. "At least you've been given a second chance."

Matt's jaw flexed. He wasn't sure how he felt about his father poking around his life when he was a kid, but he sure as hell didn't like it now. Especially if he was watching Jenifer.

Russo raised his hands. "Don't worry. I won't cause you any trouble."

Matt kept his guard up, regardless. "What about you? Do you have a family?"

"Just the people you see here tonight."

"You don't have a wife? Kids?"

His father shook his head. "No wife. One kid," he said without hesitation.

Matt suppressed a smile. Not sure why the acknowledgement pleased him as much as it did. "And what does your family think about me?"

"They knew very little about you for years, though I suspect recently my mother has had my nieces search for you on the internet. I know she keeps a picture of you hidden in a drawer. You're her only grandson. You have no idea what it took to keep her away from you tonight."

This time, Matt turned his head toward the dining room. He wasn't sure how, but he would find a way to talk to his grandmother. "So, what next?"

"This is it. I run a clean operation these days, but people have long memories. It's better for you this way. I live in New York now. I'm only here another week or two. I don't think you'll have any trouble after tonight, but I'd appreciate it if you didn't tell your mother you saw me. I imagine she wasn't too happy to hear from me after the fire."

Matt snorted. His life was exactly as crazy as he thought it was. "You know it sounds strange that you're afraid of my mother?"

Russo reached out his hand, hesitated, then pulled Matt in for a long embrace. "I'll give you some advice, kid. There is no force on earth more terrifying than a woman protecting her child."

*J*t was well before midnight when Matt and Jenifer walked out to the parking lot ahead of Nate and Caroline. Caroline had seemed almost relieved to leave. Matt knew enough to understand seeing Rachel with another man tonight might have dulled some of Nate's charm.

Jenifer clutched the collar of her wool coat as the cold wind whipped through her hair. He clasped her hand, ready if she slipped on the ice. He hadn't had a chance yet to tell her what he and his father talked about. "Did anyone ask where I was earlier?"

"No. But you'll probably get some questions at work tomorrow." Her hand tightened around his. "Are you all right?"

"I will be." Behind them, voices suddenly raised in concern. Matt turned around and saw his grandmother on her knees on the icy pavement. He couldn't understand what she said in Italian. He did recognize the defiance in her voice as she pushed away the hands that tried to help her up. Her clever, deceptive eyes locked on Matt, and she refused to get to her feet.

"Oh my God." Jenifer freed her hand. She pushed him toward his grandmother as Nate and Caroline caught up to them. "You need to see if she's all right."

Concerned the fall might not have been entirely on purpose, Matt left Jenifer with Nate and rushed to his grandmother. When he crouched down to see if she was all right, she pushed against him to stand on her own. Her arms went around his neck, strong and fierce, as her family watched on. His father frowned but didn't interfere.

Matt held on to her tight. "Are you all right?"

She tipped her head back to look up at him. Tears glistened in her eyes. "I am now."

"Me, too." His arms wrapped around her as another piece of his life fell into place. He looked around at those who'd stopped to help, and he grinned, unrepentant, at his father.

Let them talk.

21

*D*ays after the New Year, Matt finished his coffee in Jenifer's kitchen, reading a new text from his grandmother. It was eight in the morning. Jenifer and Robbie had left for school by the time Nate got there to help move them into Matt's house.

Nate rocked his chair back on two legs and crossed his arms over his chest while they waited for Henry to get there. "Is Jessie still texting you?"

Matt raised his eyes and nodded. Her text messages had stopped after her visit to the hospital, then started up again after news of the wedding broke. "She claims now that we never should have broken up." He stopped reading the message from his grandmother and scrolled back through his old texts. He wanted to make sure Jessie's were deleted so Jenifer wouldn't see it. "The one I'm reading now is from my grandmother. If I'm getting it right, she's asking about the wedding. Something about a torta and bouquets." He was getting better at translating her liberal use of Italian in her text messages, but considering he didn't understand a word of Italian and her limited use of English, the margin for error seemed pretty significant.

"Do you think your father is going to say something about you talking to her?"

It didn't seem likely Russo would try to interfere from what his grandmother had told him. Not that he would object to another meeting with him. "He knows I have her address and I sent her flowers. If he has a problem with her having my number, I'm sure I'll hear about it."

Nate dropped his chair back onto the floor. "When was the last time you heard from Jessie?"

"Last night. She knows about the baby and the wedding. She sent messages last week telling me we'll never be over."

"What's that supposed to mean?"

Matt poured more coffee and then told him about the picture Jessie had shown him at the hospital.

"And you think she's sticking to the story she ended the pregnancy because she's jealous of Jenifer?"

"It seems that way. I stopped blocking her number, hoping she'll break down and tell me more. I added my information and an estimated birth date to two adoption search registries, one in Michigan and the other in Florida. I don't know what else I can do."

"Jenifer knows all this?"

"She helped with the adoption registries, but no, I haven't said anything about Jessie's latest text messages. She's sick every morning. I don't want to pile this on top of her, too."

Nate's eyebrows wrinkled as if he didn't agree. "I saw Kyle yesterday. He mentioned Jessie's still asking questions. He thinks he's on your hit list, so for sure he hasn't said anything. I doubt anyone has, but she might have overheard people talking about you at Ernie's."

Matt couldn't do anything about that. The wedding in two weeks wasn't a secret. Neither was the baby. Everyone at the firehouse knew, and it made sense the guys could have been overheard talking about him. But he didn't like it.

When Henry finally got to the house, Matt grabbed his coat,

ready to get started. Nate stood. His chin dropped when he looked outside. "What's Rachel doing here?"

Matt went to let them in as Rachel got out of Henry's truck and followed him up the sidewalk. "I don't know. Is it a problem?" He didn't expect to see Rachel there either. Even Jenifer was at work after he'd convinced her not to waste a day off while she wasn't feeling well.

"No." Nate shoved his hands into the pockets of his jeans, staring unconvincingly out the window. "Why would it be a problem?"

"No reason." At least not one they would discuss as Henry strode up the sidewalk ahead of his sister. Rachel was twenty-five, but Matt knew she might as well be the same gangly fifteen-year-old with braces and braids when it came to any interest Nate had in her.

Rachel's cheeks were flushed from the freezing air when she got inside. She pulled off a knit hat and brushed a hand through her dark-blond hair. Her blue eyes were dancing when she gave Matt a hug. "Henry told me what you guys are up to today. I want to help." She waved behind him at Nate. "I'm so happy for you—getting married, adopting a son, having a baby."

"Thank you." Matt kissed the top of her head. "Jenifer will be sorry she missed you."

"I'll see her at the wedding. I talked to her a couple days ago, and she said it was okay if I bring a date. I hope that's okay with you, too."

"Sure." Matt shook his head for her to leave her boots on when she started to take them off. "Is it the ex-boyfriend we met New Year's Eve?"

"That's him." The low note in Henry's voice made his disappointment clear as he closed the front door behind him. He shrugged at Rachel when her look told him to be quiet.

"We're still working out the *ex* part." Rachel leaned around Matt to look at Nate. "Are you bringing someone to the wedding?"

Nate hesitated, tugging on his ear. "No."

Matt caught Nate's brooding expression when he grabbed his jacket by the door.

Henry's eyes darkened. He cocked his head at his sister and pointed at a cardboard box by her feet. "Why don't you carry that over to Matt's house? We'll follow you with the sofa."

Matt bent down to put on his boots. Nate zipped up his jacket. After Rachel went outside, Henry pointed a finger at Nate. "You need to cut that shit out."

Nate frowned. "What shit?"

"You're thinking about my sister, and I've got enough problems with her taking back the asshole who cheated on her."

Matt's jaw flexed. He didn't know anything about the cheating. It reminded him too much of Patrick and what he did to Jenifer. Rachel was a sweetheart. It was no surprise she would make the guy suffer a little and then give him another chance. Matt wished he'd known before he shook the man's hand when they met. And then agreed to let him come to the wedding.

Nate straightened with a hard look at Henry. "I don't cheat." It looked to Matt like Nate was done denying his attraction to Rachel and went straight to defending his honor.

Henry backed off, looking disgusted with himself. It wasn't like him to start an argument, not with his friends. "That's not what I'm saying. You're eleven years older than her. Jesus, Nate, she's a kid compared to you."

Thinking that wasn't entirely true, Matt kept his thoughts to himself. Rachel had told him stories over the years that would keep her older brother up at night. She had a wild side Henry didn't know about. Still, a gentleman or not, Nate measured his relationships in weeks or months. It was easy to see why that was a problem for Henry.

"I got it." Nate didn't look at either one of them when he went to pick up the end of Jenifer's leather sofa. Matt took the hint and let the subject drop as he went to lift the other end.

Henry opened the door for them. "I'm sorry," he said as Nate walked by. "Sometimes I say stupid shit."

Nate nodded, but Matt got the sense he didn't think Henry had said anything stupid at all.

~

*J*enifer brushed snow off her car after school, hoping to catch Nate and Henry at her house before they finished moving her across the street. Matt planned to have her house empty by the time he went to work tomorrow. He wanted to make sure it was ready to put on the market next week. They had a lot to do before the wedding. They had a lot to do, period. And they were just getting started.

Nate's Jeep and Henry's truck were parked in front of Matt's house when she and Robbie got there. She grabbed her tote from the back seat and let Robbie out of the car. A cold, brisk wind made her breath catch as she pulled Robbie's hood over his head. Across the street, her house looked strange in the dark. A beaten path through the snow led from her old porch to Matt's front door. Through his windows, she could see Rachel coming down the stairs.

Jenifer shrugged off her coat by the door and dropped her bag as she took off her boots. She noticed the heat in the house was turned up when she gave Rachel a hug. "I wish I knew you were going to be here. I would have stayed home to help."

Rachel smiled at the soft swell of Jenifer's belly. "They barely let me do anything. I doubt it would have been worth your while. If you want, though, I can help you unpack while Matt's at work tomorrow."

Jenifer helped Robbie with his jacket, then hung up their coats in the closet. "That'd be great." She looked toward the kitchen when she heard Matt and Henry on the basement stairs.

Matt came out looking for her, his gray plaid flannel shirt half tucked into a pair of ripped jeans and packing tape stuck to the bottom of his sock. "You're home."

His grin, his words, they sunk in her chest and melted her heart. He sounded like he'd waited all day to say that to her on their first official night living together.

But it was the way he said *home* that stirred the butterflies in her belly as she followed him into the kitchen.

Robbie dumped his backpack at the bottom of the stairs, then stayed close to her side, looking a little uncertain despite having been in the house dozens of times.

Nate came in through the back door, kicking off snow and stuffing his gloves into his coat pockets. He raised a hand and Robbie went to give him a high five. "You got yourself a big backyard," he said to Robbie. "What are you going to do with all of that space?"

Robbie's eyes dropped to the large vinyl flap at the bottom of the back door, then back up at Jenifer. "Can we get a dog?"

Jenifer shook her head emphatically and said, "No," at the same time Matt said, "Maybe."

She turned her head and looked at him like he was out of his mind.

"You know, if you like labs, I know a good breeder," Henry said, shooting his sister a look asking her *what* when she shook her head at him.

Matt, damn him, grinned at Jenifer. "How about we let you know?"

Jenifer steered Robbie out of the kitchen before Matt went and promised him a dog. "Let's go upstairs and see your new room."

The distraction worked, for now. Robbie carried his backpack halfway up the stairs while Jenifer thanked the guys and Rachel before they left.

Matt grabbed his keys and started out the door with Nate. "I'll pick up something for dinner and be right back."

Sweeter words were never spoken.

After Robbie showered, Jenifer sat on his bed and combed his wet hair. They'd had little to do to get his bedroom ready before he moved in. The walls were already painted dark blue and when Robbie had asked him, Matt moved his old bookshelf with his baseball trophies next to the dresser under the window. He tacked his collection of baseball pennants on the wall over Robbie's bed. A Spider-Man poster hung on the back of the door.

Robbie tipped his head back and looked at her. "Do you think I can get new Spider-Man sheets for my bed?"

Jenifer held the comb in the air. He had Matt's queen-size bed. Did they even make queen-size Spider-Man sheets? "I don't know. I'll have to see if I can find them."

When she finished with his hair, Robbie jumped off the bed and grabbed his slippers at the same time she heard Matt come home. Robbie rushed downstairs to see what they were having for dinner.

Matt had her sit at the dining room table before he set the pizza down and went to get plates from the kitchen. "Before you say anything, no, this is not the way I plan to make dinner when I'm home during the day and you're not."

God love the man, the last thing she would ever do is complain about a meal someone else put together for her.

After dinner, she sank exhausted into the leather sofa from her house, noticing the black and white portrait of her and Robbie hanging over the fireplace. The living room felt larger with her smaller furniture than it had with his oversized sectional. He'd sold all of his living room furniture, but they kept the dining room set his mother had left behind when she moved. What was left of Jenifer's furniture was stored in his garage, waiting to be sold. The only purchase they'd made together so far was a blue floral area rug for the dining room. The rug complemented the mocha-colored walls he'd recently finished painting. He'd confessed he liked the new wall color she had picked out, but the rug was still growing on him.

Matt sat and lifted her feet onto his lap, covering her with a blanket. She closed her eyes as his warm hands massaged her toes, pressing slowly up under her pajama pants to her knees.

Robbie curled up half-asleep in the leather chair across from them, watching a Marvel movie.

"Did you get any more texts today?" she asked.

His hands went still. "What?"

She opened her eyes. "From your grandmother. Did she send you another text today?"

"Oh, yeah." He pulled his phone from his pocket and showed her the text from that morning.

She sat up, laughing quietly. The message began with *Good morning* in English and ended with what they'd learned was *I love you* in Italian. "Are you going to invite them to the wedding?"

He took the phone and set it on the coffee table. "No, my grandparents are leaving for Florida until April. My father is going back to New York in a couple of days."

She didn't push him. Her parents were in Arizona waiting for her sister to have her baby. His mother and Ben had planned a big vacation with his daughter and her family to Europe months ago. The wedding would be small and intimate, exactly the way they wanted it.

"I'll finish cleaning my house this weekend and give the real estate agent a call on Monday."

He gave her foot a squeeze. "I wish you wouldn't go over there by yourself."

"I won't overdo it. I'm just tired tonight."

"Then let me finish up over there when I get back from work on Sunday."

If that's what he wanted, fine. She would give in this time. She could finish unpacking here with Rachel over the weekend.

A soft snore from the chair had Matt rising to his feet. "I'll carry him up to bed. Then we can go to bed, too."

She stood and folded the blanket on the sofa and started to turn off the lights. His phone pinged from the coffee table before she went upstairs. She picked it up, expecting a message from Nate or Henry. Instead, she saw a text from Jessie. She didn't open it. All she read was the start of the message: *We'll never really be over.*

Matt stood at the top of the stairs. "Are you coming to bed?"

She sank down on the sofa without answering. Her stomach knotted. How in the world could she have forgotten about Jessie?

Matt came back downstairs. "What's wrong? Are you okay?"

She handed him his phone. He read the screen but didn't open the rest of the message. "Jen—"

Tired and frustrated, she tried not to get upset about something he had no control over. "Have you gotten other texts from her?"

He sat next to her, turning the phone over in his hands. "Yes. She found out about the wedding and the baby."

Jenifer remained silent.

"What are you thinking?"

She glanced over at him nervously. "Is she right?"

He fell back against the sofa and shook his head. "No. You know that."

"What if she had your daughter, and she knows where she is now?"

Color rose in his face. "I'm not going to be blackmailed."

Jenifer swallowed hard and rubbed her temples, wishing she'd never looked at his phone. "I'm sorry. Forget I said anything."

"Please don't let her get to you." He rose and pulled her to her feet. "I love you. I want to marry you. Remember that, all right?"

"I love you, too." She leaned into him, and he kissed the top of her head.

"Then let's go to bed, okay?"

She let him take her hand as she followed him upstairs. This was her home now. Her life. And most importantly, he was her man.

22

att slid his tie under his collar as he walked into the bedroom. His heart almost stopped. Facing away, Jenifer slipped her arms into an elegant white cocktail dress. Delicate beading and a deep open V at the back of her wedding dress accentuated her soft curves and slender legs. Captivated, he couldn't tear his eyes away from her if he tried. How something so simple could bring him so much pleasure astonished him.

She must have sensed him there before she smiled over her shoulder. Lifting her long, wavy hair from her neck, she dropped her head. He could barely breathe as he made his way to her. Lightly tracing his fingertip over her silky skin, he pressed a soft kiss to the curve of her neck before he slowly zipped up her dress.

Her head fell back against his chest with a soft sigh. "You are playing with fire, Mr. Barnes."

Slowly, deliberately, he skimmed his lips under her ear. "I'm showing you my appreciation." He moved his hands to her shoulders, turning her to face him. He sat on the edge of the bed, careful not to wrinkle the charcoal-gray suit coat beside him, so she could smooth his collar over his new gray tie.

Nudging his knees apart, she stood between them and straightened his tie. She smelled like a mix of sweet, creamy vanilla and warm hazelnut. She smiled and their gazes met. "You are an incredibly handsome man."

He slid his hands over her hips and drew her closer. "I am a lucky man." He kissed the gentle swell of her belly, his voice deepening with love and adoration. "A very lucky man."

Her breath caught and, reluctantly, he dropped his hands. She was right. This was a dangerous game. Much more, and he would make them late for their wedding.

Reaching behind him, she picked up his coat from the bed. "It's almost four o'clock. We have to go." She sent him a smile full of promise and held the coat for him as he shrugged it on. "You can show me how lucky you are tonight."

Speechless, he went to pick up their suitcases for the weekend. He started out to the hallway as she stepped into a pair of white beaded heels.

"I'll meet you downstairs," she said, sticking her head into Robbie's room. "I just want to make sure he didn't forget anything else."

A gray-striped tie, the smaller version of the one Matt wore, lay on the floor by the front door. Elizabeth had called to tell them Robbie left his tie at home. Matt picked it up and carefully tucked it into his pocket before he went to put their suitcases into the car. When he got back inside, he wiped off his shoes and blew into his hands. He gave her heels a disapproving look as he helped her put on her coat. "Maybe you should wear your boots. I don't want you to slide on the ice." He thought to go look for the boots she'd packed in the car for the weekend and then saw her shake her head.

"Not in this dress." She reached for his arm. "I'll hold on. I promise."

He frowned. He didn't like it, but he tucked her hand in his arm anyway.

She smiled, teasing him. "You said you like my heels."

"I like them fine." Hell, he fantasized about them. "Just not in the snow."

Fortunately, the parking lot was clear and dry at the restaurant where the wedding was taking place. Nate's Jeep was parked by the front door next to Henry's truck. Robert's Cadillac was there, too. Henry's parents were probably with him and his wife, Lauren. Matt couldn't tell if Rachel had arrived yet or not.

Matt got out of the car first. "Wait for me." He came around to open Jenifer's door, looking behind him as an afterthought.

Jenifer pulled on her black leather gloves and took his hand. "Something wrong?"

He shook his head. "This is probably stupid, but I keep thinking my father is going to show up."

"It's not stupid since he's done it before. Maybe it would have been better if you had invited him."

Maybe. He'd considered it. Especially after he found out his mother couldn't come to the wedding. It irked him that he wanted his father to be there and that he'd been too afraid to invite him and risk more rejection.

With his nose pressed against the glass, Robbie waited at the front door dressed in a gray suit and white shirt with the top button undone. He pushed open the door when he saw them and grabbed Jenifer's hand. "Come on," he said and pulled her toward the back of the restaurant. "Everyone's here."

Matt took hold of Jenifer's free hand and followed them to the banquet room. He looked over at the tall stone fireplace on the back wall in the main dining area. It was early yet. A dozen or so cloth-covered tables set for dinner were empty. Across from the fireplace, a pair of mahogany doors opened to the small banquet room where their wedding and reception would take place shortly.

Robert and Elizabeth were first to greet them. "Thank you for inviting us," Robert said, shaking Matt's hand before he gave Jenifer a hug.

"Thank you for being here." Matt waited for Jenifer to tuck her gloves into her coat pocket before he helped her take it off.

When she had first told him she wanted to invite Patrick's parents to the wedding, he wasn't sure they would come. He thought it might be too awkward for them. Instead, they'd said they were happy to be there and offered to watch Robbie for the weekend.

Elizabeth kissed Jenifer's cheek. "You look stunning. The cake and flowers are beautiful, too."

Matt turned at the same time as Jenifer. Beyond the long dinner table in the center of the room was a white two-tiered wedding cake decorated with light-pink roses and pale-purple peonies. Beside the cake sat a bouquet of pink roses and purple peonies that matched exactly the flowers made of icing on the cake.

Jenifer arched a brow, silently asking if he'd ordered the flowers and cake. Matt shook his head and draped her coat over his arm. They had agreed to keep it simple. No flowers, and dessert from the menu.

At the mention of cake, Robbie let go of Jenifer's hand and ushered Elizabeth over for a closer inspection. Robert excused himself and walked with them across the room.

Matt thought back to the text from his grandmother. "I think the flowers and cake are from my grandparents," he said. "I didn't understand a message she sent a couple weeks ago."

Jenifer set her white clutch on the dinner table. "We should call her." Across the room, Henry waved. Beside him were Lauren and his parents, the Rev. Hank Miller and his wife, Barbara, talking to Nate. Matt looked around for Rachel, but he didn't see her yet.

"We will." He looked back at the fireplace, burning bright as waitstaff put the finishing touches on the banquet room. The ceremony would be starting any time. "I'll hang up our coats and be right back."

"Hurry." Jenifer smiled before turning to one of the servers waiting to ask her a question.

Matt went back through the dining room and kept an eye out for Rachel as he turned the corner into the coatroom. Behind him, he felt a hand on his shoulder. He thought it might be Rachel, and he turned around and smiled.

Jessie smiled back at him. Her fingers brushed his arm and he jerked away "What are you doing here?"

Defeat showed on her face as her hand dropped to her side. "I'm leaving. I came to say goodbye to you."

Matt narrowed his eyes. "You're doing that now?"

She held up the keys in her hand. "Now is when I'm leaving."

"Okay then." He gave her a half-hearted smile, noting she was dressed in jeans and a short puffy coat like she was ready to hit the road, and not crash a wedding. "Goodbye."

"I want to leave on a good note, Matt, not a bad one. I don't want you believing that I had our baby and never told you."

He studied her face. "Did you?"

Jessie stuck her hands into her jacket pockets and slowly shook her head. "What would I have done with a baby at eighteen?"

"Give her up."

"You're wrong." Jessie took her hands from her pockets and zipped her jacket. "I didn't have the baby."

He didn't know what to believe, except that she would never tell him anything different and that he wasn't blameless for the mess they were in. "I'm sorry, Jess, for not being a better man when you needed one."

"I'm sorry, too." She moved closer, then kissed his cheek. "For always leaving, when what I should do is stay."

Robbie was by himself next to the fireplace when Matt walked back into the dining room. He dropped a cherry into his mouth, and pink-colored pop dripped from his straw onto his suit coat when Matt went to stand next to him. Matt's mood lightened when he picked up a napkin from one of the tables and handed it to Robbie. "Your mother is going to kill you."

Looking down, Robbie quickly wiped away the pop. "It's all gone," he said, still inspecting the damage.

Matt took the tie from his pocket, lifted Robbie's collar, and knotted his tie for him. "Are you ready to do this?"

"Are we going to get married now?"

Laughing, Matt put his hands on Robbie's shoulders. "You bet. Let's go find us a bride."

~

*J*enifer's blood pounded in her ears as she rushed back to the banquet room ahead of Matt. He was not Patrick, she reminded herself, but the kiss still made her heart ache. Her eyes stung. Not for a moment did she believe Matt would encourage Jessie. She trusted his reasons for letting her get close to him. But for the life of her, she couldn't imagine what they were.

Elizabeth's voice cut through the din in Jenifer's mind. "Did you find Robbie?"

"No." Jenifer looked around the room for him again, hoping he had come back. She'd thought he had followed Matt to hang up their coats. When neither of them had returned, she'd gone to look for Robbie. And found Matt with Jessie.

Rev. Miller, Henry's father, approached her with a warm, friendly smile. "If we can find your groom, Jenifer, we can begin." As he said this, Matt and Robbie returned.

She took a deep, steadying breath when Matt caught her eye as he came in the door. He passed Robbie off to his grandparents before he came over to shake Rev. Miller's hand. "Thank you for doing this."

"My pleasure." Rev. Miller adjusted the clerical collar he wore with a crisp white shirt and dark suit. He took a pair of wire-rimmed glasses from the inside pocket of his coat and put them on. "What do you say we get started?"

As everyone gathered, Matt took Jenifer aside. He lowered his face to her ear. "I'm sorry I was gone for so long."

She clasped his lapels and pretended to straighten his coat. "Is everything okay?" More than anything, she needed to hear nothing would spoil this moment.

He covered his hands over hers. "Never better. I promise."

23

*J*enifer accepted a silver knife from one of the servers, thinking it was an absolute shame to ruin such a beautiful cake.

Beside her, Rachel took a few pictures of the cake. "Do you want me to get Matt?" she asked, shooting a look at her brother and Matt across the room.

"We'll give him a few more minutes," Jenifer said, setting the knife down. "How are you?"

"I'm fine." Rachel waved a hand in the air. Tall and willowy in a black fitted maxi dress, she appeared to have regained her confidence since arriving at the ceremony late, and alone. "I'm sorry I didn't get here earlier. You look beautiful, by the way."

"Thank you. You do, too. I'm glad you made it." Jenifer glanced at Matt, still talking to Henry. After a second, he looked over and winked, then clasped Henry's shoulder before making his way over to her.

He set his empty champagne glass on the dinner table and went to stand beside her. "Are we ready to cut the cake?"

She nodded and picked up the cake knife. They waited for pictures before pushing the knife through a cluster of pink roses.

Afterward, he put his lips close to her ear. "I love you, Mrs. Barnes."

Her pulse quickened at the catch in his voice. "I love you."

"Would it be all right if we left soon?"

"Are you going to tell me where we're going?"

"No." He touched her cheek, then gave her a smile when her mouth turned down. "It's still a surprise."

As far as honeymoons went, theirs would be brief. It wasn't the right time for an elaborate vacation. Not when the highlight of Jenifer's day was a two-hour nap. Next year was soon enough. For now, a weekend alone seemed like bliss.

At seven thirty, Jenifer zipped Robbie into his coat and waited while Matt paid the bill.

"Mr. and Mrs. Barnes." The manager, an older gentleman with a round, friendly face and short gray moustache, put up a hand when Matt tried to give him his credit card. "A gentleman came in this afternoon. He paid your bill and asked that we give this to you."

Matt took the sealed envelope with their names written in an elegant script and thanked the manager. He put the envelope into his coat pocket as Robert and Elizabeth met them at the door to take Robbie home.

Jenifer didn't say anything as she slipped her hand through his arm and they followed Robert and Elizabeth out to their car. She would wait to ask him about his father until after they were alone.

"Mom?" Robbie gave her a puzzled look as he held Robert's hand in the parking lot. "Is my name Barnes, too?"

Jenifer looked at Matt, then released his arm. With two careful strides across the snow-packed parking lot, she caught up with her son. "No, honey, your name is still Nichols."

"Even if Matt's my dad?"

Once they got to Robert's car, Matt crouched down in front of Robbie. He looked him in the eyes. "I will always be your dad, even if your name is Nichols. Is that okay with you?"

Robbie seemed to think about it, and then nodded, "Sure. Okay," he said before he climbed into the back seat of the car.

Robert looked between Matt and Jenifer. "You're not going to change his name after you adopt him?"

Matt rose, shaking his head, and looked at Jenifer. She shivered in the cold air and put on the black leather gloves from her pocket. "Robbie has Patrick's name. Your name. We aren't going to take that away from him. Or from you."

A cast of light from a nearby lamppost illuminated the deep lines scored on Robert's face. "I don't know what to say."

Jenifer hugged him. "You're here tonight. That's enough." She understood that they'd lost too much already, and probably expected to lose a whole lot more after Matt adopted Robbie.

Beside her husband, Elizabeth's eyes teared up. Jenifer pressed her lips together, fearful she might start to cry, too.

Matt leaned inside the car before Jenifer to say goodbye to Robbie. "Be good. I love you."

After they got to their car, Matt handed the envelope from his pocket to Jenifer before he put on his seat belt.

"Do you think this is from your father?"

"Yes, but I don't know what it means. Does he want to have a relationship or keep pretending he's not my father?"

"Do you want me to open it?"

She took his shrug for a yes. Using her phone for a light, she unsealed the envelope and opened a greeting card that read *For My Son, With Love.* She read aloud the neatly handwritten note inside.

Congratulations on your wedding. I'm proud of you, son, and the man that you've become. I wish you and your beautiful wife a lifetime of happiness.

Love,
Your father

. . .

*J*enifer wiped the tears from her eyes. She tucked the card back inside the envelope when Matt reached out his hand. "He's trying," she said.

He stuck the card into the console between their seats with a beleaguered sigh. "You're tired. Try to sleep. We'll be there in about forty minutes."

Thinking he needed the time to himself, she rested her head back against the seat and closed her eyes.

It seemed only seconds passed before she woke to a burst of freezing air. Matt leaned inside the passenger door. "We're here." His eyes dropped to her heels. "Where are your boots? I'll get them for you."

She glanced at his feet and saw he was standing in four inches of snow. "They're buried in the trunk."

He grinned. "Well, then, you're not going to like this."

She narrowed her eyes and instinctively braced her hands on the edge of her seat. "I'm not going to like what?"

Chuckling, he slid a hand under her knees and wrapped his arm around her back, lifting her up against his chest.

"Wait!"

"What?" His arms tightened around her. "There's too much snow. Besides, it might be icy. And if I just hold your arm, you'll be in snow up to your knees."

She checked out the snow-covered ground one more time and snorted. "Ankles," she said, shivering as she gave up and put her arms around his neck. "Not knees."

Snow crunched under his own less-than-sensible shoes as he carried her up a long narrow driveway. Bright stars sparkled in the clear night sky. Lights inside the sprawling shake-shingle home cast a warm, welcome glow. Matt shifted her in his arms and turned the knob of a red front door, then set her on her feet inside a spacious two-story foyer.

"I'll be right back." He made a quick inspection of the downstairs before he went out to the car for the suitcases.

Jenifer unbuttoned her coat and peeked up the winding staircase. Beyond the foyer was a wide-open great room in shades of blue and white at the end of a long hallway. Drawn to the tall windows at the back of the house, she found an outdoor light and admired the white-landscaped banks of Lake Michigan. Behind her, a white slipcovered sofa and matching overstuffed chairs flanked a tall brick fireplace. In the center of the room, a vase of red roses and a bottle of sparkling water sat on a large leather ottoman.

She turned around when Matt came back inside. He left their suitcases at the bottom of the stairs where he hung his wool coat over the railing.

He met her at the windows, slipped his arms inside her open coat, and treated them both to a deep, lingering kiss. "Are you cold?"

"No." A rush of pleasure washed over her as she shrugged out of her long black coat. Beyond the heat of his kiss, the house was warm and comfortable. He had to be uncomfortable in his suit and tie. Nevertheless, she turned toward the fireplace. "But would you mind a fire?"

He took off his suit coat and laid it over the back of one of the chairs with hers. "I'll turn it on."

"The house is beautiful. How did you find it?"

Matt turned on a switch by the windows and the gas fireplace flickered to life. "My mother and Ben rented it as a wedding gift."

Setting the mood a little bit more, Jenifer went to the sofa and dimmed the lamp. "Will you dance with me?"

"What song would you like?"

She smiled, knowing her answer would please him. "Surprise me."

His eyes darkened. He searched through his phone until Etta James' voice filled the room. As "At Last" began to play, he tossed the phone onto a chair and held out his arms.

No moment had ever felt more perfect than when his hand

pressed low on her back and they began to dance. She relished his warm breath on her skin, his heart beating fast against her chest. He was her greatest love, her second chance. She was his miracle, his champion. His lover, his wife.

As the song played, she reached up and loosened his tie. "Do we stay down here or go upstairs?"

Breathing deep, he slipped the tie from his neck, draping it over the sofa behind her without looking away. "Stay here."

Her hands stroked over his chest. "We can move upstairs later."

"Later?" He grinned like a sinner, his eyes a wicked blue as he watched her unbutton his shirt.

"Yes." She tipped her head back, touching her tongue to his lips, and felt his arms cinch around her waist. "But only if you're very good."

His response was a kiss delivered soft and slow, deepening with promise, making her insides tremble. He lowered the zipper of her dress, his thumb grazing her heated skin as the dress pooled at her feet. She unbuttoned his pants, then tugged his shirt free and let it drop to the floor. Without breaking the kiss, he tunneled his hands into her hair and kicked off his pants.

Her breath came in quick, short bursts as his eyes caressed her body. The white silky lace and high leather heels. He guided her backward, her legs touching the sofa before he lowered her onto the soft, deep cushions, skillfully disposing of the lace. Settling her beneath him, he trailed hot, damp kisses over her sensitive skin.

Her mouth went dry as her heart pounded against her chest. "Oh, God, please don't ever let this end."

He linked their hands and raised them over her head. "Never. I'm yours, Jenifer Barnes. Forever."

～

*J*enifer woke with her back pressed against Matt's chest, covered with a soft blanket as firelight flickered in the dark. The leather ottoman was pushed off to the side. Sofa cushions lay strewn across the floor. One of her heels beside the sofa had lost its mate. And Matt's tie hung innocently over the side of a chair.

Matt stirred beside her. He turned onto his back, taking her with him, and tucked her head under his chin. "We should probably go upstairs."

She lifted her arm and let it flop back onto his chest. "I can't get up. I think you broke me."

He angled his head with a smirk. "I'm pretty sure it was you who broke me."

"I don't know." She bit back a smile and pushed up to an elbow. Her gaze skimmed over his long, lean body as she pretended to look for damage. "You don't look broken to me."

"Maybe you should try again."

"Hmmm. Maybe." She dragged a hand dramatically through her tangled hair and closed her eyes as if she were thinking about it.

His large, warm hands slid under the blanket. He touched his lips to the soft skin beneath her ear. "If you're too tired, I could carry you upstairs and tuck you into bed." His mouth opened on the curve of her neck. "Or I could—"

She tipped her head back and let the blanket slip away as he whispered all the ways he would please her.

And please her he did.

~

*M*att opened his eyes to a sliver of sunlight between the curtains and his wife sleeping soundly on his chest. If he turned his face just a little, he could kiss her bare shoulder. It would wake her like any act of intimacy always did.

But if he eased out of bed slowly, careful not to jar her, she would probably sleep for at least another hour. His feet touched the floor without so much as a sigh out of her.

Downstairs, he pulled on a pair of jeans and a T-shirt from his suitcase. He made coffee before he put the cushions back on the sofa and folded the blanket, then turned on the fireplace and picked up their clothes before he started to make breakfast. The property manager had stocked the refrigerator for the weekend. The roses and sparkling water in the living room were from him, delivered to the house yesterday afternoon.

By the time he fried the bacon and poured coffee, it was snowing again. Big, heavy flakes blew in the wind and stuck to the trees. It was the kind of day one burrowed under a blanket in front of a warm fire, reading or sleeping. Or making love.

Jenifer surprised him when she hooked a finger in his belt loop and looked over his shoulder. "You made bacon?"

"Scrambled eggs, too." He turned his head and kissed her. "How long have you been up? I didn't hear you come downstairs."

"Not long." She leaned back against the black granite countertop barelegged, wearing his blue fire department T-shirt. Pinching a piece of bacon from the plate next to the stove, she took a bite, then pointed it at him. "You're getting pretty good at this cooking business."

He snatched her wrist and ate the rest of the bacon. "I am a man of many talents."

"Indeed, you are." She reached overhead for a coffee cup and his T-shirt rode high above her hips, exposing even more soft, delicate skin.

His throat tightened as she poured herself coffee. He imagined stealing back his shirt. Lifting her onto the edge of the counter. Her slender legs wrapping around his waist. Her heels digging hard into his back.

She smiled at him and pointed her cup at the stove. "You're burning the eggs."

"Shit!" He grabbed the frying pan off the stove and turned off the burner. Sure enough, the eggs were brown on the bottom when he scraped them with a spatula.

She patted his butt and picked up a plate he'd set on the counter. "They're fine. Let's eat."

"Forget it. They're burned." He went to throw them down the garbage disposal.

"No, you did good." She put a hand on his arm and took the spatula away from him. She scooped out a healthy serving of dried eggs and dropped a couple pieces of bacon onto her plate. "Did Rachel say anything to you about what happened to her date yesterday?"

Matt recognized her attempt at distraction and scraped the rest of the eggs onto his plate without commenting on them again. "She didn't say anything to me," he said, sitting next to her by the fire, "but Henry said she had an argument with her ex."

"Nate looked uncomfortable during dinner."

"That's because he has a thing for Rachel he won't talk about. He'd expected her to be with the ex, who I imagine he hates because of the cheating. And he probably would've been just fine with her showing up alone if she hadn't looked so upset when she got to the restaurant."

Jenifer sipped her coffee, frowning over the top of her cup. "I don't like that other guy."

"Me neither."

"Tell Nate not to give up. Rachel likes him."

"Yeah? How can you tell?" He didn't know how she wasn't cold wearing only a T-shirt, and he grabbed the blanket from last night and covered her legs.

"By the way she looks at him."

"Henry's not a big fan of the two of them together."

"I know." She laughed and set her plate on the ottoman he'd moved back into place. "You guys don't have as many secrets as you think you do."

"I don't want any secrets between us." He reached over and set his plate next to hers. "I have to tell you something."

She fixed the blanket over her lap and waited.

"Jessie was at the restaurant yesterday. Before the ceremony. I didn't tell you because I didn't want to ruin our wedding day."

Jenifer's gaze turned cynical. "What did she want?"

"To say goodbye. She said she was leaving for Florida."

"Do you believe her?"

Shrugging, he said, "I don't know. I hope so."

"So she just showed up to say goodbye?"

"No." He looked down at his hands. "She said she wanted to leave on good terms. Told me she didn't have the baby. I went along with her."

"How did you go along with her?"

"I didn't debate it." He sat back and met her eyes. "I wanted her to leave, so when she kissed me goodbye, I let her."

The last damn thing he expected was for Jenifer to smile. "I know. I was there."

His eyes went wide. "Why didn't you say something?"

"For the same reason as you. I didn't want to spoil our day. I trust you."

Matt pulled her in closer, lacing his fingers with hers. "Not a day goes by I don't wonder how I got so lucky to be in your life."

She let out a long, deep sigh and leaned her head against his shoulder. "I love you."

"I love you. Always."

24

By early April, scattered snow showers alternated with hard, pouring rain. A steady wind had blown open the storm door at the back of the house and loosened a hinge. Another gust would break it entirely. Matt was late getting home from work, so Jenifer hitched up the sleeves of his sweater and went down to the basement to find a screwdriver. Poking around her toolbox from the old house, she heard Matt come in the front door.

"Where's Mom?" he asked Robbie.

She couldn't understand Robbie's muffled response, but she grinned after Matt came to the top of the basement stairs.

He gave her a nervous smile. "I have a surprise for you."

Her grin froze in place. Only one possibility came to mind.

"We talked about this, remember?" He took the screwdriver out of her hand when she met him at the top of the stairs. "You'll love him. I promise."

She would, for sure. Only she had thought the *surprise* was coming once her maternity leave started.

Robbie had no idea what was happening when he came into the kitchen to find them. "What surprise?"

"Wait here." Matt opened the back door and inspected the

broken hinge before he headed out to the driveway. He reached into his truck, but she couldn't see what he took out.

Robbie watched mesmerized from the window, then almost bolted outside in his socks before Jenifer caught him by the belt loop. "We got a dog?"

"He's a puppy." Matt came into the kitchen, shrugging off his wet uniform jacket with the dog on a leash. Only the rather large-looking puppy was having none of the leash. Robbie leaned over to pet him. The puppy jumped up onto his hindlegs and knocked him down.

Right behind Robbie, Jenifer scrambled backward against the counter as both the dog and the boy skittered across the floor at her feet. She gaped at Matt. "That is not a puppy."

Matt darted a look at the dog. "He's six months old. He's still young."

Jenifer's eye twitched at the unruly golden retriever-mix that had Robbie pinned on his back.

"He'll be a great dog. You'll see."

Giggling, Robbie frantically avoided the long, wet tongue bearing down on him as the puppy stretched out on top of him.

Jenifer rubbed a hand over her mouth and tried not to smile. Okay, the dog was cute. Clearly, Robbie loved him already. But still, why get him now, instead of waiting for summer? "Where did you find him?"

Matt straightened and for the first time since he got home, he appeared a little more confident. "The shelter, just like you asked. He'd been there for months. One of the guys at work told me about him."

She eyed the dog with renewed interest. The shelter had been her one stipulation. A young, rambunctious dog made sense to her now. Not just anyone would adopt him. The big lug needed a home.

Robbie struggled to his feet, his big hazel eyes imploring her. "We can keep him, can't we? Please, Mom?" The dog suddenly seemed aware of his precarious position, and he dropped to the floor with a thud. And stayed there. Matt gave her a similar look, but he said nothing.

After a few seconds, she nodded, kneeling down to give the dog a belly rub. "What are you guys going to name him?"

Robbie peeked under the dog's hindquarters, maybe to confirm he was a boy, and then looked over at Matt. "What do you think his name should be?"

Jenifer had an idea. "What about Tobey? You know, from Spider-Man?"

The puppy sat up on his haunches. His tail thumped hard on the floor. Matt held out his hand and helped Jenifer to her feet. "I like Tobey."

Robbie petted the top of the dog's head with a grin. "Me, too."

~

*T*wo weeks later, spring had arrived full-force and a muddy backyard pitted man against beast. Or woman, if the man was at work. Between beast and boy, dirt and mud had become a way of life.

The beast in question whined from his crate close to midnight. Jenifer groaned and dropped Matt's pillow over her face. He was at the firehouse. Tobey's crate was in the small bedroom at the top of the stairs. The dog usually slept better after a long run with Matt on the nights he was home. Otherwise, Tobey stored up his unlimited energy like an ion battery.

"Tobey," Jenifer hissed through her teeth, and the whining stopped for a beat before starting up again. She tossed the pillow aside and gave him a few more seconds to settle down before she would have to get up with him.

Without thinking, she grabbed her phone and started to send Matt a salty text about his dog, then changed her mind. The truth was, she loved that dog now as much as he did. A missed call on her screen got her attention, and she listened to the voicemail.

Holding her breath, she listened to the message a second time. It was from the Florida adoption registry. They had her number, not Matt's. He'd been concerned months ago he would have to change his cell number again because of Jessie. The woman who left the message asked him to return her call.

Half tempted to wake Matt with a text, she sank deeper under the covers and hugged his pillow against her chest. He didn't talk about the search for his daughter often. When he did, she could tell he was afraid to let himself hope she existed.

What would he do now?

The next morning, he was on a call when Jenifer tried to reach him. She didn't want to leave a message, but it was Friday and if she didn't get another chance to talk to him while she was at work, he would have to wait until Monday to return the phone call.

The day dragged by when she didn't hear from him by the time she got home from school. Tobey started to bark as soon as she and Robbie got in the house. Robbie raced upstairs to let the dog out of his crate. "Can I take him for a walk?"

Jenifer shook her head. Even if she let him, Tobey would take Robbie for a walk instead of the other way around. He was still young and destructive. He had to stay in his crate when no one was watching him. One of their neighbors was kind enough to walk him the days Matt was at work. "He just wants you to play with him."

"Can I take him in the backyard?"

"Sure. Just make sure you dry his feet when you come back inside."

A minute later, Tobey barreled past her as she walked into her bedroom. She couldn't wait to get out of the turquoise maternity dress. It hung like a circus tent. But there wasn't much to do about it. She'd outgrown almost everything she owned but leggings. Considering Matt was equally responsible for her lack of wardrobe, she pulled his blue GRFD T-shirt over her head to wear with her only clean pair of black leggings. Lying on the bed, she closed her eyes and listened for Robbie to come back in the house. When the back door slammed open, she heard Robbie shout at the dog to sit. Tobey didn't like his paws dried off any more than Robbie liked to do it. She started to get up to help when she heard Matt come home.

He was already on his knees wiping the floor with a towel when she got to the kitchen. He rarely ever raised his voice, but he had a way of letting you know he was unhappy, and at that moment, he was not pleased with Robbie.

"You need to try a little harder," Matt said with his back to Jenifer. "He's not going to just sit there and wait for you to dry him off. You have to hold on to him, too."

Jenifer leaned against the doorway until he looked up. He sank back on his heels and dropped the towel, appearing to brace himself for his own lecture about puppies and pregnancy.

Now wasn't the time.

She reached out her hand to help him up. "Did you get my message today?"

"This afternoon." There was real anger in his voice, and this time it had nothing to do with the dog. He held her hand and pushed to his feet without her help. "I called back and gave permission for the woman who contacted them to call me."

Jenifer picked up the towel Matt used to dry the floor and hung it back by the door. "Did they tell you anything?"

Matt nodded and then looked past her shoulder at Robbie. "I'll tell you about it later."

After dinner, Robbie picked out a movie, *Ice Age*, and they watched it together. Matt hardly said a word and then took Tobey for a run after the movie ended. Jenifer crashed on the sofa, waiting for him after Robbie went to bed. She didn't mean to fall asleep, and she didn't hear him come back.

Matt crouched next to the sofa, and she opened her eyes. "You should go to bed."

"Will you tell me about the phone call first?"

With a pained expression, he pushed a hand through his hair. "A woman saw what we posted on the registry. She recognized Jessie's name and said that's the name of her daughter's biological mother."

"Do you have her number?"

"No. I have to wait for her to call me." His voice filled with anxiety and frustration as he stood and helped her up. "Why don't you go to sleep? I'll be up in a little while."

Later, the light in the hallway woke her when the dog came into the room and jumped on the bed. She cracked her eyes open, looking for Matt, but he wasn't there. She heard him talking downstairs as Tobey curled up next to her. She opened her eyes again a little while later when the dog jumped down and Matt came into the bedroom. He picked something up from the floor. His jacket. Maybe shoes.

She rubbed sleep from her eyes and squinted at the time. It was almost one in the morning. "Are you going out?"

Tobey stuck his head around Matt's legs and pulled at the leash in his hand. Matt turned around, holding the doorknob. "I'm taking the dog for a walk."

"Are you okay?"

He nodded and looked over his shoulder when the dog started to go downstairs without him.

She dropped her head back onto the pillow. "You better go get him before he eats the sofa."

"I love you," he said and closed the bedroom door behind him.

It was easy to see he was shielding her again, the way he always did. Protecting her from the wreckage of his past, while he was still buried deep beneath it.

25

*M*att yanked on his coat by the door and hooked Tobey to his leash. Anger heated his blood, bloomed into rage. Rage with himself. With Jessie. She had looked him straight in the eye and lied about the abortion.

During the phone call after Jenifer had gone to bed, a woman in Florida said she and her husband had adopted a baby girl from a young woman named Jessie O'Connor the year Matt had graduated high school. Jessie had told them she'd moved from Michigan and she didn't know who the father was.

His heavy boots pounded the sidewalk in the dark, his pace quick, even for the dog trotting beside him. He counted his mistakes. Doubting Jessie, letting her go without learning the truth. Young and stupid, he didn't understand the value of patience at eighteen. That paternity didn't have a shelf life. That it would have been wise of him to ask for the test after the baby was born.

Goddammit, this was all his fault.

He came to a stop at the end of the block and gave Tobey a minute to poke around a lamppost. Lights from windows up and down the street reminded him he wasn't the only one awake. But not his wife. He'd be damned if he would disturb what little sleep she got now. Morning was soon enough to share with her what he'd learned tonight. What he would not do was unload all of his anger and frustration on her.

He took out his phone and sent Nate a text. *You up?*

Seconds later, *I'm out. What's up?*

Matt watched Tobey bury his nose in the grass, sniffing at the lamppost. The second he hit Send, he knew it was a lousy idea texting Nate on a Friday night. *Forget it. Talk to you later.*

Heading home now. You want me to come over?

Yeah. Thanks. Matt gave Tobey a few more seconds and then started back to the house.

~

*M*att sat in the living room after Nate got there and told him about his daughter. "I handled this all wrong."

"You think Jessie would have kept the baby if you'd believed her?"

"I don't know." Matt leaned forward, pressing his elbows on his knees. "We never got that far. If I had believed her, maybe."

Nate shook his head and sat back in his chair. "You're thinking like a thirty-three-year-old man who knows the truth. Not an eighteen-year-old boy with reasons for doubt."

"Doesn't matter. I asked for a paternity test when I should have waited."

"You didn't think you could have kids. And you said it yourself: you guys were over before she knew she was pregnant."

Matt rose and went to look out the window. He still remembered the shock and disbelief when she'd told him she was pregnant. "I should have done things a lot differently back then."

Nate frowned. "If you'd married her, you would be divorced by now; you've said so yourself."

"I know it wouldn't have lasted. But at least I would have my daughter now." Matt's head came up. "Where's Tobey?"

"Right here."

Matt's heart sank as he got up to meet Jenifer at the bottom of the stairs. The last thing he wanted was to dump this on her in the middle of the night. "I'm sorry. Did we wake you?"

She shook her head. "No, Tobey came in again and jumped on the bed."

Matt stared hard at the dog as Nate started to leave. Nate's mouth lifted with a small apologetic smile. "Still our fault," he said, petting Tobey behind the ears. His gaze shifted to Matt. "Talk to you later."

It was almost two a.m. Matt went to turn off the lights and lock the door, hoping to tell Jenifer everything in the morning.

No such luck, he discovered, when she didn't budge from the stairs. "What's going on?"

With no other choice, he caught her hand and walked over to sit with her on the sofa. "I got a call after you went to bed from the woman who contacted the adoption registry. Her name's Andrea Bishop. She's a widow living in Florida with her fifteen-year-old daughter, Emily."

Excitement showed in Jenifer's eyes. "Your daughter?"

He nodded. His shoulders relaxed. The hopefulness in her voice soothed his pent-up anger. He opened the picture of Emily that Andrea had sent him and showed it to Jenifer. Recognition swept over her face as she studied the tall, slender girl with long dark hair. She was dressed almost entirely in black with heavy makeup that highlighted her bright-blue eyes. His eyes.

Jenifer looked closer, enlarging the picture. "She's beautiful." Her gaze lifted to his. "She looks just like you."

"She does." She looked like Jessie, too, with her high cheek-bones and short, turned-up nose. The olive skin came from him. The stern, unsmiling expression reminded him of Jessie.

"Are you going to talk to Jessie?"

"No." He forced himself to take a deep breath and then gently held her face in his hands. "Whatever I do, I'll do with you. Always."

~

The next morning, Jenifer woke to an empty house and went downstairs. Robbie was nowhere in sight. Matt's truck wasn't in the driveway. Even the dog was gone. The sand-colored drapes in the living room fluttered in the warm breeze. The T-shirt she wore was her own, snug around the middle, after she'd already gone through all of Matt's old T-shirts. Her leggings were on inside out, but at least her bare feet weren't cold.

The kitchen showed more signs of life—milk in a cereal bowl and an empty coffee cup in the sink. A glass of orange juice sat on the edge of the counter and a breeze through the kitchen window blew a napkin from the table onto the floor.

Her empty stomach rumbled after what turned out to be a short, sleepless night. Matt had tossed and turned beside her until the sun came up and she'd felt him get out of bed.

She hadn't meant to eavesdrop last night when she'd heard voices in the living room. After Tobey had woken her again, she'd gotten up to check on Matt. That was when she overheard him sharing his regrets about Jessie and the baby. His daughter. Her heart ached, wondering if he wished he could go back and change things now that he knew she was real.

Jenifer opened the refrigerator and heard Matt's truck in the driveway. She slid a glass dish aside and reached for the milk. As she did, the dish toppled off the shelf and hit the top of her foot before she could catch it. Startled by the sharp pain and broken glass, she grabbed for the counter to keep from falling. The orange juice crashed to the floor and more glass shattered at her feet. Flailing, she planted her foot and glass pierced her heel. Blood gushed as she stood on one foot and tried to catch her breath.

"Don't move!" Matt's voice sounded with panic as he rushed through the door. He stepped over the broken glass and picked her up, carrying her to one of the kitchen chairs.

Her foot jerked in his hands when he examined the cuts. "Hold still. There's still a big piece of glass in your foot." He grabbed a towel from one of the drawers. "I'm going to take it out. Just breathe."

She squeezed her eyes shut and held her breath at the sharp pain before he wrapped her foot with the towel.

"Hold this. Tight. I'll be right back."

Seconds later, he crouched in front of her, his medic bag open on the floor. He removed two smaller pieces of glass from her other foot and used another towel to stop the bleeding.

She leaned against the back of the chair and looked at the blood on her feet and ankles. "I need to wash that off before Robbie sees it."

Matt grimaced at his bloodstained hands. He stood, untied his boots, and toed them off. "I'll carry you upstairs to the bathroom."

"I can walk." She pushed to her feet and winced.

"Sure you can," he said, scooping her into his arms. "After you get cleaned up and I bandage the cuts."

Worried and bemused, Jenifer looked down at the food and broken glass all over the kitchen floor. "Where is Robbie? And Tobey?"

Matt nodded at the reminder on the refrigerator door for Robbie's baseball fundraiser event that morning. "He had to be at the field by nine."

She groaned. "I forgot."

"Don't worry about it. He's fine." He shifted her in his arms. "Tobey's out in the backyard."

Upstairs, he sat her on the edge of the bathtub to turn on the faucet. She pulled off her T-shirt and dropped it on the floor. He steadied her as she dragged off her pants, careful with her feet, and then helped her into the tub.

She leaned back and soaked in the warm water as he washed his hands, then leaned against the side of the vanity, watching her for a moment. She could see the dark shadows under his eyes.

"Can we talk?" he asked.

The helplessness in his voice made her sit up and inch forward to give him space.

Catching on, he dragged off his clothes and left them on the floor with hers. Water sluiced over the side of the small tub when he squeezed in behind her and then pressed her back against his chest.

She sank deeper into the water and rested her head on his shoulder. "Will you tell me more about what you learned last night?"

His hands closed over hers, and he rested them on her firm, round belly. "Andrea Bishop said she and her husband adopted their daughter from Jessie in a private adoption in 1998. She was under the impression Jessie didn't know the baby's father and that she gave the baby up after waiting too long to have an abortion."

"Does she believe that you're Emily's biological father?"

"I don't know. She asked a lot of questions. About Jessie. Dates she and I were together. Why I didn't look for Emily before now."

The last part put her back up. She tipped her head and looked over at him. "You told her you didn't know, didn't you?"

He pressed a kiss on top of her head, stroking his hand over her belly. "I did."

"Was she looking for you?"

"Emily? No." He went still for a long moment when the baby moved beneath their hands. "Andrea was looking because she's worried about Emily. Her adoptive father died when she was younger. As she's gotten older, she's started to feel abandoned. Friends, school, everything in her life is suffering. I think Andrea needs help, but she doesn't know where to find it. And she doesn't trust me yet."

"Do you think she'll let you talk to Emily?"

"I didn't ask. I didn't want to push. I was happy when she agreed that she and I could talk again."

He rubbed his hands over the goose bumps traveling over her arms. She didn't know if they were from the cooler water or the bleakness in his voice as he spoke of his daughter's father. After a few more minutes, he stood, reached for a towel, and knotted it around his waist before he grabbed another one. He gave her a hand out of the tub and wrapped the second towel around her.

Standing on the ball of one foot and the heel of the other, she held the towel to her chest and met his eyes in the mirror over the sink. "Do you regret how your life has turned out?"

He put his hands on her shoulders and turned her to look at him. "No. Why would you ask me that?"

"Because you lost your daughter."

He tipped up her chin to look at him. "I'm sorry that I didn't believe Jessie. I regret losing Emily because of it. But I do not, could never, ever regret falling in love with you. I told you once we were meant to be together. I swear to God, I believe that more every single day. Don't you?"

She shivered, tightening the towel in her hand. "I do."

"Stay here. I'll be right back."

He returned to the bathroom with a black hoodie and gray sweatpants, both his, along with his medic bag. After she pulled on the clothes, he gestured her to the side of the tub again and dressed the cuts on her foot.

She leaned forward and rested her forehead on his. "What are you going to do?"

"There's nothing I can do."

"If Emily's mother thinks she feels abandoned, she might look to you for help. Maybe that's why she was looking for you in the first place."

Matt put the rest of the bandages away. "Then we wait and see. I need Emily to know that I wanted her. Her mother needs to know I won't cause her any trouble. I lost my daughter a long time ago. There's no challenging the adoption or suing for any rights. Talking to Emily, meeting her, is what I hope for most."

"I'm sorry for all of the pain you're going through." Jenifer put her arms around his neck, drawing him close.

"Don't be. I need you. I need us. You've given me everything I've ever wanted. I just need you to promise me something."

"Anything."

"Promise you'll always believe in me."

26

$\mathcal{A}$ndrea Bishop had obviously done her homework. Jenifer expected no less from a desperate mother reaching out to a stranger. Despite Matt's assurances early on that he would not challenge Emily's adoption, Andrea told him she had consulted an attorney and was told it was all but impossible for him to take Emily away from her. Since then, she had come to gradually accept him as an ally, though it wasn't until early May that she warmed to the idea of letting him speak to Emily.

Andrea asked his permission before giving Emily his number. She had warned him not to expect a warm reception, then pleaded with him to be honest but sensitive if Emily did call him.

Four days after Andrea had passed Matt's number to her daughter, Jenifer found him in the living room with his face in his hands after she got home from school.

He raised his head and held out his hand, inviting her to sit with him on the sofa. "Emily just called. We talked for about fifteen minutes."

She eased down beside him, sighing as she toed off her flats and sank into the leather cushions. "What did she say to you?"

He put his hand on her belly and smiled when the baby kicked. "It felt a little bit like a test. Like she was checking to make sure I gave her the same answers her mother did." He gazed at her belly as if he were playing the conversation back in his head. "She asked my name, where I live, where I work." His smile faded. "She wanted to know if I have other kids."

But for lack of a piece of paper, Matt had a son he loved. And soon, a baby who would steal another piece of his heart. Jenifer knew he considered Emily his daughter, but how did he tell her that without crossing a line with Andrea?

She groaned as he shifted so her legs were on his lap and he could rub her tired feet. "Do you think she'll tell her mother that she called?"

"I don't know. If I don't hear from Andrea in the next couple of days, I'll tell her."

As it turned out, Andrea called Matt that night. Jenifer sat with him on the back deck as he talked to her on the phone. It seemed he'd passed Emily's test. She asked to meet him. It sounded as if Andrea had invited Matt and Jenifer to visit Florida at the end of the school year. He shook his head, looking disappointed. "No, I'm sorry. We can't fly in June. My wife is pregnant." He glanced over at Jenifer. "Maybe we could come down this fall."

Jenifer shook her head at him. Fall was too far away. "Invite them here," she whispered.

His brows pinched as he mouthed back, "Are you sure?"

Jenifer made a face as if he had to be kidding, and he grinned. Andrea accepted the invitation, and by the end of the call, they'd made plans for her and Emily to visit the first week of June.

Matt leaned over and gave Jenifer a kiss. "Thank you for making that work."

They both looked when she heard Robbie stick his head out the back door and Tobey snuck outside. Matt patted his thigh and the dog came to sit beside him.

Robbie stood on the deck steps, looking out to the backyard. He wore his glove on his hand. "Can we play catch?" Even though the sun was still bright, it was almost time for bed and the question came out more as a plea.

Jenifer raised her brows and gave Matt a look, asking him to say something to Robbie about Emily's visit. He was excited about the baby and becoming a big brother. But without any certainty Matt would have a relationship of any kind with Emily, they'd held off telling him about her. Now he would have to know.

Jenifer motioned Robbie over to sit on her lap. "Come here for a minute. We want to talk to you about something."

He tipped his head, clearly considering what was left of her lap.

Matt rubbed a hand over his grin. She fought her own smile and slapped his leg before she settled Robbie on her knees. "You two aren't funny."

Matt grew serious when he turned his attention back to Robbie. "I have someone I want you to meet in a few weeks."

Robbie listened as Jenifer put her arms around his waist and rested her chin on his shoulder. "Who?"

"My daughter. Her name is Emily. She lives in Florida, and she's coming to visit with her mother soon."

Robbie wound a strand of Jenifer's hair around his fingers as he seemed to think about that for a second. "But you said before you aren't a daddy."

Jenifer's heart squeezed at his small possessive voice. She lifted her gaze to Matt and knew he had heard it, too.

Matt held out his arms and Robbie got down, then climbed onto his lap. "I've never met Emily. She was born far away."

"So you *are* a daddy?" He made it sound as if he had been replaced by another child.

Matt's mouth opened, then closed with a silent sigh as he shot a desperate look at Jenifer over the top of Robbie's head. The adoption was months away. With the baby, and now Emily, it was possible Robbie felt as if he were falling between the cracks. He didn't understand the importance of a piece of paper. Matt didn't need one to be his father.

Jenifer silently agreed with her husband.

Matt angled his head so he could look into Robbie's big hazel eyes. "I'm not one yet. Not really. But I would like to be your daddy starting now. Would that be okay with you?"

Robbie wrapped his arms around Matt's neck, gazing at him as if he hung the moon and the stars. Matt hugged him hard against his chest. "I love you." Matt looked up at Jenifer, held her eyes, and for the second time that night, he whispered, "Thank you."

~

*R*obbie moved into the nursery temporarily the Saturday Emily and Andrea were arriving. Jenifer knew he wasn't pleased. "It's a baby's room." He stood in the doorway with his hands fisted on his hips. He pouted at Matt next to him. Tobey lay sprawled at their feet. "Why can't Emily sleep in here?"

Matt raised his eyebrows and pointed to the twin-size bed. "Because you have a big bed, and she's sleeping with her mother. Do you want to sleep with us?"

Robbie frowned and dropped his hands. "No."

Jenifer grinned over her shoulder. She put the last of Robbie's clothes into the dresser next to the crib and bumped the drawer closed with her hip. Matt had cut it close with his bluff. Not long ago, Robbie would have taken him up on the offer to sleep with them. "Tobey can stay in here with you; how about that?" She tossed a few baby things into a wicker basket and hid it in the closet. "Dad will move the crate up here before we leave for the airport."

Matt waited for his answer.

Robbie narrowed his eyes, pursing his lips, and Jenifer could almost hear the gears grinding in his head. "Can he sleep with me, instead of in the crate?"

"No," Matt said the same time as she did. Tobey would turn the house upside down if he was out of the crate all night.

Matt followed her out to the hallway and tossed the last of the dirty sheets and towels into the hamper. "I'll move the crate." He gestured to Robbie. "Grab your jacket—it's raining. And then we'll head to the airport."

Jenifer caught Matt's hand before he could go downstairs. He'd spoken to Andrea before they got on the plane that morning. He had been quiet ever since. "How are you doing?"

He let out a long breath, shaking his head. "I don't know what I'll do when I see her."

She squeezed his hand, knowing that whatever he did, he would get it right. "You'll know when it happens."

The rain had stopped, and the sun broke through the clouds before they arrived at the busy airport. Two lanes of traffic jammed the terminal and a steady flow of pedestrians in the walkways slowed progress. Cars double-parked at the curb caused a bottleneck at baggage claim. With nowhere to wait, Matt dropped Jenifer and Robbie off so they wouldn't have to walk, then went to park the car.

A teenage boy sitting on a bench outside the terminal doors gave up his seat when he saw Jenifer. He reminded her of a young Nate when she smiled and thanked him as she sat with Robbie. After a few minutes, she turned around when she heard her name called out. A woman in her mid-forties pulling a black wheelie bag started toward her. A young girl with unmistakable eyes wheeled her own suitcase and trailed behind.

It was Emily. Jenifer's heart stammered with recognition. Emily looked entirely different from the picture Andrea had sent Matt in April. Her straight, shoulder-length hair was a natural brown instead of the near-black Jenifer remembered. Her face was tan and makeup-free. Instead of black, she wore a pale-pink blouse with jeans and brown leather sandals. There was no doubt in Jenifer's mind that she was Matt's daughter.

Jenifer shifted her gaze, searching anxiously for Matt as Robbie stood up. She rocked forward and tried to get to her feet.

The woman hurried over, leaving her suitcase next to the bench, and offered her hand. "Jenifer? I'm Andrea Bishop." She smiled and helped Jenifer to stand. She pointed a short distance away. "That's my daughter, Emily."

Jenifer covered her mouth and tried not to cry when she saw what was about to happen. Emily smiled hesitantly, looking around at all the people in the crowded terminal. She didn't see Matt, but Jenifer knew the moment he saw her.

"Emily?"

Her hand fell away from the suitcase, her eyes wide, before she turned to look at him.

"Emily," Matt said again, and this time, as he approached, he held out his hands. She seemed frozen in place until he stood in front of her, and she let him fold her into his arms.

Still holding Andrea's hand, Jenifer watched Matt gaze down at his daughter. He spoke quietly to her for a minute, and Jenifer noticed Andrea's eyes fill with tears.

"She was nervous to meet him, but excited, too." Andrea let go of Jenifer as her eyes moved anxiously from her daughter to Robbie to Jenifer's swollen belly. "I hope she will be as important to him as he is to her."

If only she knew, Jenifer thought, in tears herself. "I believe she is already." Jenifer looked over to see Robbie scowling like Tobey when Matt gave attention to the neighbor's dog. It would have been cute, the sweet, little pout on his face, if she didn't think his feelings were so hurt.

"Come here." Jenifer sat back down on the bench and took him into her arms as Matt and Emily made their way over to them. "Daddy loves you very much."

Andrea winced, her face filled with worry.

"It's okay." Jenifer rubbed a hand over her belly and smiled. "We're only getting started."

Jenifer noticed Emily's watery eyes as she walked with Matt to where Jenifer and Andrea waited on the sidewalk. Jenifer caught his attention, tipping her head at Robbie. He put his hand on Robbie's shoulder as Andrea greeted him. Emily shook Jenifer's hand before she turned to Robbie, who stared up at her with what appeared to be jealousy.

Emily seemed to take his animosity in stride as she smiled at him and asked, "Are you Robbie?"

He gave her a curt nod and pulled his bottom lip in. "Is Matt your dad, too?"

Emily's eyes shifted to Matt before she turned back to Robbie. "He's my father. My dad died."

Robbie's expression softened as he shoved his hands into his front pockets. "My father died, too."

Jenifer caught the curious look Emily sent her mother. She wondered if Matt had told them he wasn't Robbie's biological father.

Andrea barely lifted a shoulder. Apparently, he had not.

Jenifer worried as Robbie seemed to regard Emily in a different light. As a sort of comrade-in-arms. She thought of his friends. Kids he knew with only one parent. There were two of them. But both sets of parents had divorced. She lifted her eyes to Matt. Had Robbie believed that he was the only one to have his father die?

A similar awareness seemed to come over Matt as he squeezed Robbie's shoulder. He looked over at Andrea. "You'll discover there are all kinds of fathers in this family."

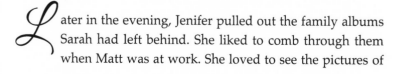

*L*ater in the evening, Jenifer pulled out the family albums Sarah had left behind. She liked to comb through them when Matt was at work. She loved to see the pictures of him as a young boy, and later as he got older. It looked like he'd had a terrific childhood, just like he said. She hoped showing the pictures to Emily would bring her closer to Matt.

She stacked the albums on the coffee table while he showed Andrea the house. Robbie brought Emily upstairs to his bedroom. The streetlights were barely on by the time they got back downstairs, but Jenifer couldn't keep her eyes open any longer.

She yawned, waving Matt into the dining room while Andrea and the kids started to pore over the old pictures on the living room floor. "I have to go to bed."

"I'll walk you up."

After she said good night and they went upstairs, Matt sat on the side of the bed, grinning as she took out his fire department T-shirt to wear to bed. "Why do we even bother putting that shirt back into my dresser?"

She smiled and shrugged, until she noted with some dismay that her favorite T-shirt of his was becoming too small. She gave it a little tug to stretch it out. "How are you doing?"

"It's surreal," he said, lying back against the pillows and drawing her down next to him after she got into bed. "She looks like me. She has my eyes." He turned Jenifer so she lay with her head on his chest, his hand on the side of her belly. "She's so sweet and warm and amazing."

"She is. You make beautiful children." She touched her lips to his neck. "I can't wait to meet the next one."

"I wouldn't have found her without you."

"It must be strange," she said, "to suddenly be the father of three children."

He sighed and kissed the side of her head. "Two children. Robbie and whoever you have cooking in there."

She turned onto her side after he got up and covered her with the blanket. "Three," she said. "Emily will fall in love with you. You'll see."

~

*a*t the kitchen table the next morning, Jenifer found Robbie shoveling chocolate chip pancakes into his mouth and Emily grilling Matt while he drank coffee. She loved how he'd made pancakes for his kids and then gave them every bit of his attention while they swapped stories.

"You played baseball?" Emily sounded pleasantly surprised as she doused her own pancakes with syrup.

"I played in high school and college." He looked up and winked at Jenifer in the doorway.

Emily put the syrup down, then folded her arms on the edge of the table. "Were you good? What position did you play?"

Robbie almost choked on his pancakes. "Did you see the trophies in my room? Those are all his."

Matt thumped Robbie's back and waited until he stopped coughing. "I played first base. I was okay." He pushed a glass of orange juice in front of Robbie. "We won a conference championship when I was in college."

Emily sank back in her chair, her blue eyes dancing. "I'm a pitcher. My team went to states last year."

"She's a natural," Andrea said, coming in from the back deck, then glancing down at her coffee when she seemed to realize what she'd said.

Jenifer smoothed a hand over Robbie's hair as she came all the way into the kitchen. "She very well could be, but I wouldn't rule out the effects of a positive influence." She gave Matt a quick kiss. "Tell you the truth, I'm counting on it."

Over the next several days, Matt kept Emily and Andrea busy while Jenifer and Robbie were in school. He'd taken the week off and shown them around Grand Rapids, toured the firehouse, and then spent a couple of afternoons with them on the boat.

At the end of the week, Matt's truck wasn't in the driveway when Jenifer and Robbie got home from school. She thought he was still out shopping with Emily and Andrea when she found him stretched out on the sofa with his arm dropped over his face.

Grinning, she dropped her tote bag by the door and kicked off her sandals. "Tough day?" He'd taken Andrea and Emily to the mall after Jenifer had pointed out to him Emily wore the same outfit a couple of times during the week.

His head lolled to the side to look at her. "She tried on the same three pairs of jeans four times. I needed a haircut by the time we finally left the mall."

Jenifer pressed her lips together and smiled. "What did she finally decide?"

He sat up and gave her a crooked grin. "She didn't. I did. I told her to get all three."

She laughed and dropped down beside him. "That's a bit excessive."

"So her mother said." His humor faded. "Andrea wasn't comfortable with all of the shopping, but I could tell she let me do it for Emily."

"Andrea's a good mother." That was evident enough. Hopefully knowing Emily had someone who loved her more than anything else in the world helped ease the pain Matt felt over losing her.

He blew out a long breath. "She works two jobs. I think they do okay, but I don't know..." His voice trailed off.

Jenifer rested her head on his shoulder. "Are you going to offer to help?"

"I wanted to talk to you about it first."

"I know your relationship is a bit unorthodox, but she's still your daughter. I'm good with whatever you decide to do. It's Andrea you have to convince." She leaned into his hand as he rubbed her back, remembering his truck wasn't in the driveway. "Did they go somewhere after you got home this afternoon?"

"Andrea asked if she could borrow the truck to take Emily out to dinner. I think they needed some time alone." His strong hands moved to her shoulders, kneading them as her eyes slowly closed. "If you're up to it, we could grab dinner out. Maybe go to a baseball game. The Whitecaps are playing at home tonight."

She smiled and rocked up to her feet with a little push from behind. They wouldn't have many more opportunities to spend time alone with Robbie before the baby was born. "Sounds fun. I'll change my clothes and we'll go."

∾

*T*he game ended late. It was ten o'clock at the end of the ninth inning, and they still had a long walk back to the car. The warm night had brought out the fans in droves. Jenifer lumbered across the parking lot holding Robbie's hand. Matt kept watching her as if he feared she would drop the baby before they got to the car. "I should have picked you up in front of the stadium."

"Look at all the traffic." She yawned, waving her hand in the air. "We'd be here another hour if you did."

A few minutes later, they were in the car, inching toward the exit. Robbie's eyes closed the minute his head hit the back of the seat.

Jenifer closed her eyes, too, listening to Steely Dan on the radio when they finally got onto the highway. Tomorrow was Saturday. They could Skype with Sarah and Ben for the first time with Emily in the morning, and then she would make a run to the store. Afterward, they would go to the lake. It was going to be warm again. They could eat dinner on the boat and the kids could…

27

att slammed his foot on the brakes. He threw his arm across Jenifer's chest. Front and side airbags exploded like mortars. Struck from behind, their car spun into oncoming traffic. They were hit again before their car collided with a guardrail. Glass shattered. The force slammed Jenifer forward, then back again.

Pain shot through Matt's arm with the impact. Using his left hand, he reached over and unbuckled his seat belt, clutching his right arm against his chest. "Jenifer?"

Her breathing was ragged, her face bleeding from the broken glass. She was trapped, pinned back in her seat by the passenger door. Her eyes were closed, but her head flinched when he said her name.

Fear punched in his chest at the blood, her blood. "Don't move."

Robbie was pushed forward and twisted between the front seats. He was unconscious, still secured in the booster seat that had kept him from being thrown from the car. He was breathing. Matt pressed his fingers to his neck. His pulse was strong. Leaning over him, Matt found Jenifer's pulse and then pressed his hand to her abdomen.

Nothing.

His mind blurred as he tried to shut down his emotions. He had to get them out of the car. He needed backboards, neck collars. Equipment to cut Jenifer's door. He wiped blood from his eyes. Cursed at the arm against his chest. He couldn't do it alone.

"Robbie," Jenifer whispered.

Her broken voice threatened to tear him apart. "I'll get him out. I'll get you out." He put his hand on her shoulder. "I love you. Just be still."

He stared at Robbie, trying to decide how to free him. He needed to be boarded. Without knowing if the fuel tank had been compromised, he didn't know how much time he had to get them out. He didn't dare move Robbie unless it was absolutely necessary. He opened his door and saw two other vehicles involved in the crash. A teenage boy had gone to the aid of an elderly man still trapped inside his car. A young woman tried to calm the third driver. Traffic on either side of the road had come to a standstill.

"Matt."

He reached over and touched Jenifer's hand. "I'm right here. Everything's going to be okay. Just hang on."

"I love you." Her head lolled, and his heart slammed against his chest.

Sirens wailed in the distance. Given where they were and the severity of the accident, he was almost certain his company would respond.

Minutes later, Matt shouted for two boards when he caught Nate jumping out of the truck and then come running toward him. Behind Nate, Kyle hurried around to the back of the truck.

"Jesus, Matt," was all Nate said as he signaled for more help. He reached inside the car. "Jen, honey, it's Nate," he said as he assessed her condition through the broken window. Matt's throat tightened when she didn't respond.

Kyle rushed to the car with Henry and two backboards. Matt

took a breath and tried hard to steady his voice. He touched Jenifer's shoulder, hoping she could hear him. "We're getting Robbie out now."

Kyle and Henry signaled for Matt to move out of the way. He was no good to Robbie with one arm, and he climbed out of the car to give them room to work.

"Here." Nate threw a blanket at Matt to cover Jenifer as he prepared to pry open her door. Kyle and Henry freed Robbie from the back seat, boarded him, and rushed him to a waiting ambulance. The generator powering the hydraulic cutter blasted through the air.

Matt got back into the driver's seat. He checked Jenifer's abdomen for movement and lost his breath when a tiny foot nudged his hand. Jenifer started to shake. Her breathing grew more labored. Matt shot Nate a look telling him he would tear the car door off himself if they didn't get her out now, shouting over the generator, "She's going into shock!"

Nate shook his head and shouted back over the keening of mangled metal as it was ripped away, "Just stay with her!"

Nate and another firefighter wrenched off the car door and prepared to extricate Jenifer. Nate pointed to the sky, signaling they were airlifting her to the hospital. "Go check on Robbie."

Torn between his wife and his son, Matt froze, then rushed over to Robbie.

He got to the ambulance as the night sky flashed red and blue against the orange glow of flares alongside the road. He saw Robbie's leg stabilized and an IV taped to his arm. "Is he conscious?"

A paramedic slammed the back doors closed. "Is he your son?"

Matt clenched his jaw. "Yes, dammit. Is he awake?"

"No." Matt didn't know the paramedic, who signaled for another one to check Matt. "We're taking him to Children's."

A hand grabbed Matt's good arm when he attempted to run back to Jenifer. "Stay here. Let them do their job." He resisted and the first paramedic helped restrain him. "You're going to get in the way over there."

Matt cursed at both paramedics when he heard the chopper in the distance. Sharp, burning pain radiated down the arm he still held against his chest, but he'd be damned if he didn't go back to check on Jenifer.

Henry shouted at the paramedics over the roof of Jenifer's car, "Let him go!"

Matt broke free and ran back to the car as the ambulance transporting Robbie hit the siren and sped off. "I'm right here," he said as they boarded Jenifer and lifted her onto a stretcher. He stayed alongside her and held her hand, hoping she could still hear him. "You're being airlifted. I can't go with you. I'll meet you at the hospital. I love you." He kissed her forehead before Nate and Henry lifted her into the helicopter.

"They got her, Matt!" Nate shouted over the wind and loud choppy noise of the propellers as the helicopter lifted into the air. "You gotta go."

Matt's heart pounded, blood throbbing in his ears. He had to get to the hospital. Jenifer's car was smashed. He turned in a circle, searching for Rescue 5 in the chaos.

Henry came running over and started pushing Matt toward the ambulance where the paramedics had held him up.

Hell no. "I don't need a damn ambulance. I need the truck."

Kyle stood next to the paramedics. They waved Matt over. Kyle pointed up and called out, "You got lights and a siren. Get outta here."

One of the paramedics jumped in back with Matt. The other climbed into the driver's seat. "Where are we going? Children's or Butterworth?" asked the driver, who seemed better informed now about the situation.

Matt scrubbed his hands over his face. He'd never felt so divided in his life. "Butterworth." He pulled his phone out of his pocket with his good hand and called Robert.

"There's been an accident," he said when Robert answered.

"They took Robbie to Children's. I need you over there. Jenifer's going to Butterworth."

Robert's voice was all but drowned out by the blare of the siren. "What happened? Are they all right? Are you hurt?"

Matt choked back his fear as he looked down at the blood on his clothes and told him what happened.

"What about the baby?"

"The baby was still moving before they took Jenifer from the car." Matt could hear Robert relaying what he said to Elizabeth in the background. "Will you call Jenifer's parents? And call me as soon as the doctors tell you anything about Robbie?"

"We're out the door now. We'll call Tom and Kate, and then call you as soon as we know anything. I want you to do the same."

Rachel was pacing at the entrance to the emergency department when Matt arrived at the hospital. He jumped out of the back of the ambulance and rushed meet her. "You're working tonight?"

She put her hand on his good arm. "Yeah. Henry called. Come on." She tried to steer him into an exam room, and he pulled away.

"Not now. I have to find Jenifer."

"Not like that, you won't." Her eyes darted to the blood on his clothes as she pushed him past a set of fire doors and into an empty exam room. She pointed at a chair. "Sit. Don't move. I'll be right back."

No way was he going to sit. Rachel had thirty seconds before he would leave to find Jenifer. It didn't take her that long to come back with a pair of green scrubs in one hand and a clipboard in the other.

Rachel made him sit on the end of the exam table. "I asked about Jenifer before you got here," she said, taking a pair of scissors from her scrubs and carefully cutting away his T-shirt. "She's having an MRI to check for brain swelling."

A vise-like grip closed around Matt's throat as he had to force himself to remain still. "Will she need surgery?"

Rachel pulled away his T-shirt and threw it in the trash. She wet a washcloth with warm water and gently wiped his face. "It wouldn't surprise me." She glanced at the clipboard on top of the scrubs she'd set next to him. "You need to fill out the consent forms."

He nodded with a sick, shaky feeling in his stomach. "And the baby?"

She handed him the scrub top and talked to him like a friend, not a nurse. "You have a second set of forms there, in case they have to deliver the baby early."

He managed to get the shirt over his head and pull it over his bad arm. "I have to go upstairs. I need to be with them."

"I know." Rachel helped him with his shorts and into the scrub pants. "Then you're going to let me X-ray that arm, okay?"

He'd almost forgotten about the arm.

Matt sat alone in a small, empty room waiting to talk to another of Jenifer's doctors when Robert called. "Robbie's in surgery. We didn't get to see him first. The doctor said the damage to his leg is extensive but that he doesn't think he has any other serious injuries."

"Will you stay with him until I can get there?"

"We won't leave him. How's Jenifer?"

Matt felt sick to his stomach. His family was hurt, in two different hospitals, and all he could do was wait. "She has a head injury. She needs surgery to relieve the pressure on her brain. I spoke to the neurosurgeon. I'm waiting to meet the obstetrician who's going to first deliver the baby."

"Are you by yourself?"

"No." Matt stood when Nate and Henry walked into the room behind a tall, dark-haired woman in blue scrubs and a scrub cap. "I have to go. I'll call you as soon as I know anything more."

"Mr. Barnes? I'm Dr. Lang. I'm one of Jenifer's doctors this evening." She reached out her hand to him. "I'll be delivering her baby prior to the surgery to relieve brain swelling."

Matt sank back into his chair. He dropped his head in his hands. Nate sat beside him. Henry clasped Matt's shoulder. "Two surgeries? You agree this is safe, too?"

"Jenifer is thirty-six weeks along, correct?"

Matt raised his head and nodded.

"Then I believe, as does the neurosurgeon, that a caesarean delivery is safest for both mother and child. We'll be better able to assess the baby's condition following the accident, and Jenifer's body will have the advantage of devoting all of its energy on her recovery."

Matt focused his thoughts on one word. Recovery. "Can I see her?"

Dr. Lang smiled with regret. "We're moving quickly, Mr. Barnes. I believe she's already being prepped for delivery. Someone will come find you as soon as the procedure to relieve the swelling is complete and she's moved to recovery."

It was Rachel who returned after less than an hour. He got to his feet beside Nate and Henry before she hugged him. "You have a sweet little baby girl. She's beautiful and healthy, and it doesn't look like she suffered any injuries at all from the accident. They took her to the NICU as a precaution. She'll be ready to see you soon. It shouldn't be too much longer before you can see Jenifer, too."

His gut wrenched as he reached for the door. "I just need a minute."

Finding a small alcove at the end of the hallway, he squatted against the wall and stared down at the gray speckled floor. This was not how it was supposed to be. Jenifer shouldn't have been alone when she gave birth to their daughter. He should have been by her side, holding her hand, telling her he loved her. That was how it should have been.

After a short while, Matt heard heavy footsteps coming down

the hallway. He looked up. Nate held out a hand. "Come on, time to get up."

A wave of despair nearly crushed him. He couldn't move. Barely breathed. "How do I see the baby without Jenifer?"

"We're not going to see the baby. We're going to see your wife."

28

*J*enifer lay unconscious in the ICU. Matt sat beside her bed, elbows on his knees, his head in his hands, listening to the clock ticking on the wall. Her eyes were swollen closed and her face cut from shattered glass. A white bandage covered her head and a breathing tube was taped to the side of her face. He studied her heart monitor, adjusted the breathing tube, and then braced his hands on the bed rail and dropped his head.

He was alone. His mother and Jenifer's parents were still on their way to Michigan. Nate and Henry had returned to the firehouse after Matt talked to Jenifer's doctors following her surgeries. It was two o'clock in the morning, and he could barely keep his eyes open anymore.

He leaned over the bed and lowered his lips to her ear. "We have a little girl. You did such a great job. She's safe and healthy and waiting for her mommy to wake up and hold her."

The doctors told him they didn't think she would wake before morning. Rachel had tried to talk him into going home to get some sleep. But unless he went to be with Robbie, he wouldn't leave Jenifer alone until she woke and he knew she would be all right.

"I'm waiting for you, too." He stroked his hand over her hair and swallowed hard to keep his voice from shaking. "I love you. I need you to come back to me."

Rachel returned with a pillow and blanket. She set them on the table next to Jenifer's bed. "Any change?"

"Nothing." He smoothed his hand over Jenifer's blanket, tucking it into her side.

Rachel checked the monitors, then read her chart at the foot of the bed. "Have you seen the baby?"

He sat again, rubbing the back of his neck, torn over going to the NICU alone. "No. I keep hoping she'll wake up, and then I'll go. I've talked to the nurses who are taking care of the baby. I'll go in the morning."

"Okay. Get some sleep. I'll check back in a little while." Rachel put the pillow behind his head and covered him with the blanket before she left.

The steady sound of Jenifer's heart monitor brought him a small measure of comfort as he stretched out in the chair beside her. He closed his eyes and laced their fingers on the side of the bed.

A nurse looked in on Jenifer several times during the night. Each time, he'd checked on her, too, hoping to see a change. Once, around four in the morning, he was asked to leave, and he'd dragged himself to the cafeteria in search of coffee.

He was almost asleep again as sunlight filtered through the metal blinds behind the white curtain around the bed. Someone touched his shoulder. He kept his eyes closed, hoping whoever it was wouldn't ask him to leave again. When he felt a tap on his arm, he let out a breath and turned around.

Rachel was standing behind him. She shook her head and put a finger to her lips. She nodded toward Jenifer, insistent, and pressed the call button. Matt caught the small movement. If he hadn't stood and looked down at her face, he might have missed it. It was her eyes. She was trying to open her eyes.

~

*J*enifer tried hard to lift her hand. The rest of her body felt helpless and heavy with sleep. A dim light and quiet murmur of voices pushed their way through the darkness that enveloped her.

A soft, familiar voice whispered, "I love you, Jenifer. Please. Open your eyes."

Matt.

She tried to do as he asked, but the light hurt from behind her eyelids and she shut them tight. Suddenly, the light was gone.

Matt whispered again, "Squeeze my hand if you can hear me."

Her eyes fluttered. She tightened her fingers, then filled with despair when the warmth of his hand disappeared. The light returned. Different hands and unfamiliar voices frightened her.

Matt's voice came from farther way. "You're okay. I'm right here."

She squeezed a different hand on command, and then flinched at a sharp prick on the bottom of her foot. Soon, the room went dark again.

"She's waking up." A strange voice started to fade away. "Give her a little more time."

Jenifer felt a scratch on her cheek, a soft kiss on her lips. "Sleep," Matt said, holding her hand again. "We'll be here when you wake up."

~

*J*enifer opened her eyes to sunlight slanting through the metal blinds, casting a swath of light over Matt, slumped in his chair with a white cloth over his shoulder. He was sound asleep. She spotted a bouquet of pink tulips next to her bed. Tape on her arm made her skin itch. The tube in her nose startled her. Panic rose in her chest. Instinctively, she lifted her hand, expecting to touch her swollen belly, and she gasped.

Matt shot out of his chair. He stumbled against the side of the bed and, for an instant, he grinned like a loon as she gaped at him.

She didn't understand. His arm was in a cast. His face was cut and bruised. Her head throbbed and her whole body racked with pain. Her thoughts jumbled together as bits and pieces of the accident floated at the edge of her mind. Fear and apprehension knotted in her stomach. "Where's Robbie? The baby?"

Matt leaned over and held her face in his hands. "Robbie's safe. The baby's okay." He brushed his thumbs over her cheeks. "And you're awake," he said, smiling down on her.

She turned her head from side to side, looking for them. "Where are they?"

Matt pushed the call button next to her pillow. "The baby's here. Robbie's at Children's Hospital." He shook his head when tears streamed down her face. "He's okay, I promise."

A nurse came to the door and smiled when she looked at Jenifer. "I'll call the doctor and let her know you're awake."

Jenifer looked back at Matt. "What happened to you?"

He held up his cast. "Broken arm. That's all."

"How long was I asleep?"

He inclined the bed and helped prop her up against the pillows. "Less than twenty-four hours. But it was the longest day of my life."

She touched a hand to the bandage on her head and winced. "Who's with Robbie?"

"Your parents, or Robert and Elizabeth when your parents are here."

Jenifer blinked hard, but the tears didn't stop. She closed her eyes, trying to remember Matt or Robbie in the car, but she came up blank. "How badly was he hurt?"

Matt slid his chair closer to the side of the bed and sat. "He broke his leg. He needed surgery last night, but the doctors say he's okay."

"The baby's okay?"

Matt squeezed her hand and pressed it to his lips. "The baby wasn't hurt in the accident. But you needed surgery. They delivered her first." He got up and parted the curtains at the foot of the bed. He wheeled a clear bassinet with a pink label *Baby Girl Barnes* to where Jenifer could reach out and touch it.

Mesmerized by the tiny bundle he lifted with his good arm, Jenifer could barely breathe. "We have a little girl?"

She watched Matt gaze intently at his daughter. A beautiful, unexpected treasure. "She needs a name," he said, nestling her into Jenifer's arms.

Jenifer cradled her baby girl. Grateful she was safe and healthy. She kissed the tuft of downy soft hair and touched the round, chubby cheeks and precious little lips pursed into a kiss. She looked like her daddy with bright-blue eyes. And reminded her of Matt's father. "What if we named her Anna?"

Matt raised his eyebrows and smiled. "You want to name her after my grandmother? Why?"

Jenifer touched her cheek to the top of Anna's head. "It seems fitting. You wished for a grandmother, hoped for a child, and now you have both."

~

*M*att borrowed his father-in-law's car and left the hospital after Jenifer fell asleep again. When he got home, Tobey started barking from up the street. Emily fought to hold him back on his leash. Her eyes grew huge as Matt got out of the car.

"You can let him go," he called out.

Emily dropped the leash and ran behind the dog as he charged toward home. When she reached Matt, she threw her arms around his neck, and he squeezed her tight as Tobey circled between their legs.

"You said you were okay." Her tone sounded accusing as her eyes moved to his cast.

He kissed the top of her head and then tilted back to look at her. "I *am* okay."

Her eyes narrowed. "Why are you wearing scrubs?"

Raising his good arm, he took a step back and tried to look offended as a way of distracting her. "What? You don't like them?" He turned around as a car he didn't recognize parked behind him in the driveway. His mother got out first, followed by Ben.

Emily stayed behind Matt. He noticed she didn't let go of his hand.

"Matt." His mother seemed to try hard not to stare at Emily. She touched his cast and then brushed her fingertips over the cuts on his face. "You're hurt, too."

He moved her hand from his face without letting go. "It's nothing." He pulled Emily into his side as Andrea came out the front door. "Mom. This is Emily. Emily, this is my mother, Sarah."

His mother appeared awestruck as she clasped Emily's hands. "You have no idea how wonderful it is to meet you, Emily."

Emily looked overwhelmed as she leaned in closer to him. "Hello."

"Let's get you into the house," his mother said, putting her hand on his back, "and you can sleep for a little while before we go see the rest of your family."

Andrea introduced herself once they got inside and then went into the kitchen with Emily. Ben took charge of Tobey and went to finish his walk.

Sarah went with Matt to sit in the living room. "You're going to need help when Jenifer and the kids come home. Ben and I talked about it, and I'm going to move back to Michigan. He'll commute for a few months until he retires, and then he'll move home, too."

Matt frowned at her upending her life because of him. "Mom—"

Her lips firmed. "This is what I want to do. You and I have been given a special gift. I'm not about to waste it."

Emily returned a few minutes later with a sandwich and chips. She set them on the coffee table in front of Matt. "I made this for you." Her dark-blue eyes flicked over the cast on his arm. Her chin quivered. "Do you think I could go see Jenifer and Robbie before we leave?"

Matt rose and gave her a hug. His mother's hand touched his back. "I think they would really like that. Jenifer and Robbie love you." He tipped up her chin and kissed her forehead. "And I love you, too."

∼

*T*he next day, Matt went to Children's Hospital when Robbie was discharged. Matt's mother and Emily were waiting for them at Butterworth. Jenifer had been moved from the ICU into a regular room, which was good because he had a surprise for her.

It took some finagling to secure Robbie and his leg cast into the back seat of the truck. He had to be uncomfortable, but he wanted nothing to do with going home before he saw his mother and new sister at the hospital.

Robbie dead-eyed him in the rearview mirror. "You promise we're going to see Mom, right?"

Matt grinned at him. "I promise. But she doesn't know, so this is going to be a big surprise."

Robbie had his own surprise coming, too. For some reason, he thought he'd missed Emily before she went home. He had no idea Matt's mother was in town, too. He thought he was just going to see his mother and the baby before they went home.

At Jenifer's hospital, Matt managed a wheelchair for Robbie and, playing around, he wheeled him backward down the hallway so he couldn't see Emily or his mother waiting for them.

"Are you ready to surprise Mom?" Matt asked, stepping away so Emily could take the handles of the wheelchair from him.

Robbie started to say something over his shoulder, and his eyes lit up when he saw who was pushing him. "Emily!" His mouth fell open at the sight of Matt's mother. "Grandma Sarah!"

There was a lot of excitement in the elevator as they started up to Jenifer's floor. Matt had made sure to call before they got there so she would have the baby in the room with her. He put his finger to his lips as the elevator doors slid open and Robbie began to squirm in his wheelchair.

Matt went into the room first. Anna was asleep in the bassinet next to the bed. "Is it all right if I brought company?"

Jenifer's eyes lit up when Emily pushed Robbie into the room. Robbie's expression filled with fear when he looked at the bandage on her head.

Jenifer sat up and held out her arms. "I'm okay, honey. It's just a little boo-boo."

Matt heard her breath catch at Robbie's full leg cast as Emily pushed him closer to the bed.

His mother walked in behind Emily. Her eyes filled with joy as she went to look inside the bassinet.

Matt squeezed Emily's shoulder before he came around to lift Anna and settle her in her grandmother's arms.

Jenifer patted the bed. "Will you let Matt bring you over to sit with me for a minute?" she asked Robbie.

Robbie nodded and tried to push up to his good leg like he thought he could get onto the bed all by himself. He started to teeter, and Emily steadied him.

Matt picked him up and sat him on the bed. Jenifer put her arms around him and tucked him in close.

"Do you want to hold your baby sister?" his mother asked Emily.

Emily's eyes went wide as she went to sit in the chair next to Jenifer and Robbie.

Matt scooped up the sleeping baby and laid her into the arms of his oldest daughter. He crouched in front of both his girls. His heart stuck in his throat.

"She's a miracle," he whispered to Emily. "Just like you."

29

$\mathcal{T}$he next morning, a jet took off at the airport as Matt parked at the curb inside the terminal. Emily hopped out first and went to take their suitcases from the back of the truck.

"Call me when you get home," Matt said, closing the tailgate behind her. Steeling himself, he opened his good arm to say goodbye.

Emily wrapped him up in a hug. "I will. Will you let us know when Jen and the baby come home?"

He kissed her cheek, hoping they would be home soon. "Yes."

Emily turned her head to look at her mother, then lifted her eyes to him. "Do you think I could come see you over Christmas vacation?"

Matt gazed at Andrea over the top of Emily's head. He had already asked if he could see Emily again and she'd agreed. She had also allowed him to reimburse her for the airline tickets, and she didn't balk when he'd asked if he could send Emily packages. He would tell her another time that he was making plans to set money aside to help with college.

Andrea met his eyes for a moment and sighed as if she were

giving away a piece of her heart. In a way, he supposed, she was. "I think we can work something out."

He smiled, though it made his heart ache to tell Emily good-bye. He tipped up her chin with his finger. "I'm going to miss you. I love you. I want you to remember that."

Emily blinked hard and then handed her phone over to her mom. "Will you take another picture before we go?"

Matt lifted his blue fiberglass cast in the air and shook his head. His face was still cut and bruised from the accident. "Are you sure you want a picture of this?"

"Yes." Her expression turned shy but solidly determined. "I love you, too. I'm lucky." She turned them both to face her mother. "Some kids think their dads are heroes. I want to show everyone that my father really is."

∽

Two weeks later, Jenifer laid Anna on the changing table in the nursery. Warm sunlight spilled through the bedroom windows before dusk. She listened to Matt carrying Robbie up the stairs and into the bathroom. It was no easy task. She envisioned Matt's good arm around Robbie's waist, one of Robbie's arms around Matt's neck, and Robbie's other hand dangling his crutches at his side as they slowly made their way up the stairs.

Robbie's crutches thudded against the wall in the hallway and slid to the wood floor outside the nursery. "Why can't I take a shower instead of a bath?" It was the same question he asked every night since he'd come home from the hospital. That, and how long until he could ride his bike again. He was in good spirits, though, with all of the extra attention from his grandparents and friends from school. Being a new big brother helped too.

"Because I don't want you to slip and fall." Matt stayed firm, and seconds later, Jenifer heard the tub start to fill with water.

Matt stuck his head into the baby's room. "How are you

236

doing?" His soft, dark beard was thicker than usual, his skin tanned from working outside while he was on medical leave. Anna had spit up on the front of his gray T-shirt and narrowly missed his basketball shorts before they'd brought the kids upstairs.

Jenifer finished changing Anna into light-yellow pajamas dotted with white daisies and little white socks. Anna stuck her tiny fist into her mouth and kicked her chubby legs in the air. "She's getting hungry. I'll have to feed her soon."

Matt looked over his shoulder to where she could see Robbie sitting on the bathroom floor, putting on the plastic bag to keep his cast dry. "Do you want me to help you guys downstairs? The tub's still filling." He gestured with his head toward the bathroom. "I can give you a hand. He'll wait a minute."

"No." She picked up Anna and laid her on her shoulder as they got comfortable in the rocking chair Matt's grandmother had given to them. "We're fine. We can wait."

Matt came in to give them both a quick kiss on the cheek, then went back into the bathroom. He worried about her getting around the house. Her head didn't hurt as much anymore, and her balance was almost back to normal, but he still carried Anna on the stairs for her.

After the water stopped, Jenifer could see Matt leaning against the vanity through the bedroom door after he helped Robbie into the tub. "I think we exhausted your mother tonight. She looked relieved to go home even before your father left," she said.

Matt pulled his collar out and sniffed his T-shirt. He made a face at what probably smelled like sour milk, then pulled off the shirt and tossed it into the hamper. "I think the reason for that is because she's still getting used to seeing him around. Just like I am."

"You're happy, though, aren't you?" She pressed her cheek to Anna's head and breathed in the scent of fresh powder and warm, clean cotton. "I mean, I know it's awkward for your mom, but at least your father is willing to be in your life now."

Matt folded his good arm over his cast. "It took the accident to finally get him to come around, but I'm glad he's trying."

"Are you going to tell your mother he owns the loft she's living in?"

Matt's eyebrows pinched together. He shook his head almost comically. "Nope. Never. The sooner she buys a house and moves out of that place, the safer I'll feel."

Jenifer chuckled. She patted Anna's back as the baby squirmed against her shoulder. "She loves that loft."

"She sure does. My father made certain it was too good a deal to pass up. But she can be stubborn. If she finds out I let him help without telling her, she'll kill me."

Jenifer thought there was a pretty good chance he was right. She also believed keeping any more secrets from his mother was a bad idea. "You should still tell her. He's been very kind, especially taking my parents to dinner before they left and spending so much time here with your grandparents. She'll see how much he loves you. Give her a chance."

"Maybe you're right." Matt reached down and handed Robbie a bar of soap from the sink. He tilted forward to look at her again. "What did the attorney say when you talked to her today?"

"We can finalize the adoption any time. She kind of put things on hold after the accident but said we can schedule an appointment to sign the paperwork when we're ready."

"I'd like to take care of that soon."

"That's what I told her." She slanted him a grin. "She'll let us know when we can meet with the judge."

Anna lifted her head and let out a hungry cry. Jenifer grabbed a cloth from the wicker basket on the floor and draped it over her shoulder, then settled in to feed her.

Matt went to grab a bath towel from the linen closet and dropped it on the floor next to the tub. Jenifer watched as he knelt on the floor and helped Robbie shampoo his hair and wash up before Matt helped him out of the tub again.

A few minutes later, Robbie was in his pajamas watching the Yankees game in the living room. Matt came back upstairs into Anna's room. He sat on the edge of the twin bed, then flopped onto his back and closed his eyes.

Jenifer watched him for a minute as Anna fell asleep against her chest. With his arm bent over his head, he stretched out his legs and let out a long, exhausted breath.

She rocked in her chair, biting back a smile. "Matt?"

A low rumble sounded deep in his throat. "Hmmm?"

The end of another long, tiring day was probably the wrong time to ask, but she couldn't help but wonder. "Do you ever want more children some day?"

His head lolled to the side as his eyes cracked open. "You want more kids?"

She arched a brow with a noncommittal shrug, waiting to hear his answer first.

He rose up to his good elbow. His blue eyes turned soft and serious. "I think I've pretty much exhausted my luck. Why? Do you want another baby?"

His warm, tender gaze pulled at her heart. "I don't know." Maybe it was the challenge of beating the odds that made her want to leave their options open. Or maybe it was seeing what a wonderful father he was to Robbie, Emily, and Anna. "I just think maybe we shouldn't try to stop it from happening."

The corners of his mouth turned up with equal parts joy and disbelief. "You want to leave it up to fate?"

Somewhere along the way, she'd fallen more in love with him than she had ever imagined. The love he returned changed her life forever. "I do. I believe that fate's always going to be on our side."

ALSO BY SUZANNE WINSLOW

Keep reading for a preview of
Bailout, Smoke and Fire Book 2
Nate's Story
Early 2021

CHAPTER 1

Intervene

August 2013

After a ten-hour shift in the ICU, Rachel Miller maneuvered her way through the crowded, glass-enclosed walkway, headed for home. The tall overhead bridge connected the Grand Rapids hospital to an adjacent parking garage. On the street below, the evening traffic had slowed to a standstill. The early August sun heated the inside of the tunnel as a steady stream of hospital personnel and visitors passed in both directions. A blur of strangers until she passed through the glass doors into the garage and a flash of red hair sent a shiver up her spine. Two car rows ahead, she spotted Nate Doyle walking with his back to her alongside a second firefighter. They were friends of her brother. When she was a teenager, Nate had been her much-older, red-headed fantasy. It was embarrassing, now, to remember how she'd followed him around like a lovesick puppy. Eventually, he'd started to avoid her. Sometimes, despite becoming friends years later, she wondered if he still did.

"Rachel?" A familiar voice called her from behind as Nate rounded a corner and disappeared inside the hospital.

She pressed her lips together, letting out a small sigh before she reluctantly turned around. "Jack."

Jack Greene gave her a nervous smile as the glass doors closed behind him. He stuck one hand into the front pocket of his gray trousers. In his other hand, he carried the expensive leather briefcase she had given him for his birthday last year. His expression softened. "You look great."

She studied the familiar handsome face she had tried hard to forget for months. His dark-brown eyes rested on hers. The sun had streaked his short blond hair. His deep sexy voice was natural, the strong, athletic build hard-earned. Altogether, he could charm the panties off a virgin, something she'd learned firsthand their freshman year of college.

"Thank you." She touched a hand to her short blond pony-tail, glancing down at her purple scrubs and black athletic shoes. Standard nurse attire. And the same charming Jack. "Did you work at the hospital all day?" After they broke up, she assumed she would see him at work from time to time. He was a successful pharmaceutical rep. He'd gravitated toward sales the way women had gravitated toward him during his years on the lacrosse field. Their on-again, off-again relationship had finally ended seven months ago, after she discovered he'd cheated on her a second time.

He nodded, switching his briefcase to the other hand. "I had appointments all day; otherwise, I would have come by the ICU to see you. How've you been?"

"Good. I've been busy, too." She peeked at her watch, partly out of curiosity and partly in an effort to move him along.

He pointed to the small purple earrings she wore. "How are sales?" he asked, referring to the jewelry business she'd started about the same time they'd broken up.

She gave him a quick smile for remembering. "Online sales are up. Consignment's next." If she could find the time. Reminded of time, she glanced down at her wrist again.

He cleared his throat as if he knew she was trying to put him off. "Would you like to have dinner with me? We could talk, catch up."

With a quick shake of her head, she stuffed her water bottle back into her bag. "I don't think that's a good idea."

"Are you sure?" With what appeared as chagrin, he adjusted his perfectly straight gray-striped tie. He clicked his key fob, and she noticed his car up ahead.

"I'm sorry, Jack. I'm happy to see you, and I hope things are going well. But I need to cut this short and head home." She glanced over his shoulder, surprised to see Nate heading their way as she took another step toward her car.

Nate wore his uniform—dark-blue pants and a matching short-sleeve button-down shirt. Medium height with a broad chest and wide shoulders, he was built like a wrestler. She could see his fair skin was burned from the summer sun. His hair, a deep, rich auburn, looked as if it had seen the inside of a helmet recently.

Jack stayed beside her, keeping to his old habit of walking her to her car. He put his hand on her arm. "Rachel?" Sadness and regret sounded in his voice. "Are we really over this time?"

She turned to face him, hoping to make her point without sounding cruel or vindictive. She didn't hate him, but he wasn't getting another chance either. Her heart needed a rest. "Yes. Jack," she said, lifting her chin. "We are really and truly over."

He dropped his hand. "I love you. If you would try one more time, I promise, I'll prove it to you."

Rachel reached up and rubbed at the dull ache starting behind her eyes. Without thinking, she raised her voice. "It's too late. I'm seeing somebody else." She knew the second the words were out of her mouth, Jack wouldn't believe her. She was a terrible liar.

Jack opened his mouth as if to say something and then closed it when Nate came up behind him.

Nate slipped his arm around Rachel's waist as if he had done it a hundred times before. She had to hide her astonishment, especially when he pulled her into his side. "I'm sorry I'm late, babe." He leaned closer, his vivid green eyes locked on hers. Arching a brow, he gave her a second to stop what she guessed would happen next.

Not a chance.

The moment his warm, soft lips took hers in a quick possessive kiss, her heart nearly stopped. How many times had she imagined him holding her like this? Kissing her? Her fingers tightened on his arms. She swore the corner of his mouth lifted as he held her upright, and then he shifted his gaze to Jack.

"We've met before." Nate reached out a hand to her bewildered ex-boyfriend. "Nate Doyle. You're Jack, right?"

"Jack Greene." Jack appeared as stunned as she felt when he shook Nate's hand.

Nate nodded, still holding his hand to her back. "That's right. New Year's Eve. And then, I think we missed you at that wedding a couple weeks later."

Rachel almost choked as Nate subtly pointed out the argument that had led to her attending a mutual friend's wedding without Jack. It wouldn't be a stretch for Jack to believe Nate knew he had cheated on her, too.

There was no missing the shame and regret reflected in Jack's eyes. "You have a good memory." He nodded at Rachel before heading to his car. "It was good to see you again. Take care."

Nate stayed at her side until Jack got into his car and drove off.

Dumbfounded, Rachel crossed her arms and studied Nate's face, her heart still pounding in her chest. "What was that all about?"

He dropped his hand and took a step back. "I'm sorry." Worry lines furrowed between his brows. "I was just leaving the hospital, and I heard what you said. I was trying to help." The lines across his forehead deepened. "*Are* you with someone else?"

"No." She took a deep breath and thought about the kiss. "Maybe we should talk about this."

"I can't. Not now." He held up the hand he'd pressed against her back. It was the first she noticed the bandage. "I have to get back to the firehouse and check in with the captain. He needs to know I'm cleared for duty."

"What happened?" She tried to examine his hand, but he pulled it away.

"Nothing. It's a minor burn." He gave a quick look over his shoulder like he was searching for an escape. "I have to go. Matt gave me a ride. He's probably waiting back at his truck. I hope I didn't do anything to offend you."

She wanted him to stay, talk to her. Not avoid her— again.

Nate didn't say anything after he climbed into the front seat of Matt's truck and stared out the window, thinking about Rachel.

Matt was already behind the wheel with the air conditioning on and an oldies song playing on the radio. The bright-green fiberglass cast on his right arm rested on the center console. Last month, he almost lost his family in a car accident. His wife, Jenifer, had been eight months pregnant and had to be airlifted to the hospital. Their son suffered a leg fracture, and their daughter had to be delivered early. Fortunately, everyone was recovering well. "What's wrong?" he asked at last.

"Nothing."

"All right." Matt shot him a doubtful look, then turned out of the parking garage, headed back to the firehouse. "Did you finish the application for the lieutenant test?"

Matt was a lieutenant with the heavy rescue company. Nate worked under him. Any time the lieutenant's test posted, Matt would encourage Nate to apply. He hadn't been interested in a promotion before now. He enjoyed his job. Then, a few months back, Matt got married, adopted Jenifer's son, and grew his family. All of which prompted Nate to think more about what he wanted out of his career, and his life. Becoming a lieutenant would give him more responsibility, a raise, and a move to a new firehouse. It was the move that had held him back for a long time, but not anymore.

"I did it right after the job posted this morning."

"Go ahead and pick up the study material. Start reading the manuals. I'll give you a hand, if you want."

"You think I'll get selected?"

The corner of Matt's mouth pinched. "You've got ten years in, plus you exceed the criteria. Just start studying." He gestured to Nate's hand. "What did the doctor say?"

Nate barely glanced at the bandage. "I'm cleared. What about you? When are you off light-duty?"

"I got another week until the cast comes off, so sometime after that."

"Hmm." Nate looked out the window again, his mind back on Rachel.

"Are you going to tell me what's going on?"

Nate kept his eyes on the road. "I did something stupid a little while ago."

"When? I've been with you all day."

Nate hesitated, then dropped back against the seat and told him about Rachel.

Matt raised his brows when Nate finished. "You kissed her?"

It wasn't exactly a vote of confidence from the guy who knew all sides of Nate's dilemma.

"I saw her walking to her car when we were leaving. I just went to say hi when you stopped to talk to Jenifer's doctor." Nate leaned back against the seat, wondering how big of a mistake he'd made with Rachel. "She was telling that guy, Jack, we met New Year's Eve that they were over. She told him she was with someone else. It looked to me like he didn't believe her. All I wanted to do was back up her story. What would you have done?"

His best friend of ten years gave his answer with a single sidelong glance.

Nate frowned, frustrated. "Okay. Fine. You've got Jenifer. But did *I* do something wrong?"

Matt shrugged. "I guess that depends on your motive."

"What do you mean, motive?" Nate had meant to help a friend. A woman he cared about. That his response was to kiss her was relative to the situation. At least that's what he told himself.

"Come on. I know you have a thing for Rachel. All I'm saying is, if you did it to get a taste of forbidden fruit, then yeah, I think you just opened up Pandora's Box. If your motives are as altruistic as you say," Matt shrugged, then snorted out a laugh. "Forget it, you still opened the damn box."

Matt was right. Nate did have a damn *thing* for her, but it didn't start until after she was out of college. But by then, she was with Jack, so Nate continued treating her like a sister. Her older brother, another firefighter, preferred it that way. "Do you think she'll say anything to Henry?"

"No. Why would she? She likes you, too."

"Sure, years ago." Back when he'd had to thwart her efforts to push his buttons. "Even if you're right, it doesn't matter. Henry thinks I've been with half the women in Grand Rapids. He isn't going to be happy if he finds out I kissed her."

"Henry needs to remember she's twenty-five. You're thirty-eight. No one expects you to be a virgin." Matt grinned at him. "Besides, my math puts you at less than half of Henry's estimate."

Nate shook his head. "You're both wrong." He dated successful, career-minded women who were no more looking for a serious relationship than he was. He was honest. He wasn't looking for a happily ever after. He'd tried that once and failed. And no, he did not sleep with all of the women he went out with. "Rachel wanted to talk to me afterward."

"What did you say?"

"I told her I had to go. Besides, I don't need to start any trouble with Henry."

"See?" Matt pointed at him. "That's the box I was talking about."

"The box is shut tight," Nate muttered, mostly to himself.

"I don't think Rachel is going to tell him anything. Even if she does, she'll give him the whole story, including how the ex-boyfriend made a play for her." Matt snorted. "He can't stand the guy, so I bet if he has to pick between the cheat and you locking lips with his little sister, he might just buy your hero story."

Nate looked back out the window. He believed it was more likely Henry would see right through him.

ACKNOWLEDGMENTS

So many wonderful people have helped me write this story. Lucinda Race—thank you, my friend, for your patience, honesty, and immeasurable faith. Your guidance has been invaluable.

Joyce, Stefanie, Marie, James, Jim, Megan, Cassandra, Bruce, Rachel, Trish, Carol—your voices are on these pages and in my mind, always.

Tom, Troy Fire Department-Battalion Chief and friend—God bless you and keep you safe every single day. Thank you for answering a litany of questions, sharing your stories, and reading whatever I sent your way.

Casey Hagen, cover artist—thank you for understanding my vision and bringing it to life. Thank you to my editors. Mackenzie Walton—it's my hope Matt is a better man and Jenifer a stronger woman because of your insight. Kimberly Dawn—may your gift for grammar be my saving grace.

Jody Kaye, Judy Kentrus, Melanie A. Smith—you answered the call for guidance, offered your support, and I am truly grateful.

Thank you to my daughter, Kim, for answering countless medical questions, sometimes several times a day.

Thank you to my sons, Bill, Stephen, and Eric for fielding questions on everything from genetic diseases to baseball.

And, to my husband, Mark, who understands what a blank stare means, and keeps me sane, even when I drive him absolutely crazy.

ABOUT THE AUTHOR

Suzanne lives with her husband and their rescue dog, Murphy, in the suburbs of Upstate New York, though she never gives up hope of living in New York City one day.

For more information about Suzanne and her books, visit www.suzannewinslow.com.

Thank you for reading my novel. I hope you enjoyed the story. If you did, please help other readers find this book:

This book is lendable. Send it to a friend you think might like it so she can discover me too.

Help other people find this book by writing a review.

Social media links

Facebook
https://www.facebook.com/AuthorSuzanneWinslow/

Instagram//www.instagram.com/suzannewinslowauthor/

Website https://www.suzannewinslow.com

Made in the USA
Middletown, DE
24 August 2021